COLD COMFORT

COLD COMFORT

A NOVEL

DON BREDES

Harmony Books · NEW YORK

Published by Harmony Books, New York, New York.
Member of the Crown Publishing Group.

Random House, Inc. New York, Toronto, London, Sydney, Auckland
www.randomhouse.com

HARMONY BOOKS is a registered trademark and the Harmony
Books colophon is a trademark of Random House, Inc.

Printed in the United States of America

Design by Elina D. Nudelman

Library of Congress Cataloging-in-Publication Data
Bredes, Don.
    Cold comfort: a novel / by Don Bredes.
ISBN 0-609-60687-5 (hardcover)
    1. Police—Vermont—Fiction.   2. Brothers—Fiction.
3. Vermont—Fiction.   I. Title.
PS3552.R363 C65 2001
813'.54—dc21
                                        00-063280

ISBN 0-609-60687-5

10   9   8   7   6   5   4   3   2   1

First Edition

for Eileen

ACKNOWLEDGMENTS

This novel would never have seen the literary light of day without the insightful advice and steady encouragement of my old friend, Howard Mosher, a writer's writer if there ever was one. Tony Ganz was instrumental in helping me get the manuscript into the hands of the best editor on earth, Shaye Areheart. I owe them both more than I can say. To many others who generously offered me their time and expertise I want to convey my deepest appreciation, among them: Sid Adams, Dante Annicelli, Tom Buckles, John Dillon, Lyle Edwards, Kathy Hedstrom, Tom Klein, Gary Moore, Evan Perron, Roland Prairie, Herbert Spellman, Chip Troiano, and Jane Woodruff.

The gods of the hills are not the gods of the valleys.
Ethan Allen

Sophie Hannah's
next novel is forthcoming
in Spring 2013

Read on for the first chapter of

Kind of Cruel

My last stop that September morning was Sullivan's General Store and post office in Tipton village on the shore of the lake, the only store between the border and Allenburg, fifteen miles to the south. It was the height of foliage season, and today's sunny forecast had evidently inspired the tourists. Half a dozen vehicles with Quebec tags were lined up at Sullivan's single pump, blocking the delivery dock. Often enough you'd see Canadians driving twenty miles out of their way just for the American gas, but seldom a whole caravan like this. I had to idle on Lake Street and wait for an opening.

In its heyday, when I was a boy, Tipton had a full-serve Gulf station with four pumps, three food stores, including an IGA with carts, two decent restaurants, a four-story hotel overlooking the water, a famous summer camp for girls, a lumberyard, a funeral parlor, a grain dealer, and an opera house. A paddle-wheel excursion boat used to steam the length of Arrow Lake between Tipton and Iceville in the summertime, and any day of the year you could board a train in the village and ride to Boston or Montreal.

The Lakeview House burned to the ground the winter I turned ten—late one February night, the last winter my father was alive. The glow woke us. It was sixteen below. We bundled up, the three of us, and drove down from the farm and stood with most of the town for what seemed like hours out in the icy street watching it burn. The roof tumbled in all at once. That signaled the beginning. Railway service ended the next spring. Within the year the gray granite station house was dismantled for the stone. The girls' camp went bust about the same time. Later, by the early eighties, the last of the mountain's pulp and sawlogs had been cut off, and one after another family farms everywhere were going under. For Tipton what really clinched it was the interstate, which plowed through a few miles to the west when I was in high school, draining off all the town's through-traffic. Even the ornate Victorian bandstand, centerpiece of the green, was gone, flattened last year when a dead elm blew down on top of it. So, besides an ornate limestone watering trough, gift of the Civil War Widows, now filled with yellow pansies, there was little left that recalled those high-stepping times. The older generation lamented the decline. For me, after a couple of reversals down around Boston, where I'd spent half my adult life, it was this Tipton, bypassed and forgotten, that I'd come back for.

It was a pretty village still, twenty-odd frame houses and a few of brick, all well-kept, with wide porches and rolling lawns. The two-story town hall with its squat steeple stood at one end of the green between mammoth white pines. At the other end were the library, painted yellow, and two simple clapboard churches, one Baptist, one Presbyterian. The green overlooked the southern tip of a wild, deep lake that lay between the granite facade of Mount Joseph on the east and the steep, forested slopes of Ferdinand Gorge on the west. The lake, Arrow Lake, was ten miles long and nowhere more than a mile wide. It spanned the border some eight miles to the north and drained into the great St. Lawrence.

South of the village the wooded hills were interspersed with cropland and rocky pasture. It was here, a year ago, that I'd taken up truck farming on the twenty-eight acres my mother had left me. Twice a week every week from May to October, I was on the road in my pickup, distributing produce to outlets in eight or nine nearby towns. Now and then I helped out at the farm a mile up the road, my dad's old place, where my half brother raised Christmas trees, made a little syrup, and ministered to one of the few remaining dairy herds in the county.

I N Sullivan's Store, on wooden apple crates set against the back wall underneath the brass grid of postboxes, I laid out red and green cabbages, acorn squash, a heap of onions, bunches of leeks, carrots, beets, and parsnips, and a bushel of the last of my late corn. The corn, a bicolor hybrid, had come in exceptionally well, bright and creamy and not too sweet. For a first-year operation, in fact, I'd done more than all right with everything I'd put in the ground—except for the potatoes, Green Mountains and Kennebecs, which were good-sized and plentiful but too scabby to market.

At the register Peg Gonyaw sold Snapples and chips to a couple of women in leather jackets and city boots. The taller one, a honey-blonde, eyed me up and down, whispering to the shorter one, who lowered her sunglasses to take me in. Pretty bold, this pair. Montrealers, if I had to guess. I'm six and a half feet tall (my mother's side; she was lanky, a Swede), with my father's thick French hair and dark eyes. Now and again I'll draw looks.

The door jingled as Pepper Desautels sidled in. Pepper lived above the store.

"Morning, Pepper," I offered.

A half-raised hand was all the greeting he mustered as he shuffled past me, making for the Megabucks machine on the counter. I stepped back so Peg could help him with his tickets. He was getting up there now, Pepper, and fighting emphysema. I hated to see him throw away money he didn't have on this god-awful state-sponsored gambling.

He was shuffling out the door again when I said to Peg, "How can you stand this contraption?"

She regarded me. "You're grumpy today."

"I'm serious. Say the word and I'll drag it out of here and heave it into the lake."

"Owners might not appreciate that."

"The hell with the owners. Government's got no business suckering people."

"You kidding me? That *is* their business!"

Cy Sullivan had sold the store a few years ago to a group of investors. It was managed now out of the Northwoods Realty office down in Allenburg, though Cy's fading snapshots of anglers with their trophy catches still checkered the wall behind the register.

The two women hadn't left. They lingered under the big front window, thumbing through a *Vanity Fair,* chattering to each other.

"I got one for you, Constable," Peg said under her breath. "You want to clean house, how about running them hookers back up across the line?"

"What makes you think they're hookers?"

"Some cop you are. They been working out at the Lodge all summer."

"They're performers, Peg."

"Same difference," she scoffed. "Reggie never would've stood for half the crap goes on out there, that's for damn sure."

It seemed everyone who'd known my dad knew him better than I did. Reg Bellevance had been town constable for twenty-some years. He'd died when I was ten—barn lung leading to stroke. My memories of him were hazy, though my unreasoning anger at the loss of him was as sharp as ever. "Reg was pretty much live-and-let-live, from what I hear."

"He was a God-fearing and decent man," Peg insisted. "He didn't take no guff. You couldn't drop a ice cream wrapper on the sidewalk but he'd have you picking up trash all up and down Lake Street if he seen you do it."

I had nothing to say to that. God-fearing and decent weren't attributes I'd lay claim to. "They're not hurting anybody," I said, glancing at the women again. Straight Arrow Productions was a legitimate business, hard as it was for some in this town to stomach. "Take it from me, Peg, porn's all right. It's a channel for stray lust—every bit as useful as lightning rods on a haybarn."

"Bull," she said.

In the 1880s a New York textiles magnate named Cooley built a mansion out on the point northeast of the village, three stories with wraparound porches and a tower on either end, no fewer than twelve fireplaces with marble mantels, and a chandeliered ballroom. He had carriage barns, horse barns, a billiard hall, a greenhouse, and a railroad spur for his private car. After Cooley's heirs decamped in the twenties, the estate became the Arrow-Wind Camp for Girls. The daughters of industrial barons summered there on the lake right up until the early sixties, when the wilderness experience fell out of fashion, and the camp went under. In the seventies the refurbished main building became a bed-and-breakfast, the Arrow Lake Lodge, which catered mostly to Canadians. It never caught on, although somehow the name stuck. The current occupant was a downcountry ex-con named Keith Quimby, who had turned the second floor into an erotic-film studio. His production offices occupied the upper floors, and he himself lived in one of the towers. The Quiver Club, a saloon that featured his porn stars as exotic dancers, did a lucrative business in the old dining hall on the ground floor.

"I'll have a box of thirty-eights, too, Peg."

"Goin' plinkin'?" she called from behind the sporting-goods case.

"Got to collect a vicious dog."

"Yeah? Whose?"

"One of Madeline Rand's rottweilers. Damn thing bit Cad Latham's little girl in the leg yesterday evening. Broke the skin right through her jeans."

Peg clucked. "You take care, Hector."

Although I had profound misgivings about this venture, I smiled and gave the cartridge box a shake. The last time I'd held a loaded gun in my hand I'd killed a man with it. Three years ago, when I closed the blue Smith & Wesson box and put it in the bottom of my police academy footlocker with my uniforms and dress oxfords, I truly believed I'd never set eyes on it or anything else in that footlocker again. Not till I was a sentimental old granddad anyway. But I dug out the Florsheims last fall for my mother's funeral, and now, just an hour ago, I'd unboxed and oiled the old .38 and tucked it into a heavy leather glove behind the bench seat of my pickup.

Madeline Rand had arrived in town four years ago with two boys, seven and nine, a station wagon full of clothes, and a pair of blunt-faced dogs that looked like Dobermans on steroids. She had eight or ten of the animals now—for protection, she told me last March when I'd gone up there to remind her that the town required all dogs be licensed and vaccinated by April 1 each year. This time, I said carefully, her compliance would be required. First she'd heard about it, she said. I nodded and looked around at the season's accumulation of excrement in the snow-covered yard. The dogs were all inside. "There's another thing, Madeline. If you're inbreeding these animals for cash, as I believe you are, then you're not just ignoring the law. You're engaging in a dangerous and despicable practice, do you understand? And if you don't put a stop to it, I will." To that she said nothing.

The truth is I prefer to have as little to do with dogs as possible. So even though Madeline never did square up with the town, I let the matter slide. Then ten days ago or so my nearest neighbor, Otto Morganthau, called me to report that a pack of ferocious canines up on the Rake Factory Road had run out after him and his wife as they were passing by on mountain bikes. He was sure they'd have been mauled if they hadn't been headed downhill. I didn't doubt him. That night I phoned Madeline and told her she was going to have to keep her dogs restrained from now on.

"Like hell I will!" she said. "The whole county lets their dogs run. Dogs got rights same as people."

"People come first," I said. "You need to cooperate with me on this, Madeline, or you run the risk of seeing those animals destroyed."

"Don't you threaten me!"

"Tell you what. You restrain the dogs, and I'll ask the selectmen to forgive you your fines, which—"

She hung up on me. But when I drove out the next day to check, I was relieved to see she had the larger animals collared and tied to cinder blocks and the pups indoors. So far, so good. I slipped a note of thanks into her mailbox, and I mentioned that Aubuchon's Hardware was running a fall special on chain-link kennels.

Last night Ella McPhetres called. Sophie Latham and her cousin were walking by Madeline's on the way home from picking blackberries yesterday afternoon when all of a sudden the nursing bitch comes shooting off the porch and gets the girl in the calf. Four serious punctures. It was late, I'd had a few beers, and I was angry at myself for letting the Madeline Rand thing slide the way I had. "Listen to me, Ella," I shouted, "I am goddamn sick of this town's *dogs*. I'll tell you straight out, I have never owned a dog. I have never *liked* dogs—*any* dogs—and the dogs around here, Jesus Christ, you know, if they're not off running deer, they're chasing cars, and if they're not chasing cars, they're tearing into compost heaps or shitting in somebody's salad garden. Every last one of 'em is a nuisance or a menace. You don't need a constable in this town, you need a goddamn *dog* warden." She had the sense to remain silent. "Ella, here it is. I'll follow through with the damn rottweilers, but that's the end. When I'm all done with Madeline, I'm all done with canine control."

Ella was the one who'd talked me into the post in the first place, she and my brother, Spud. *Piece of cake* was how they described it. The town hadn't enjoyed the services of a constable since Clyde Greeley moved south five years ago. Nobody in the available pool was qualified, until I moved back. As an ex-cop, I was *perfect.* "Don't worry, it's nothing like when Reg had the job," Ella promised at the time. "These days, anything ugly comes up, the state police take care of it." Spud had agreed. "A little light peacekeeping, that's all it amounts to, Heck. Serving court documents, ticketing these idiots that dump tires in the lake. . . . This 'n' that." Never a mention of dogs.

MADELINE'S place wasn't far from my cabin, two miles down past Cobb's Corner and another mile up the Rake Factory Road. It was nothing more than a deer camp—oil-drum stove, no siding, no foundation, no plumbing—that had stood empty fifty weeks a year until the summer Madeline took refuge there. When she'd moved in with those two bony kids of hers, no one believed they'd last the winter, and here they were heading into their fourth. You had to admire them for that. Tough little unit, used to hardship and rustication.

The only vehicle in the dooryard was Jack Krauss's derelict Volkswagen Fox, set up on hardwood blocks. It was Jack's hunting camp. When I called around looking for him (Jack would be liable if Cad Latham decided to sue), his sister informed me that Jack was out in Wyoming hanging drywall. She said he'd been trying to get Madeline out of that shithole ever since his marriage fell apart two years ago, but the woman wouldn't budge. He'd even gone to court last fall to get her evicted, but those proceedings took friggin' forever, and anyhow now he was out West and you had to be in Vermont to pursue it in the legal system, never mind if the woman was flat-out robbing you month after month by not paying one single dime of rent.

Even before they could see me, the big dogs threw up a deafening clamor as I approached the porch. She had them confined around back of the place. There was nobody home, it seemed. Madeline had boxboard tacked to the window frames, so you couldn't see inside. On the porch was a rotting sofa, and sitting on that were a broken box of galvanized roofing nails and a couple of fifty-pound sacks of Purina Dog Chow. No firewood anywhere that I could see. Couple of five-gallon gas cans. I hoped she wasn't heating the place with one of those god-awful kerosene space heaters.

I found the mama dog behind the shack tied to a butternut tree by a length of half-inch plastic rope and chain. She was lunging right into the air at me and roaring her head off. The rest of them, six or seven, roiled around in a dusty snow-fence pen, roped to their cinder blocks. They made one hell of a racket. The way the lathered-up mama dog was heaving herself against that flimsy rope, I was afraid she might break loose and run off on me. Then I'd really have a situation. And little Sophie Latham would have to endure a rabies series.

You didn't want to spoil the head if you could help it. I sidled in as close as I could, my heart pounding. She was in such frenzy that I knew I wasn't going to get a clean shot. Point and squeeze was all you could do. I shut my eyes and fired.

The dog writhed around in the dust. Lung shot. I put another slug just behind the shoulder. And another. She shuddered and lay still, her teats steaming, blood spilling from her jaws. I closed my eyes again and sat there crouching in the dog stink, the gun dangling from my finger, sweating like crazy, feeling sick. The clamor was hysterical now around me.

Finally I straightened and stood up, disgusted with myself. What a turn I'd come to in my pitiable life. Executing dogs. A car was approaching, rumbling up the steep washboard. I pocketed the gun and wiped my blood-flecked knuckles on my pants. As the dog noise subsided some, I could hear crows grawking overhead. Butternut leaves spun down on a gust of wind.

I walked around front. An old Gremlin beater pounded up over the rise and pulled in beside my Powerwagon, with Kevin Hepplewhite's daughter Donna at the wheel—eyebrows plucked into perfect arches, white blade of a nose, bleached scrolls at her temples, pink Boca Raton T-shirt with shoulderpads. Was she already old enough to drive? She looked closer to twelve than sixteen.

Madeline and the boys were down in Connecticut for a few days visiting relatives, Donna said. She'd been feeding the dogs. I told her about the incident with the Latham girl, and we shook our heads, contemplating the spilled blackberries all around us in the road. Donna couldn't guess how that could have happened, unless the girls had been teasing her, which, knowing Sophie Latham, she wouldn't be surprised. During the day Queenie usually stayed right up on the porch with her pups.

"Untied?"

The girl nodded. "When she's feedin' 'em, sure." She was still looking down.

"I had to destroy the dog, Donna. I'm sorry."

"You what?" Her chin trembled. "You mean you *killed* Queenie?" She began to cry.

"It's not your fault, Donna. "

"But she— It was the *pups* is all it was. She was just trying to protect her *pups*."

"I'm sorry, Donna. Once an animal bites somebody, the animal has to be tested, and that's it. Look, I'll break it to Madeline, OK?"

After she'd calmed down enough to feed the other dogs and drive back down the hill, I got the dead dog into a GLAD bag and drove it down to the Small Animal Clinic in Allenburg. I took the long way through the wooded hills, hoping the beauty of the season might offer a little solace.

I was tilling in cornstalks when Rita, the woman from the clinic, called. "The rottweiler tested negative for rabies" was all the message she left. After the first twinge of guilt, I reminded myself the dog was a biter. And the Lathams would be greatly relieved, which was the main thing. Just the same, Madeline would probably sue me and the town for abuse of office, destruction of property, and bringing needless misery into her children's hearts. Not that she'd get far, but it would be front-page controversy in this neck of the woods. I was trying to stay out of the papers, above all, so I decided to call Otto Morganthau and have him write up a supporting complaint based on the bike-chasing incident.

As the phone rang, I stood in my front doorway looking out toward their house. They'd built a really magnificent glass A-frame high in what used to be my dad's sugar orchard. You couldn't see the place from here until the leaves were down, but from the south end of the garden if you looked up the view cut, you could see its shining facade in the yellow-orange maples.

It kept ringing. They were probably outside.

I was about to press OFF when someone answered.

I returned the phone to my ear. "Otto?"

"Who is this?" the voice croaked.

"Hector Bellevance. Is Otto there, please?"

"Heck! Jesus God, Heck! It's me! Spud!"

"Spud?" What did I do, dial the farm? "Sorry, Spud—I was trying to reach the Morganthaus."

"Hector," he whispered, "they're *dead.*"

"Who?"

"The Morganthaus! Somebody *killed* them!"

"What do you mean? How do you know?"

"I'm here! I'm at their place. Somebody *shot* them, Hector. Jesus Christ Almighty! They're *dead.*"

"Don't touch a thing. Understand? I'll be up in two seconds."

2

The Morganthaus' red Audi was the only vehicle at the end of their long drive when I pulled in. By the drift of leaves across the wipers, it hadn't been moved for days. Spud must have walked down. I slid out of my pickup and studied the ground and the curving path that led to the glass house. The small back deck lay in a sea of hostas and ferns. As I paused to steel myself for the scene below (it had been a long time), two jets tore along above me, side by side, trailing bright bands of vapor.

I crossed down through a bed of ankle-deep myrtle, along Gaea's winding fieldstone path to the kitchen door, a sliding panel in a wood frame. It was open a foot or so. I peered in. The stench hit me like a slap. I turned fast and walked away until I caught the deck rail with the heels of my hands. They were with me again, the Jamaican whore, her face pulled apart by pliers and her arms flayed, the smashed boy whose dad was some Mafia chief. They made him watch them beat the kid to pieces with crowbars before they shot him. The others, too, the Dumpster babies and the floaters. None of them would ever leave me, I had accepted that.

I tucked my nose into the crook of my arm and slipped into the kitchen.

I'd first been here about a year ago. I came up to introduce myself after I'd moved into my mother's cabin. It was a pleasant visit. I liked Otto. He was relaxed, cordial, wry, interested in my plans for the land, the truck farm. We chatted about my mother, and windsurfing, and the growing moose population. Gaea, more reserved, brought us beer, cold shrimp, ham with sharp mustard, and chunks of dark bread, out on the front deck. She joined the conversation just briefly, making a wistful comment about the years they'd spent living on the water. I thought she seemed wary of me, though later I chalked that up to her uncertainty with English. She and Otto conversed exclusively in French. Gaea was born in the Middle East—Lebanon, if I remembered—raised in Greece, schooled in Switzerland. What stood out most about the visit was this woman's poise and beauty, her naturally graceful manner. I found myself feeling jealous of how settled they seemed as a couple. It got to me, the private looks they traded, the French phrases I only half-understood. After I went home that day, I decided to keep my distance from those two, for my own good. But as it happened, over the next several months they made no effort to socialize. We'd wave and smile when we passed in the road, and once or twice this summer we exchanged pleasantries at the beach. But they proved to be quite a private couple all in all. I couldn't recall their ever having company up here.

The pine trestle table was set for two—with silver, cloth napkins, long-stemmed goblets, an open bottle of Chianti. The room was too hot, and I saw why. The electric oven was on, and its door was broken open. Gaea had gone over backward across it when she got hit.

She lay faceup. Shot multiple times from the throat down through the torso. Machine pistol. Her face was covered with blowfly maggots. Flies swarmed everywhere, over her and upon something in a loaf pan on the counter, the supper she'd been about to bake. Casings lay under the table along the mopboard. I stooped over and picked one up. Nine-mil.

Foreign manufacture. Probably jacketed, military stuff. The wall behind her had taken a dozen slugs. Guy just walked in and started blasting. I leaned in over her to turn the oven off.

She had been the fittest woman I'd ever laid eyes on—smooth muscles, tight, honey-colored skin with no fat under it anywhere. Head of wonderful, twisty golden hair. The hair was all that was left. She was bloated and gray, in a leathery mat of her own blood. She had a white fleece bathrobe bunched up under her hips. Arms outflung. Legs akimbo like a frog's. Golden crotch spread open.

The scene was days old. Close to a week, by the insect action and the lividity. Execution, if I had to guess. The killer, no doubt, was far away.

"Spud?" I called out.

Nothing.

Otto was in the open area between the living room and the dining space on a rumpled, blood-soaked kilim, butt in the air, arms flopped out in front of him like a Muslim. Back of his head was shot away, brains sprayed down his lean, brown back. More flies at work.

He'd been coming this way. From the couch. I could see his reading glasses on the floor near the fireplace, where he'd flung them. Charge the shooter was about all you could do if you were going to do anything. That was Otto, a doer to the end.

First few rounds caught him in the gut, sent him glancing off the arm of an upholstered chair. He was moving, though. Took the last burst in the face to stop him. Another dozen or so casings glinted on the oak floor. He had on khaki hiking shorts, no belt, no shirt. Underneath his doubled legs his bare feet curled toward each other like a baby's.

"Spud?"

The stairs were two-inch-thick planks cantilevered out of a single rough-hewn beam. I went up. The bedroom, at least twice the size of my living room, was awash in the shifting light of the sugarwoods. All the way to the peak of the house the roof was a checkerwork of skylights framed in bleached wood.

Spud had his face buried in the Morganthaus' king-size mattress.

"Christ, man. What the hell are you doing?"

He lifted his dark head, but didn't look at me. At twenty-eight, he was eleven years my junior, less sharp-faced now than he used to be as a boy, but still with the angular cleft chin, clear forehead, and broad shoulders he was given by his father, Felice LaClair. Felice had been a handsome kid my mother fell hard for in her senior year of high school. He was shipped to the Korean peninsula as a mechanic the summer after graduation, and while he was overseas, Agnes, pressed by her parents, finally accepted courtly, steady Reg Belle-vance, scion of Montcalm County's original settlers. Felice returned, heartbroken, as my mother would tell it, and married Ella Caswell. He left her ten years later for my mother when Reg died, even though she'd vowed never to remarry.

I pulled him up. "Come on. Let's get out of this place."

"They said for me to stay put."

"Who said?"

"I called the troopers."

"Well, hell, you don't have to stay *here*. Those guys don't want to process this scene with you in the middle of it."

He followed me out onto the deck. We sat in damp canvas butterfly chairs, both of us silent for a while, breathing in the clean air. The pond down in the hollow between my cabin and the Morganthau property held the last light of the after-noon. Extending above the ragged fir stand south of the vil-lage, the Baptist church spire was rosy, and beyond that a stretch of Arrow Lake gleamed like a steel blade under the cliffs of Mount Joseph. There was a lot of bird activity—

crows, nuthatches, goldfinches, tree sparrows, doves, jays—
otherwise it was still.

"How could this happen here?" Spud said.

"This can happen anywhere, believe me."

"It makes no *sense*. Why would somebody want to kill
them?"

After a moment I said, "Did they ever give any intimation
that they might have been trying to hide from something?"

He sagged as he turned this over. "No. Who knows? They
didn't seem to be too worried about anything."

The summer that the Morganthaus built this place my
mother wrote me about it. She said it seemed strange, with
all the spots they had to choose from, that they hadn't picked
one with a view. Then, the following spring, Otto had a
twenty-acre swath of my dad's prime sugar orchard clear-cut
from the deck here all the way down to the pond. The view
he gained was narrow, but it was high and long—out across
the softwoods skirting the village and up the length of the
lake to a flat blue slice of French Canada in the notch
between the north slope of Mount Joe and the wooded hills
surrounding Iceville, in Quebec. To Agnes the cut was hide-
ous. It was incomprehensible, as if some lunatic barber had
run his clippers down the middle of her son's head.

"What brought you down here, Spud?"

"See, Otto—" He cleared his throat. "Otto was building
this sauna. You know, up on the quartz ledge. And I was curious to see how he was coming with it. Last weekend I helped
him carry the materials up there, the Sakrete and all, but
when I came back, it was still sitting there just where we left
it. Well, that didn't seem right. So I thought I'd come on
down to the house, see if he was sick . . ." He paused and
dropped his voice low. "When I looked in and I saw her laying there the way she was, all shot to hell, the first thing that
jumped into my head was *Otto*."

"That's understandable. They fight? Do you know?"

He shrugged. "Who doesn't?"

I sighed. "Well, looks like some kind of payback to me."

"Payback? For what?"

I shook my head. I didn't know the Morganthaus. I'd heard some scant talk of them, mostly from Agnes and Spud. They were from Montreal by way of Fort Lauderdale, where they kept their sailing yacht. "Spud, why'd you go up into their bedroom?"

"The phone was ringing. And I didn't want to go back in the kitchen."

"When I called, you mean?"

He nodded. "How long's this gonna take, Heck?"

"How long is what gonna take?"

"It's just . . . I have *cows* to milk."

We caught the rush of tires on the gravel road below. Down the view cut we saw two state police cruisers flicker past the roadside popples beyond the pond.

"You go on up to the farm, Spud. I'll deal with the troopers."

He looked relieved. "You sure?"

"Yeah, go on. They'll be up a little later—you can count on that."

"OK. Thanks." He hopped off the deck and loped away through Gaea's myrtle, disappearing in the trees like a deer.

The cruisers roared in underneath the maples. Car doors thunked. Shoes cracked across the deck.

"Hotchkiss!" a deep voice barked. "What'd I tell you? Go back out there to the road and seal off the damn driveway!"

"Can't I get a peek first?"

"No! No peeks. Go do what I fucking asked you to do. I don't want any more vehicles in here. That means Cahoon, that means the ME, I don't care who, they *walk* in. Also, everybody stays out of the driveway and off the footpath. You see something on the ground, I don't care what it is, do not pick it up. Photograph it and flag it. Got that?"

The sliding door banged against the stop. "Ding-dong. A-vonnnn!"

Somebody made a loopy whistle. "Pew-*eee*!"

These guys were already out of their depth. The Vermont State Police was a small force. Competent and dedicated, for the most part, but spread thin. And there were no seasoned homicide people, few specialists of any kind, really. Of course, they didn't see many homicides to begin with, and the ones they did see were hot-blooded all-in-the-family, by and large.

"All right, all right, all right. Stand back now. Anybody want to vomit, take it outside, got that? OK? OK, first off, to repeat myself, nobody touches anything. Is that understood? We got one chance to do this the right way." An Instamatic whirred. "Ainsley, wait. You keeping a photographic log?"

"Yes, sir."

"Thank you. Now, everybody, if you move, watch where you set your brogans. Walk slow and careful."

A steel measuring tape clacked on the tiles.

"Damn, Sergeant, but this is *bad*."

"Breathe through your mouth, buddy, that's all."

"Quite the beaver, hey, Ed?" someone said.

"What's wrong with you, Gooms," another cop said, "you never seen a natural bush before?"

"Hey, hey, lookee here, boys. Anybody hungry?"

"Put that thing down!" the sergeant yelled. "Christ Almighty! What'd I just fucking *say*? Don't they teach you bozos *anything* anymore?" He blew into the air. I could feel the tension where I stood in the next room. "All right. All right." He paused. "Listen to me. From now on everything's for the record. Stay focused on what you're here for. Everybody got it? Good. OK. Now, here on the kitchen floor of the Morganthau household we have one female, age thirty-five to forty-five, about five-five, hundred ten or so pounds, blond hair, dark complexion . . . What is she? Jewish? Darryl? Any idea?"

A minute later a trooper came around the half-wall between the kitchen and the dining area and stopped short at the spectacle of poor Otto. He was trim and slight, early twenties, with a fussed-over head of smooth, sandy hair. I was standing in the doorway facing him, larger than life, but the trooper was fixed on the body and thought he was alone in the room. I watched him as he worked his black investigation gloves tighter on his fingers. "Yo!" he croaked finally. "Sergeant Evans? I got the husband out here!" He fingered a small notebook out of his shirt pocket.

I spoke up. "Excuse me there, Officer."

He jumped.

"Easy now, easy does it," I said, showing my palms.

He had his hand on the butt of his auto. "Don't move. Who are you?"

"I'm Hector Bellevance. I'm a neighbor. Brother of Preston LaClair, who called this in a short while ago."

"OK, so that would be your Dodge truck parked up above then, sir?"

"Yes, it would."

He called out, "Sergeant? I also got a neighbor in here. It's his pickup out back."

The sergeant came around the pass-through and stopped to grimace at Otto, hands on his hips. He sighed. "What do you think, Darryl? Look at that. You think they *arranged* him in that back-asswards position?"

"I would tend to doubt it," the trooper said seriously.

"Sergeant Edmund Evans," he said, coming toward me. "Acting commander, Troop B Barracks." He was a burly man, thick arms and shoulders, a good-sized gut, graying hair cut close, early forties, with small, shrewd hazel eyes turned up at the corners. Knobby nose. Big, square, clean-shaven jaw. White cotton shirt open at the collar, no necktie, corduroy field jacket, black-and-silver running shoes.

"Hector Bellevance," I said. "The log cabin you passed down opposite the beaver pond, that's me."

"OK. So, you know these people?"

"Not very well, no."

"What are you doing here, Mr. Bellevance?"

I let him know that I was the new constable in town and then went on to explain about Madeline Rand's rottweilers and the incident with the Morganthaus so he'd understand why I'd been calling the house. "I was trying to reach Otto, and my brother, Spud, answered their phone. He farms the place up at the end of the road, and he'd come down to look in on them. He was a friend of theirs. When he got here, he found them dead, so he called the police."

Spud had known the Morganthaus since Agnes sold Otto a forty-acre piece of Reg's maple stand about eight years ago. Actually, it might have been Otto who kept the forty acres and sold *her* the rest of the farm. The particulars were never quite clear to me. But somehow, with Otto's cash greasing the exchange, Agnes and Spud managed to reacquire the family farm from a local realtor, Gavin Ingalls, who had picked it up at auction not long after Reg died. Ingalls had been letting the place out on tough terms for years until Agnes (or Otto) talked him into letting it go. Anyway, the deal benefited all parties. Spud and Agnes got the family farm back at a good price, and Otto got the use of the land without the burdens of owning and maintaining it.

"So you're saying you called here and your brother picked up the phone."

"That's right."

"What was he doing here?"

"He was looking in on them, as I said. They were friends."

"OK. So where's he at right now—your brother?"

"His place. He had chores that couldn't wait. I told him you'd be along."

He sucked his cheek, appraising me. "OK. Seeing as how Spud's run off on us, can we talk to you for a few minutes?"

"Absolutely."

"Ainsley!" he called. "Exactly the same deal with this one out here when you're done in the kitchen. Munsinger," he said to the poofy-haired one, "listen. I'm counting on you. Don't let Goomer screw this up. We're doing nothing but taking notes and pictures till the Crime Lab gets here. Got it?"

"Yes, sir," said Munsinger, "I got it."

We walked out around the A-frame and shuffled up to the parking area, the myrtle vines grabbing at our feet. His breath whistled in his nostrils as we trudged. He was out of shape and tired and feeling sorely beleaguered. He smelled stale in that rump-sprung jacket. I felt a sudden welling of relief to be living the life I was, and no other. That was progress.

All at once he stopped. "Hold it one second. Here I am walking you up to your vehicle, and I just realized I can't let you have your vehicle. It's part of a secured crime scene—sorry."

I told him I understood.

"Keys in it?"

I shook my head and handed them to him. "Don't be long with it, all right? I'll need that truck early in the morning."

"Shouldn't be a problem. I'll try and have one of our people drop it off tonight," he said, distracted. He looked back toward the house. Trooper Ainsley was cackling in there. He rattled his head and turned to me. "Mr. and Mrs. Morganthau have any relatives nearby, that you know of?"

"Otto had a brother in Montreal," I said. "Gaea's people are over in Europe, I believe."

"Gaea?"

I nodded toward the house. "Otto's wife. She spelled it G-A-E-A."

"Gay-uh," he said, trying it out. "OK. What else can you tell me about them? Just off the top of your head."

It was a lazy question for an investigator, but the guy was beat, so I opened up for him and recounted what little I knew. Spud once told me that Otto and his older brother had been in business together in Quebec. Manufacturing. They made plastic shipping containers. Until sometime in the eighties, at least, when Otto left the business to start a new life. He left everything, as Spud told it—his Georgian, red-brick house in Westmount, his wife and two young children, his lifelong partnership with his brother—kicked it over for the love of a beautiful woman and the dream of paradise in the Caribbean. When the dream wore thin, as it was bound to, he and Gaea retreated to Tipton, where Otto built the big, glass A-frame.

"Where's the ex?" Evans had taken a small notebook from his breast pocket.

"Toronto, I think. Remarried. Kids are grown."

His pager started beeping. He snatched at it. "Waterbury," he said. Vermont State Police Headquarters. "I better get on the radio. Listen, you be home tomorrow?"

I did about half my weekly business at the farmers' market on the Allenburg green on Saturday mornings. The foliage crowd would have it packed tomorrow, too. "Show up at my place bright and early," I said. "I can give you half an hour."

"Seven too early?"

"Seven's good."

"You don't mind walking home?"

"Not at all, Sergeant. It's a fine evening."

He squinted alertly up into the blue, as if the considera-tion had just occurred to him. I knew what that was like.

The next morning was muggy and still, warm for late September in the north country. The radio was promising rain later, then a day or two of sun, and then a bad blow—a tropical storm off Bermuda was veering to the north. I was lying in bed after a restless sleep when, for a bleak moment, I felt I was back in Truro in the shingled bungalow, alone in our four-poster, grieving. I could almost inhale the stink of summer traffic filtering through the curtains on the ocean air.

I'd been sleeping well since I'd left the Cape, thanks to the quiet and the cushion of time, and I hadn't been dwelling at all on my dreams. Each morning, as soon as I opened my eyes, I was propelling myself up and into the day. Today I couldn't move. The crushing sadness held me like a blanket of chains. This hadn't happened in a long while. It was in July a year ago that she'd just walked out on me, the front door thrown open into the trellis, the cars passing on the busy street beyond, the carbon monoxide wafting in. That's what had triggered my state of mind. The cars, the smell and clamor of traffic on the dead-end road below the cabin. Mornings up here were quiet. Normally I'd notice maybe two vehicles down on the road—the Agri-Mark milk truck and Brenda LaClair's Subaru wagon—and that would be it.

In good weather I carried my breakfast to the picnic table next to the upper garden, so I could eat watching the birds at the feeders. My favorites were a pair of red-breasted nut-hatches. Over the course of the summer, they and most of the chickadees had learned to flutter in and take a wheat kernel or a dried raspberry from my cereal spoon. Today, even the chickadees were scarce, spooked by the commotion below on the road and back in the woods. While I ate, the State Bureau of Criminal Investigation's Mobile Crime Lab passed by with a two-cruiser escort, then State's Attorney Nezzie Holmes in a white Olds, and a little later the WCAX-TV news team's bristling Aerostar, then Medical Examiner Marty Griswold's long gray van. In between all the while there was a procession of curious locals in cars and trucks.

By the time Evans phoned, it was going on eight o'clock. He'd been up at the A-frame half the night, he said. Then he was handling paper until three. Now all of a sudden he finds out the forensics team is in a yank to fume the house, and he still has things he wants to get sorted and boxed and out of there before they seal the place up. Can I wait a while longer?

"Sergeant, I want to thank you for getting my truck back to me. Right now I've got it loaded with fresh produce that I'm not gonna move if I don't make tracks pretty quick. Market folds up at one."

"I know, I know, but don't run off on me, Bellevance. I need you, OK? You know how it is. Half an hour? Please?"

"Hey, tell the techs they can fume the place tomorrow. The perp's a thousand miles from here by now."

"That's Cahoon's call. He loves all this hocus-pocus."

A fume job called up latent prints. Evidence techs would fill a bunch of petri dishes with Super Glue and set them out all over the house, then tape the place up. Two days later, you went back in and found a mosiac of prints everywhere, all in white, like apple blossoms after a storm. The evaporating esters in the glue would adhere to the fingertip residues. Evans was right. It was magic.

"Makes sense, I guess," I said. "But what's the rush?"

"I know, I know. It's overkill, you ask me. Shit, somebody's got to *trace* all those individuals."

"Well, that's fine, that's the job. But I'm saying there's time. You don't want to let these lab techs muscle you off the scene."

"You know this guy?"

"Cahoon? No. I saw him on television a while back. From what I heard, the state's lucky to have landed him." Brian Cahoon was the VSP's new BCI chief. He'd started out as a trooper over in Addison County, later made FBI, and moved to Jersey and then D.C. An FBI Academy grad, he'd ended his career teaching forensic science in Quantico. He hadn't been retired to his family's place on Lake Bomoseen for long before Carl Nichols, commander of the force, pressed him back into public service to run the revamped Bureau of Criminal Investigation at state police headquarters in Waterbury. Nice coup. The state was starved for talent down there.

I occupied myself with some light hand-weeding in the blueberry plantation, trying to keep myself presentable for market day. Toward eleven, I was just about to jot the sergeant a note with my regrets when I heard a car pull into the turnout at the foot of my hill. I went to look. It wasn't Evans. Dingy white Mazda 626.

Woman with copper hair popped out on the driver's side. I recognized her. She was the slight, energetic redhead who'd caught my eye more than once in town over the past few months—at the post office, the Grand Union, the health club, the arts center. I had no idea who she was. She definitely had an arresting air about her, though. More an aura than an air. A charge. It got to you. She was pretty—quite pretty, with a freckled, oval face and keen, clear, blue eyes. Yet there was a jangly, self-preoccupied buzz to her that gave me pause. Static electricity.

I watched her as she bounded straight up the bank, swatting the milkweed out of her way with a canvas carryall. She was wearing a green cowboy shirt with snaps, a denim skirt, and black sandals. She didn't shave her legs, I noticed, when she got close.

"Mr. Bellevance?"

I nodded.

"Wilma Strong-Parkhurst. Of the *Eagle*." She had a firm hand. "This a good time?"

The dense, crinkly hair, those forthright blue eyes, the wealth of freckles, the even teeth in that wide mouth—none of this squared with the image I had of the reporter whose byline I'd been seeing in every issue of our local daily. School board wrangles, hailstorms, bankruptcies, arts events—Wilma Strong-Parkhurst was one busy scribe. I had her pictured as a doughy blonde. In overalls. With rimless glasses. It was the *Wilma*. But also the *Parkhurst*. I knew Vic Parkhurst from high school. He was 4-H, ran track. Gangly, soft-spoken, shy as a field mouse. County forester these days, avid fly fisherman.

"So you're Wilma Strong-Parkhurst."

She squinted. "Surprised?"

"Never would have put you and Vic together, that's all."

She laughed. "Where were you when I needed you?"

Glib to boot. I led her across the lawn to the picnic table.

"I just want to ask you a few questions." She sat down and flipped open a stenographer's notebook. "Police dispatcher tells me it was your brother, Preston, who reported the murders, but you were the one at the scene when the cops got there. Is this true?"

"Spud's my half brother."

"Right, but you were the one who was there when the cops arrived?"

I nodded.

"You're Tipton Town Constable, aren't you?"

"Afraid so."

"You used to run a little seafood restaurant down on the Cape. Popular spot, by all accounts."

She'd been backgrounding me. Naomi's, the place was called, and my wife had run it, not me. All I did was bus the occasional table and ride herd on the wait staff. I liked that job, though. For as long as it lasted.

"You were married to the owner, Naomi Herter. Of the Wellfleet Herters. And before that you were a cop in Beantown. First you worked Harvard Security, then you went with the city, Dorchester District. Six years later you made detective."

"You're a whiz, all right. Where'd you dig this up?"

"I wrote your mom's obit last fall. Maybe you read it."

I hadn't.

"Wonderful woman, Agnes. Much beloved. I bet half of Montcalm County attended her memorial service."

"I know," I said. "I was there."

She blushed. "Right, of course. Your eulogy was just about the most moving thing I ever heard."

I nodded. It was slides. Photos I had collected of Agnes Oliver Bellevance, age three to sixty-three. With my remarks. Agnes had taught first grade at the Tipton village school for forty-one years, right up until the day last June when she fell over in her garden, dead of an aneurysm. Ella found her the next morning. It was the way she would have wanted to go, certainly. Only not so young. She was just sixty-five and a vigorous, engaged, thoroughly wise woman.

"Anyway, I was writing that piece, and I came across a little file on you in the *Eagle* morgue."

"And you were entertained."

"I was, actually. Not too many Harvard grads end up as cops."

"What's all this got to do with the Morganthaus?"

"Nothing. Except as a former street cop and homicide detective, I was hoping you would have some insights into what happened out here."

I shook my head. The allure of the woman was fading. She reminded me of how much I disliked the press, with its blithe sense of privilege and expectation.

She chewed on her Bic. "Town clerk told me Morganthau was a retired industrialist from Montreal. You know what industry?"

"Plastics, I believe."

"How about the wife?" She flipped back a few pages. "What's her story?"

I shrugged. "All I know is she was born in Lebanon, and her family emigrated to Greece when she was little."

"Clerk says she was unusual looking."

"Gaea was a knockout, although not in the conventional sense."

The reporter looked up. "What do you mean?"

"She was completely careless about her looks. No makeup, no hairdo, you know. She was a jock. An athlete."

"OK, I get it," she said, writing. "Anything else you can offer? About either one of them?"

"I didn't know them very well."

"But your brother did. He told the police he was dropping in on them when he found the bodies."

"Spud was a friend of theirs. He'd known them for a number of years."

She closed her notebook. "I met Spud one time at a Co-op meeting. Doesn't look like you at all."

"His father was actually Ella McPhetres' ex-husband, Felice LaClair. He and Agnes were together for a number of years."

"McPhetres told me. She says your brother inherited his dad's roving eye."

"Well, I don't know about that. He and his wife just had a baby boy in April, and he's milking sixty head by himself. I don't think he does too much roving anymore."

"Hope not. They're looking at him, you realize," she said mildly, her eyes narrowing.

"Who told you that?" I asked after a moment. But, hell, of course they were looking at him. It was a measure of how long I'd been out of the business that it hadn't struck me first thing. Three years, that was all. You could lose plenty in three years.

She shrugged. "They've got to start somewhere, don't they?"

I watched from the knoll as she hurried down my mother's zigzag path, as light on her feet as a doe. She got in and cranked the Mazda. The fan belt shrieked.

As she took the turn at the bridge, it looked for a second as if she were going to sideswipe Evans's unmarked Chevy coming down the other way. I winced. He swerved toward the ditch. They cleared by inches.

A minute later Evans was plodding up the hill. At the top he stopped to catch his breath. "Christ, Bellevance, I sure would hate to have to climb up here in the wintertime with all my groceries and snow clear up to my ass."

"You'd get used to it," I said. Agnes used to keep the path packed out with snowshoes. "Looked like that little Mazda almost ran you off the road down there."

He gave a snort and glanced behind him toward the bridge. "You caught that? That's just wacky Wilma. Writes a buncha crap for the *Eagle*. Likes to test your mettle, if you know what I'm saying." He was looking around. "Some spot you got here. Those all blueberries?" He was surveying my mom's plantation, a thousand bronzy red bushes about four feet high, stretching away in long rows toward the softwoods.

"My mother put them in a few years ago, all by herself,

when she was sixty-one. Be another four or five years before they're commercially viable."

"That long, hunh? Real sharp-looking little plants, though." He clicked on his tape recorder. "Hector Bellevance's place in Tipton. It's eleven-twenty, September twenty-fifth." He looked up again. His eyes were pink with fatigue. He gazed out toward the gaudy hills, pondering how to begin. "Man," he breathed, "I always wonder what makes 'em all turn different colors like that."

"It's the failing light," I said.

"The what?"

"It's chemistry. When the sunlight diminishes, it stops stimulating chlorophyll and the green fades out, so then the leaves can show their true colors."

"No shit. Is that right?"

I offered him a plate of vanilla wafers.

He averted his eyes. "Don't tempt me. Doc says I gotta drop fifty. Kinda life I lead, you know, it just defeats the purpose—eating out of a fucking bag every day. Can't cut back that way."

"I know what you mean."

"Yeah, you were a cop once. Wilma was telling me. Big-time—made BPD Homicide, right? Then they busted you back to civilian due to a tragic incident of negligence."

I paused. "I'm not sure where you're getting that. The investigation cleared me of any negligence. I quit for personal reasons."

"The way I heard it, you killed your partner. This true?"

I studied him for a moment. He was working me, the son of a bitch. Stu Harper had been thirty years old—on the squad just four months. He'd come over to us out of Drug Enforcement after Lew Tibbits had his triple bypass. He was a sturdy, intuitive cop. A natural. Harper was ahead of me in a narrow, open stairwell. We were chasing an armed import agent toward the roof of a shipyard garage, where he would kill himself a minute later in a fall down an air shaft. My gun discharged, and the slug glanced off the banister and tore into Harper's neck. He bled to death there at my feet, leaving a wife and two kids. I assigned them my pension. Whatever else it's my fate to suffer in the years I have left, I've already been to the bottom. Which is about all you could say for it.

"I thought you wanted my help, Sergeant. Instead, here you are dicking with my head. You trying to intimidate me, is that it?"

"Nah," he said with a crinkly smile. "Never mind. Sorry I brought it up. Anyway, shit happens. So, Mr. Bellevance, yesterday when you were up at the Morganthaus' A-frame, did you by any chance search through the deceased couple's belongings?"

"Did I what?"

"You heard me."

He was just crude, the type of hardhead cop that liked to shove your face in the mess first thing, see what he could jolt out of you. Spud would have had a rough time with him the night before. Brenda, too. The last thing they needed was an investigator with a sadistic streak. "I turned the oven off," I said. "That's all."

"So as far as going through their drawers and closets and whatnot—you didn't get into anything like that."

"No. But someone did, I gather."

He nodded. "Hard to say whether they took anything. Wristwatches, jewelry, stereo, bunch of expensive camera equipment and so on—that's still there." He yawned. "What about your brother?"

"What about him?"

"Same question. There was quite a gap of time between when he went in the house and when you caught him on the phone. Ten minutes, maybe an hour. He's fuzzy on that."

"Sure he is. He was in shock. Still is, I'll bet."

"You think he mighta rummaged around in there?"

"No, I don't."

"OK. Fume job'll help us there, maybe. I hope." Evans adjusted his butt on the bench. "So Cahoon's people are putting the time of death in a window from Friday afternoon, the seventeenth, to sometime Sunday evening. Maybe you could help us narrow that down some. Do you recall any gunshots last weekend? Like from an automatic?"

"I'm afraid I don't."

"Any strange cars going by?"

"No. Friday I was in the garden all day, and you can't see the road from down there. Saturday's market day. I was in town. Didn't get home till after seven."

"Sunday what did you do?"

"Sunday it rained most of the day. I read the *Globe,* stacked some firewood. Nothing momentous."

"When was the last time you saw or spoke to the Morganthaus? Either one of them?"

"I've been trying to recall. Several days, I'm sure. You know, you get an entomologist on those blowfly maggots, and you ought to be able to narrow the range down to a few hours."

"Yeah, thanks. How'd those people get along—as a couple? You have any sense of that?"

"Not really. They seemed happy enough."

"Morganthau ever mention any personal difficulties, conflicts, fears, as far as you can recall?"

"Not to me. He walked out on his wife and kids, but you know about that."

Evans nodded and glanced at his notebook. "Besides this Rand woman with the dogs, were there any other locals that had a problem with Morganthau?"

"You don't think this was local, do you?"

He only looked at me, waiting.

"One comes to mind. Wayne Hrushka. But that was several years ago."

"OK. What was that about?"

"Morganthau hired Hrushka's outfit to pour the foundation when he built that place, and they screwed it up somehow. South side was over an inch off-level. Otto was pretty angry."

"He withhold payment, anything of that nature?"

"I wouldn't know."

Evans grunted. "What about your brother—they get along all right, him and Morganthau?"

"Sure. Spud looked after the place while they were away—watered their plants, plowed their driveway, that kind of thing."

"What about Morganthau's brother—Yves?"

"Never met him. I understand they were business partners at one time, but they had a falling-out."

"OK. You ever meet his kids? Robert and Sylvia?"

I shook my head.

Evans sighed. "We located a will in his file cabinet. Dates back to before he got married to Gaea. Notarized in Dade County, Florida. According to this document, Morganthau left everything to her—Gaea. If it stands up, the estate will revert to his kids."

"You talk to them?"

"Not yet. The thing's got to go through probate—you know. The brother is executor. But here's what's weird. We looked everywhere, and so far the estate comes to nothing but the house and their old boat. No cash, no art, no annuities, no bonds, no life insurance, no safe-deposit keys . . . zilch. I mean, neither one of them's working, and all they got in the bank's about ten grand. You know where their money might be?"

"Sorry. I'd have some people go through the yacht."

"We already have. Broward County sheriff located the boat in a drydock yard north of Miami. Nothing on board but boat supplies. Gotta be somewhere. Seriously, Bellevance. What do you think?"

"It'll turn up. How'd his brother take the news?"

"See, that was weird, too. He was real low-key, like he just woke up or something.'" Evans shook his head. "Guy lives two hours away and he's never been down here—you believe that? I had to give him directions."

"He and Otto were estranged."

"So you said, yeah. What was that about?"

"The story is, Otto met Gaea at the Winter Olympics in Japan, and they fell crazy in love. A month later he gave up everything so he could be with her—house, family, everything. Including the business."

Evans yawned again and rattled his head. With his finger he began squashing the small syrup-colored ants on the oilcloth, one after another. "Speaking of love, Constable, you got a girlfriend?"

"Why?"

"Just curious. Tall, handsome fella like yourself, living all by yourself way to hell and gone out here . . . I figure you gotta be gettin' some somewhere."

"Where're you going with this, Sergeant?"

He put his palms up. "Hey, no offense. Take me. I was supposed to get married this summer. Girl I was engaged to was working up to the Roostertail. Gwendolyn Novagroski? Maybe you met her up there. Little brunette, great shape on her. Sweet girl, too. Anyway, the invitations were at the printer's, her parents approved of me in spite of the age difference and all that BS, and we're going along, looking at houses and refrigerators and whatnot, and then, *biff bam,* she blows me off for some snowboarder. Back in March this was. Girl calls me on the phone, and it's all boo-hoo-hoo, how she can't go through with it, she's not ready, and not a thing about this fucking snowboarder. So then the next day her mother calls me to say her and this guy took off for Steamboat Springs. What a kick in the ass. And guess who's stuck with the printer's bill?"

"That's too bad."

He puffed the air. "I was at Khe Sanh. You know what I'm saying? I don't sweat the small stuff. OK, so this brings me to my point. Ever since Gwendolyn blew me off, I been a regular poon hound. I mean, I can't stop *thinking* about it." He palmed his crotch and shook it. "I don't know if you ever been out to Quimby's Quiver Club . . ."

"Not lately."

"But so you know that place is a pussy palace. Some of the babes he's got up in there . . . Seriously, where does he *find* 'em? There's this new one he brought in this last spring. Name's Cheryl. Unbe*liev*able. Girl's got these road-cone tits. You should check her out, Bellevance. I wouldn't kid you."

"I'm sure."

"Which brings me back to your brother."

"Finally."

He smiled. "No, what I'm getting at is just . . . we have similar interests, your brother and me. I seen him in there a couple of occasions."

"So?"

"Here's the connection. Early this morning I stopped and talked to your neighbor with the dogs, Madeline Rand."

"She's back?"

"She's back, and she's ripped at you, Bellevance. You didn't tell me you destroyed the mama rottweiler."

"Couldn't be helped."

"Well, you're the constable. But you got this broad out to skin you."

"I've been skinned before."

"Right. Anyway, she told me this disturbing little story. According to her, your brother had a thing for Morganthau's wife."

"What kind of thing?"

"Obsession-type thing. You know what I'm saying."

This had to be coming from more than Madeline. Who else? Brenda? I looked at him. "What is this shit, Sergeant? Madeline Rand doesn't even *know* Spud."

"So this the first you heard of it?"

"Heard of what?"

"Your brother and Mrs. Morganthau."

"You—" I stopped myself. "Why don't you just tell me what the woman said?"

"Well, it seems one of her boys was in the woods above your place late one afternoon last spring—bird-hunting, I guess he was—and this kid happened to see your brother peeping on Mrs. Morganthau in her glass-walled bedroom. While Mrs. Morganthau was totally naked."

"Great. You talk to the kid? Or just Madeline?"

"Her and the kid both. Billy. He swears it was Preston."

"Sergeant . . . all you have to do is talk with them to realize those two boys of hers are a couple of half-wits." The noon horn blared ten miles down the valley at Allenburg Tap and Die. I waited while it died off. "They'll say anything she wants them to say. And as you pointed out, the woman's out to skin me."

"You suggesting she's making this up?"

"Or the kid is. Anyway, you're barking up the wrong tree. Spud's not the guy you're after, not a chance in a thousand."

"First trees first, buddy—you know how it goes. I think the sex thing is key here." He stood and stretched. "Tell me this. Your brother have his tubes snipped, that you know of?"

"His tubes?"

"Vasectomy—you know what I'm saying."

I shook my head. "You found semen."

"Bingo."

"Where?"

"In her. On the bathrobe."

"You type it yet?"

"Tried. Guy was a nonsecretor." About a quarter of the human population are nonsecretors, which means their bodily fluids—saliva, tears, semen—can't be grouped. "But Cahoon's people determined there was no sperm in the sample."

"Christ, Evans, you find semen in the wife's body and you think my *brother's* responsible? What about her *husband*—you check him out?"

"That's being done, that's being done," he said soothingly. "It's early in this process, all right? Fact remains, Bellevance, your brother's got a lot to account for."

"Yeah? Like what?"

He pursed his lips and looked at the ground. "There's a few discrepancies. Go ask him. Meanwhile, I'm outa here." He took two steps and turned. "One thing I almost forgot. We got to pull some prints off you, if you don't mind. Just for standards, all right? Preston's coming by the barracks around two o'clock. You might as well tag along. How about it?"

"Be happy to oblige."

He gave me a nod. "Toodle-oo, Constable."

The farm had endured three hard-up tenants since my mother and
I moved in to the village when I was a boy, and yet except for
the bulk-tank tubelines overhead, the cowbarn looked just
the same as it had then, from the cobwebby hand-hewn
beamwork to the cracked, fly-smeared windows and the
scrawny mousers slinking around everywhere.

Spud was working on a water pump. At the sight of me he
groaned. "Jesus H. Christ, you, too? All these friggin' inter-
ruptions, I can't get *nothing* done around here." He flipped
his pipe wrench into the toolbox.

"Calm down, Spud. I won't keep you long."

"No, really! I mean, you wouldn't *believe* the vehicles.
They've been turning around in the dooryard all goddamn
morning! State troopers have the road to the A-frame closed
off, so these jerks are coming *here*. Right up on the goddamn
porch. People I never even seen before, everybody wantin' to
know where's the back way in."

"Double homicide's a big event for around here."

"Tell me about it." He laughed dryly, brushing his mustache out of his mouth with the back of his hand. "What I
don't get is the mentality behind why they need to get *close*
to it. What's that about?" He fingered some hand cleaner out
of a tin.

"People are crazy," I said.

"Wow, that's deep. You learn that from being a cop?"

"Among other things."

We walked out into the autumn air. Canada geese were passing overhead in a ragged line. An outboard whined down on the lake, like a mosquito. The cows made their dull comments. This year's barn swallows twittered around us, banking against the yellow sky. Getting ready to leave. Underneath all the ordinary noises was the thrum of the investigation—voices, radios, cars, a generator. Spud turned his head that way. The strain and weariness in his face were painful to see.

"Spud, you look completely whipped. You holding up all right?"

"You think I'm hurtin', you ought to see Brenda—she's more frazzled than the goddamn cows. Barely said one word to me since yesterday."

"She must be scared."

"I don't know what she is." He shook his head. "She's still got that postpartum condition going. It's bad. It's like her and the baby are in a contest to find out who can bawl the most."

Their marriage had gone off in a hurry. From the beginning Brenda begrudged Spud his devotion to the farm, though he didn't recognize it. He had her out in the barn milking every morning until she found herself a part-time job in the bakery down at Price Chopper. On weekends he still had her driving trucks. Brenda hated farmwork—the dirt, the cold, the heat, the boredom. She pitched in as little as she could get away with. Within a year, the pregnancy saved her from all the outdoor chores. Not that she was any happier stuck alone in the house. Spud complained about how short she'd become with him. Snippy. Tired all the time. At their wedding reception in the town hall a year and a half ago, Agnes had predicted that Spud and Brenda wouldn't last any longer than Spud and Cathy. Cathy was the frisky hairdresser he'd stolen from some long-haul trucker over near Burlington. That one crashed in four months, and here the poor sap was doing it all over again, Agnes said, trying to rescue another unhappy woman from herself.

I plucked a sprig of ryegrass and leaned against the yardlight, one heel propped up on the ball of my knee, trying to strike an easy, reassuring pose for Spud's sake. He was wound tighter than I'd ever seen him, which was saying something. "Tell me. How'd the cops treat you last night? Was it bad?"

"No, not bad. It was worse this morning."

"They came up twice?"

He tucked in his chin. "Yes. Now I'm supposed to go down to the barracks and do a friggin' lie detector test."

"The hell you are. What for?"

"Because. They found out that, actually . . . see, yesterday wasn't the first time I saw her in there."

My stomach tightened. "Go ahead."

He swallowed, blinking. "See . . . I know this sounds peculiar, but the first time I saw her in there, I didn't go in. All I did was I *looked* in, and I caught a quick glimpse of her in there, that's all, sprawled out on the floor like she was. . . . And I kind of jumped back. And then I just left."

"When was that?"

"Wednesday."

"For Christ's sake, Spud, that's three days ago! Why didn't you tell anybody?"

He clenched his big hands. "Because I couldn't believe she was *dead*. I didn't want to believe it. Does that make sense?"

I straightened away from the pole and sought his eyes. "It makes sense. Of course it does. Trouble is, now you've lied to the police."

"No, but I *explained* it. I didn't totally lie. See, last night, when they were up here asking me why I went down to the Morganthaus', Brenda was sitting next to me on the couch, and you know Brenda. I couldn't say, 'Uh, actually, Officer, I saw her laying there two days before.' What was Brenda going to think? I saw Gaea naked on the floor and I didn't mention it to her? So I just ran the two times together."

"Last night I understand. How come you changed your story this morning?"

"See, what happened was they found my footprints up there, up where Otto was building the sauna. So that's how they figured out I wasn't up at the sugarhouse yesterday like I said, because it rained in between, and my footprints were obviously older than one day. So that's why I need to do this lie detector. To smooth it over."

"Shit. You need a lawyer, not a lie detector."

"I *knew* you were gonna say that! Fuck it, I *explained* the situation. I don't need a lawyer. *I haven't done anything wrong!*"

"You lied! Why the *hell* didn't you say something on Wednesday?"

"I told you! Because I didn't think she was *dead*! I didn't know *what* to think. I saw her laying there and I thought maybe they were up to something kinky. Which I . . . I just . . . It's like I just needed to make myself believe she wasn't dead." He whirled around and kicked the side of the barn.

I said, "Spud, did you ever spy on Gaea? From up in the woods?"

"Oh, for— Who's *handing* you this shit? Lonnie?"

"Lonnie! What does Lonnie know about it?" Until this April, Lonnie Perkins had been Spud's hired man. Spud let him go when baby Lyle was born and Brenda quit her job at Price Chopper.

"I saw her one time," he admitted, pained.

"I'm asking you, did you *spy* on her?"

"No! It . . . It wasn't on purpose." He shook his head, chuckling strangely, that little chipmunk chitter he used to make as a kid when he was nervous or frightened and didn't want it to show. Then a tremor started up in his chin and he sobbed, once. He fought it down, jaw muscles pulsing. "You got to help me get through this, Hector," he said finally. "I'm strung out real bad. I'm so jittery and depressed, I can't concentrate, and Brenda won't hardly look at me, and now these friggin' troopers are on my case like I'm a *suspect*. Jesus *Christ!*"

"I'll help you. I want to help you. But I need you to be straight with me, Spud. Hear?"

He nodded.

"OK. Now I have to tell you something. It appears the police have reason to suspect you had a sexual interest in Otto's wife. If that's true, and if Otto called you on it—"

"He didn't call me on *nothing!*"

"Did you have an interest in her or not?"

"An interest? What's that mean, an *interest*? What's that got to do with them getting *shot*?"

"That would depend on the particulars."

"The *fuck* it would! I'm no goddamn killer! I don't even hunt!" He spun around and stormed across the road toward the house.

WE drove into the lot of the Vermont State Police Barracks B, a red-brick slab off the state highway near the I-91 exit south of Allenburg, in separate vehicles. It was just after three, but Evans and company, we soon learned, hadn't arrived. That should have tripped a little alarm in me, but I wasn't in the game yet. I was an upright citizen with an innocent brother to protect, and I didn't expect the challenge to tax me all that much.

A dispatcher pointed us toward straight-back chairs set against the wall in the main room, then brought us apple juice and magazines. "You make yourselves comfortable. Shouldn't be too long."

The waiting began to wear on Spud within ten minutes. Any farmer resents having to sit still, and Spud was antsier than most. Especially since he'd begun farming alone. He couldn't read the *People* magazine in his lap, couldn't stop craning his neck out the window and grumbling under his breath about all he ought to be getting done before it began to rain.

It was four-fifteen by the time Goomer Ainsley, the chinless trooper from the A-frame team, came through a side door. Evans would be another few minutes, was all he said. No explanation, no apology. He ushered us into an empty interview room—blue cinder-block walls, chalkboard, long, bare table in the middle—and proceeded to roll off our prints. Then he told Spud he'd been instructed to take blood and hair samples, "if you would be so kind." Spud rolled his eyes, pushing up his sleeve.

As we cleaned up, Evans came in and nodded to Ainsley, who started the tape recorder. The big sergeant dragged a folding chair over to the table. "Mind if I refresh myself?" He cracked open a can of Dr Pepper and took a swig. His Nikes, I realized, carried the tang of fresh manure— Suddenly my scalp prickled with heat. He'd suckered us down here and searched the farm. The bastard.

Ainsley had wandered off to the side of the room. He leaned on the windowsill with his arms across his chest, a silhouette against the half-open blinds.

"OK, now before we get started," Evans said, "what is your role here, Mr. Bellevance—guardian angel?"

"Close enough. Spud doesn't have a whole lot of time, Sergeant, so let's get on with it."

He grunted. "Half an hour oughta do it, hour at the outside."

"Ten minutes," I said. Spud nodded beside me. He'd promised to follow my lead. I wanted to be the one setting the boundaries here, but Evans knew I needed to hear what they had on my brother and how hard they intended to run with it. He could drag this out for quite a while, if he saw some advantage in it.

"All right. Let's not get hung up on the clock, OK?" Evans rubbed his eyes with the heels of his hands. He looked even worse than Spud. "First off, describe the Morganthaus for me, will you, Preston? Whatever comes to mind."

Ainsley yawned into his armpit.

Spud pushed his lower lip out. "How do you mean, describe them?"

"I mean describe them. Like with adjectives."

"I don't know what to say." Spud's chair popped as he shifted.

"Preston, listen to me. You were the Morganthaus' only friend in the area. You were their nearest neighbor. You had keys to their house. You did business with them. Most importantly, you found the bodies. Twice," he added with a tight-lipped smile. "You are my main man right now, dig? As such, I would like you to give me the rundown on these people. If that's not too much to ask."

"Whatever comes to mind, Spud," I said. "It's OK."

He looked into his rough hands. "Well, it seemed to me like they had the perfect life. That was the main thing about them, as far as I'm concerned. They didn't work. They had money. They were all set. They skied in the winter, went sailing in the summer . . ." He shrugged. "Shangri-la."

Evans pinched his nose. "Try 'em one at a time. You and Otto go back a ways, don't you?"

"Kind of, I guess."

"You sold him a piece of your farm, didn't you?"

"Not exactly."

"Tell me about that."

"Well, he had title to the property, except he wanted somebody else to farm it. He was looking to let it out, basically, but he couldn't find anybody. My mom finally went up and talked to him, and he agreed to sell it to us. The way it worked was Otto would keep the north-slope sugarwoods for himself, and we'd write up the deed so if I ever wanted to sell he'd have first crack. That way he got to keep the farm without having to pay the taxes on it."

"So, what you're saying is *he* sold it to *you*."

Spud nodded.

I didn't contradict him, but this wasn't how Agnes had described the arrangement to me. They'd bought it together, was how I'd understood it, from Gavin Ingalls.

"How friendly were you with the Morganthaus?" Evans went on.

"We were neighbors. They lived on my farm, was the way I thought of it, so I did stuff for them. Haven't we been through this enough times?"

"How often did you see Otto, would you say?"

"We visited now and then."

"Your wife says she didn't like him."

"She was jealous—because of the easy life they had. That's how she is."

"So, when you say 'we visited,' you mean *you* visited, isn't that right? Your wife says she never set foot inside that chalet."

He gritted his teeth. "No, I mean *we* visited. Me and *them*."

"Easy." I patted his arm.

"OK. Tell me about *Mrs*. Morganthau."

He rubbed his chin. "She was different. Kind of multicultural. Good cook, good gardener . . ."

"You 'admired' her, correct? That's the word you used this morning."

"If you say so."

"You liked her, in other words. She was attractive."

"I guess."

"Very attractive. And you like attractive women a whole lot, don't you?"

I straightened and said, "He likes cold beer, too, Sergeant. Where're you headed with this?"

"You didn't tell him?" He leaned in toward Spud. "We got a witness that says you're a backwoods Peeping Tom."

Spud flushed and drew himself up in his chair. "If you're getting this from Lonnie Perkins, all I told him was that one time when I was walking by up in the woods—this was two, three years ago—it was near dark, and the lights were on, and I saw her getting out of the shower. That was it. It wasn't like I was waiting there or anything."

"Thanks for clearing that up. You been married once before, haven't you, Preston?"

"Right. So what?"

"To a Cathy Litzinger. Of Winooski, Vermont. You ever slip around on her?"

He colored.

"She was married when you two met, isn't that right?"

"What's she got to do with this?"

"I talked to her this morning. Nice gal, loves to chat. Says hi, by the way. She tells me, middle of the day, you two used to pop into the Mallett's Bay Cabins for a little nooky. Sometimes you might even take her old man's boat out and do it on the lake."

I said, "Anytime you want to leave, Spud, just say so."

He turned to me, cheeks flushed. "I don't want to leave. I want to hear what he's trying to get at."

"You know what he's getting at. Whether you had any kind of a sexual relationship with Gaea."

"There wasn't no relationship!"

Evans squeezed his nose again and sniffed. "Your wife says she had concerns about you and Mrs. Morganthau. Echoes from her own past experience, you could say."

"Brenda's been cranky ever since the baby was born. It's one of those hormone things. They don't know why it happens, but she hasn't been too rational lately."

"You're saying there was nothing going on between you and Mrs. Morganthau?"

"I'm saying our friendship was totally innocent."

"'Totally innocent,'" Evans repeated. "Preston . . . you spend a fair amount of time at that strippers' club down on the lake, don't you?"

"I been in there."

"I know. I've seen you in there myself. You and Lonnie Perkins. Reason I ask, the manager, Keith Quimby, says he saw you and Mrs. Morganthau in there back in April sometime. What was that about?"

Spud squirmed. "We had lunch there one day. There was something she wanted to ask me."

"They have lap dancers in there and such, as you know. Pretty strange destination to take your neighbor's wife out to lunch."

"Not in the daytime it isn't. Anyway, *she* took *me*. She wanted to ask me something."

"Yeah, she did? What was that?"

"She wanted me to talk to Otto about them adopting a baby."

His brow lifted. "*That's* original."

"It was because . . . Well, she wanted a baby and he didn't. She thought I could talk to him about it." There was a quaver in his voice.

I rose, feeling my back grab. It was time to yank him. "We've had enough of this, Sergeant, thank you. OK, Spud? Let's get out of here."

"You want to leave, Bellevance, you feel free. Preston here has a prearranged appointment with my polygraph specialist."

"I'm gonna pass on that," Spud said, standing.

Evans's face went tight. "That's *dumb*, LaClair. That's real shitass dumb. You know why? Because either you do this for me now, or I'll have to get the state's attorney to convene an inquest. You don't want to sit through an inquest. Tell him, Bellevance."

"We're leaving," I said. "C'mon, Spud. Now."

Evans gave a snort and banged both hands down on the table. "One last question, OK? Then you can leave."

I looked at Spud. "You don't have to give them an answer, all right?" I had to hear the zinger.

Spud shrugged.

"We'll bite," I said.

The sergeant glanced significantly at Ainsley. He really was a son of a bitch. For all the cops who were scrupulous and deliberate and discerning, the toughest men on earth day-in, day-out, there were also the unscrupulous sons of bitches. Who were just as tough. "I would like to hear how Mrs. Morganthau's dildo ended up in your sugarhouse."

Spud paled. "What dildo?"

"All right, boys," I said, "we're all done here." I pulled at Spud's elbow, but he didn't move. *"Spud!"*

He shook me off. "Wait a minute!"

Evans beckoned to Ainsley.

With a telling smirk, Ainsley lifted a manila envelope from the windowsill behind him and strolled over to hand it to Evans. Evans unfastened the clasp and removed a Ziploc bag. He held it up by two fingers. Inside was a pink, two-pronged vibrator in the form of a monk with a rounded cowl holding a stubby candlestick.

"Recognize this item, Preston? We found it in your toolbox."

"In with your drill bits," Ainsley added.

Spud put his head in his hands and sank into the chair.

"Who signed the warrant?" I demanded.

"Larrabee."

"You prick," I said. "That must have been one hell of an affidavit to convince Avis to grant you a no-knock." Avis Larrabee was a young district court judge in Allenburg.

"What no-knock? Mrs. LaClair was very cooperative. She was there the whole time. With the baby in her arms."

Spud groaned.

"What did you come up with for cause?"

"Get serious, Bellevance. Preston gallivanted all over that house—upstairs, downstairs, in my lady's chamber. And then it took him *two whole days* to call the goddamn thing in."

"I want to see the warrant."

Evans fingered a yellow copy of the search warrant out of the same envelope.

Under "Described Property and Things," it read, "Automatic or semiauto 9mm firearm. Any documents, letters, diaries, photographs, or other papers or objects belonging to Otto and Gaea Morganthau."

"How do you know that thing is Ms. Morganthau's? You've got no damn business taking it unless you know it's hers." What's more, the fools had no doubt wiped the evidence clean of prints by dumping it into a plastic bag like that.

"So glad you asked. Ainsley?"

"It was Mrs. Morganthau's," the trooper said. "Her American Express records indicate she ordered it from the Xandria Collection catalog last December twelfth. Item number two zero one eight, Friar Knobby."

Spud's eyes were full of tears. "I don't know how it got there, if you even found it there. . . . But I'm no damn *killer*, for Christ's sake!"

"So what are you doing with her Friar Knobby in your toolbox, Preston? The world wants to know."

"Damn it! Come *on*, Spud. You don't have to take this shit."

He didn't get up. "I don't *know*. Maybe I picked it up when I was there, when I went in there. Maybe I thought it was a doll, and I picked it up. That's all I can think."

"*Maybe* you picked it up? That's how you want this to play? Picked it up for what? A *souvenir*? Little memento? Or maybe she was using it one of those times when you were out there watching her, hey?"

"You're a fucking *asshole!*" Spud rose and charged out of the room without turning. Ainsley followed on his heels.

"Better have him sit for that polygraph, Bellevance," Evans said solemnly. "One way or the other we've got to get all the pieces put together."

"You're on your own, Sergeant. From here on my brother's off-limits, you understand? He's given up everything he knows that's relevant to your investigation."

"Give me a fucking break! He *sat* on those stiffs for days. How come he did that? You know what I think? I think he went down there every day. Shit, Bellevance, if you hadn't called up and caught him there, who knows when we would've got the word."

"He was in shock, goddamn it. It happens all the time."

"You know what happens all the time? Guys get caught fucking other guys' wives, and the other guys go apeshit."

"No. Here's the truth of it. Whoever killed that couple was a pro. This wasn't about sex. This had to do with their other life, with something they were hiding from."

He shook his head. "Can't see it. Pro slips in their bedroom the middle of the night with a twenty-two. Pop here, pop there, he's all done. These two people were *hosed*, Bellevance. This was passionate and personal. Whoever did those people knew them, and don't forget the guy came in there on foot."

"Maybe that's what he wants you to think."

"Shit. They *knew* him. No, listen, some stranger barges into your house, you're gonna yell. Mrs. Morganthau didn't yell. We know this, because Mr. Morganthau sat right where he was until he heard the weapon. I think the killer was somebody they were casual with."

"It was a warm afternoon," I offered. "She probably had the door open. He could have slipped in while her back was turned."

"Unh-unh. They were upstairs having sex right before. Our guy was in the woods *watching* them and that's what sent him over. Why? Because him and the wife were slipping around."

"Christ. That's television crap."

"Somebody else was fucking her. We got forensic proof."

"Not that semen?"

"Nope. No, that was Mr. Morganthau's, you were right about that. Seems he had cancer of the testicle at one time, and all his sperms got fried in treatment."

"Which explains why Gaea wanted to adopt a kid."

"Maybe, yeah. There's one very major circumstance it doesn't explain, however. " He exhaled through his nose, puckering his mouth in anticipation of what he was about to drop on me. "Mrs. Morganthau was pregnant."

I stared at him. "How do you know?"

"Six to eight weeks. Yes, indeed."

"You *prick*. You were going to blindside him with that once you had him strapped up. Weren't you?"

He waved me out of the room. "Don't let him leave the state, Bellevance. Hear?"

"What's an inquest?" Spud asked. We were in my truck outside the barracks. A light rain was pattering on the cab roof.

"It's a goddamn inquisition," I said. "Just you, Evans, and State's Attorney Nezzie Holmes. Everything you say in chambers is sworn and admissible. If they decide you're not cooperating, they can jail you for contempt."

"Huh. They jail me and you'll be milking cows, Heck."

The hell I would. "Spud, were you screwing Gaea?"

"No!" he shouted. He slammed the dash, and a pencil jumped out of the vent. "Goddamn it, Brenda's having fits up to the house right now, I *know* she is."

"If you weren't screwing her, we can arrange for some tests that'll put you in the clear."

"Oh, yeah? What tests?"

"Gaea was pregnant when she died, Spud."

He went white. "She *was*?"

"According to that lardass of a sergeant back there."

His mouth opened and closed. He rattled his head, and that eerie grin of his flashed under the tears that had sprung out of his bloodshot brown eyes. He clapped his hands to his face. "Oh, God . . . oh, God . . ." He heaved himself out of the truck and came around to my side. I rolled the window down. He was stricken. "If Brenda walks out on me now, Heck, I mean . . . that's it. I won't last the winter up there.

You got to help me. I been through pure hell the last couple of days, Jesus Christ."

"I'll talk to her."

"Tell her to stick with me. She'll stick, if this don't get out." He started toward his own vehicle and turned back. "I'll tell you one thing flat out. I'm not admitting nothing about her, and I sure as hell won't be talking to the police again unless they arrest me, and I don't care if they do lock me up. I still won't say a single word about Gaea. They can stick their inquest up their friggin' ass."

I drove into Allenburg proper and down past the brick-front shops along Railroad Street, heading home, but just before the Memorial Bridge across the river in the direction of Tipton, I pulled to the curb. Rain flecked the windshield. I waited there, mulling over the potential for more anguish and slander and violence in this thing. Hell, it was just beginning. It was an execution—I'd seen enough of them—and like most criminal executions, the odds were it would never be solved. Not by the sorry likes of Edmund Evans, I was sure of that. I wanted to go back to the cabin, crack a Molson, and run myself a bath.

But I knew if I backed away now, not only would Evans and company focus their underfunded efforts on poor Spud until they broke him—one way or another—but the real killer's trail would fade to nothing. I couldn't sit back and let that happen. Anyway, it wasn't as if I'd have to fly to Fort Lauderdale and start hunting up assassins. Not even close. All I needed was something to suggest a more promising path for the official investigation to lurch off in. Research, that's all. Two, three days' work if I was lucky. If I started right now.

I swung into the Sunoco station and turned around. My tongue tasted like iron. My neck and chest felt clammy. My head was hot. This was all good: I was into it again. It was a feeling I'd missed—the rush, the righteous fury constricting my throat. Dangerous trait in a cop, though, hotheadedness. It hadn't always served me well. But it was a potent source of energy—you just had to contain it. Squad Three Homicide, pinnacle of my busted career: Buzzy Fine, Lew Tibbits, and me. We meshed so neatly, Buzzy's memory and eye for the odd detail; Lew's easy way with kids and women of any age, any race, any psychosis; and my cold Yankee determination. Still, with the tough ones, the stranger-on-stranger whack jobs like the Morganthaus, whenever we managed to close one of them out, what it always took in the end was luck. We caught a break. Except it wasn't ever that simple. We never would have caught the break if we hadn't been watching for it. Counting on it. Pushing toward it. That made all the difference. We hung in. That's what you did. As much as the caseload allowed.

But it was always a team thing. Buzzy, Lew, and me. That was the hesitation now. With this one, I was on my own. Like a slick-pants PI. *A fucking PI.* Over kielbasi and Beck's that gray summer day in South Boston before I left for Tipton, it was Sergeant Detective Buzzy Fine who'd said, "You know what's gonna happen to you, Hector, don't you? You'll wind up in the sticks with no professional options except become a fucking PI. No, I'm telling you. Is that how you want to end up?"

No chance, I told him. No chance in hell.

I cruised back through the heart of town, south past the Cinema Three and the Courthouse Square, then out over the tracks onto U.S. Route 5, the truck route. At the Maple Haven Motor Inn, cheapest motel in town, where it was a sure bet Evans had put up Yves Morganthau, I got the desk clerk to give me the room number. Twenty-six. There was a gray Mercedes 190 out front, Quebec tags.

I knocked.

"Yes?" The door was opened by a thinner version of Otto. Or that was my first impression. This guy was in worse shape, by far—sunken chest, good paunch on him like a melon—though he did have his brother's square shoulders, pale blue eyes, and spearing Gallic nose.

I introduced myself as an investigator working for the Town of Tipton.

Yves hesitated. "Another detective?"

I nodded. "I'm terribly sorry about all this, Mr. Morganthau. Otto happened to be a neighbor of mine. May I come in?"

The man relented with a long sigh and pulled the door wider, indicating an orange vinyl armchair across the room beside the curtained patio window.

He was a heavy smoker by the smog in the room and the jaundiced rings under his eyes, yet he dressed with care, sporting an ascot at the throat of his fine V-neck sweater. *Sesame Street* was playing on the TV.

"You'll have to forgive me if I—" He braced himself against the dressing table, overtaken by a fit of coughing. I watched him as he groped along its surface for some cherry syrup. He dosed himself from the bottle, wiped his eyes with a handkerchief, plucked a smoke from a pack on the bed table.

Pall Malls. He swayed as he flicked his lighter.

"Please forgive my . . ." It flamed. "I have"—he inhaled—"this flu, and I have just come from viewing the bodies." His voice was fluty, phlegm crackling underneath.

"I understand," I said. "Let me ask you, do you have any thoughts on the subject of why somebody would want your brother and his young wife dead?"

"No, none at all. But I blame her, if you want to know."

"Why is that?"

"It's simple. If he'd never met her, my brother would be alive today, I'm sure."

"When was the last time you saw Otto?"

"The day the two of them were married. In Fort Lauderdale. The ceremony was held in a butterfly grove. The priest played tiny silver chimes."

He tugged the drapes away from the patio windows and looked out on the leaf-littered courtyard, the empty swimming pool, stacked resin lounges, a high-voltage power corridor cutting up over hills in the rain. He clucked. "My Lord. All the world to choose from and he had to end up here."

You're the one who's ended up here, I thought. "Have you been up to see the house yet, Mr. Morganthau?"

"Not yet, no. I'm not sure I want to."

"I understand. Still, it's a spectacular piece of property. The view is breathtaking."

"So I've heard. Excuse me, please, if you will." He went into the bathroom to clear his passages.

When it was quiet in there, I called in through the door, "Before I leave you to yourself, Mr. Morganthau, I hope you won't mind taking a moment to tell me a little bit about your business."

"What business?" he called back.

"The manufacturing concern you and Otto owned together."

He reappeared and lowered himself onto the bed, carefully tugging up his trousers, not to stretch the knees. "Do you imagine that would have something to do with his murder, Inspector?"

"I don't imagine anything, Mr. Morganthau. You and Otto founded a manufacturing company. Is that right?"

"Yes. Morganthau Plastics, in 1962."

"You made shipping containers?"

"Later on. At first it was commercial packaging. There

were just the two of us in the shop in those days, and our wives. Fifteen years later we combined operations with a maritime transport concern in Nova Scotia, and at a stroke we became the largest company of its kind in the eastern provinces. In the end we were absorbed by an American conglomerate."

"Did Otto have any enemies in the business world?"

"None at all. Everyone loved Otto. Even Lucas."

"Who's Lucas?"

"Lucas Dunston. Our partner in Halifax. Lucas was crushed when Otto left."

"You mean when he quit and left the country."

"Yes . . . You've heard about this?"

"Only that when Otto met Gaea, he put everything behind him. His wife and kids must have been torn up when he left. You, too, I suppose."

Yves nodded. "We were . . . bewildered, for the most part. Our families . . . we were sharing a duplex at the time, so it wasn't as bad as it might have been. Although in some ways perhaps it was worse. His wife, Francine, was distraught for a long while. Too long. She couldn't accept that he would abandon her, after all they'd been through. And with no explanation. Just . . . poof! Had she ever known him? But . . ." he shrugged. "No one did. No one knew Otto, I told her."

"Not even you?"

"Inspector, Otto ran away when he was sixteen. I was twelve. He hopped a freight train to Saskatchewan. When he finally called home—three years later—he was working as a cart handler in the uranium mines. He broke our mother's heart. Just as he broke Francine's."

"Does Francine know about the murders?"

"Yes, of course. I telephoned her as soon as I heard." He stubbed his cigarette out inside a flying-ducks wastebasket beside the bed. This bent-over activity started him coughing again. He put a hand to his throat and rose from the bed, the other hand waving in front of him, and made for the bathroom. I took this opportunity to stretch out of my chair and flick the thumb-latch on the patio door.

When Morganthau returned, slapping his ribs and flaring his nostrils, his face rinsed, hair combed straight back, he glittered, almost restored—except for the rheumy eyes. "Would you care for a Scotch, Inspector?"

"Sorry, no, I have to be going. But let me say this. Whenever you begin disposing of the property, if I may help in any way whatsoever, I hope you'll call me." I printed my name and number on the pad by the telephone.

AFTER that smoky room, the damp night air was a relief. I got into the old Dodge and waited. The rain was sifting down through the glow of the motel's walkway lights. After some time Otto's brother emerged wearing a topcoat and beret. He hurried into his little gray Mercedes. I followed him a short distance to the center of town and watched as he pulled over just past the Golden Dragon, easily the worst restaurant in Montcalm County, where the competition was not keen. I regretted not having thought to offer him a dining recommendation. Then again, sick as he was, tasty cuisine was probably not a priority.

Back in his room I turned up nothing I might have hoped for. A copy of the will, for instance. No doubt Morganthau had what papers he'd been given with him in the car. But in the wastebasket under a mound of tissues, I found something unexpected, a message slip from the desk clerk: "*While You Were Out* . . . 3:30, Northwoods Realty, returning your call. They will try again."

Was Yves already arranging to unload the property, before it went through probate? Why the hurry? And why Northwoods? Gavin Ingalls ran Northwoods. He was the Realtor who'd snapped up Dad's farm when my mother had been forced to sell—and it was through Ingalls, with Otto's help, that Spud and Agnes had managed to reacquire it. Gavin Ingalls was no pillar of the community. He was a small-time scam artist. For years, one of his uglier practices had been to buy up failing farms and then sell them on stiff terms to hopeful farm kids itching to be out on their own. Inevitably, as the struggling farmer sank deeper into debt, Gavin's brother Marvin, an officer of the Allenburg Savings Bank, would foreclose, whereupon Gavin would waltz in and grab the machinery and the animals. He'd sell off the premium booty right away and end up auctioning the rest of the property all over again, its value declining as the untended outbuildings rotted and the hayfields grew up in spruce and chokecherry. He and Marvin also owned the Mount Joe Ski Area (ten trails, no snowmaking), which had been bumping along somehow since I'd been in grade school, even as it lost money season after season. The Ingallses periodically managed to restructure the enterprise, keeping it afloat as a tax dodge of some sort.

Whatever it meant, this Northwoods connection was worth looking into.

AT home, as darkness closed in, I fixed myself a salsa omelette and scanned Wilma Strong-Parkhurst's leading piece in the *Eagle*.

Tipton Killings Cold-Blooded, Say Investigators

Police spent today looking for clues in the double homicide of a couple found shot to death Friday afternoon in their vacation home outside the village of Tipton.

Vermont State Police Sgt. Edmund Evans said no arrests had been made nor has any motive been determined in the deaths of Otto Morganthau, 50, and his wife, Gaea, 32, described by townspeople yesterday as a friendly, athletic couple who kept to themselves.

Residents in the tiny hamlet of 200 located eight miles from the Canadian border reacted with surprise to what Evans called a "vicious killing."

I skipped to the bottom.

Sergeant Evans announced that a special agent from the Behavioral Science Unit of the Federal Bureau of Investigation will arrive in Allenburg on Monday to assist the state police in the analysis of the crime scene.

What was this? If an FBI agent was actually coming up from Quantico to help Evans hammer out a profile, this had to be Cahoon's play. He was the only cop in the state with that kind of pull. But even at that, getting support from the Bureau at this stage was unheard-of. The feds never came in on a homicide until the local talent had exhausted all the obvious avenues—usually a year or more after the fact. Even then those boys didn't travel. Their time was too valuable. You boxed up all you had and you shipped it down to them.

Unless this was a bluff. An attempt to apply a little local pressure on an unwitting suspect—with the help of an impressionable reporter. I found Wilma's home number in the book.

Her voice was on the tape: "Hi! We're out right now. You know what to do and when to do it."

I pressed OFF.

The large gravel lot in back of the Lodge was more than half-full, and it was still early, not quite nine. Clearly, Quimby's sin pit was making some bucks for him. That didn't bother me, but I did hate to see the building going to ruin the way it was, the cornices crumbling, half the porch-rail spindles kicked out into the ratty-looking yews and junipers, trash peppering the ragged lawn. Though if the rumor Ella McPhetres had been spreading around was accurate, Quimby was on the verge of selling out and heading West. Vegas or LA. When that happened, if it did, I intended to lean on the owners to see to it that whoever took over this property had a more wholesome vision for it.

Inside the door, a pair of oxlike bouncers were stationed at a wooden lectern with a cashbox on it. One of them, the younger of the two, was tall and fat, with red-apple cheeks and a stony expression. I told him who I was and that I was here on town business, not to entertain myself.

"Sorry, mister. You don't get past me without you pay the cover," he said in a high voice. "Five dollars folding money, no discounts, no exceptions."

I asked for a receipt.

Country music throbbed out of speakers hung in every corner. Off to the right on a translucent plastic stage lit from underneath, two dancers in G-strings were gyrating. Impressive talent, Evans was right about that. Quimby had to be paying well—you wouldn't find more alluring physiques in Montreal or Boston. The customers, however, were a mixed bag. Fair number of flashy playboys down from Sherbrooke in French Canada, plenty of locals—loggers and millworkers in their work clothes, loud tables of kids from the state college campus in Allenburg. A few women here and there.

I took a stool at the copper-top bar. The barmaids wore peasant blouses with loose-laced bodices. Mine was gorgeous and young, not yet twenty at a guess, with black hair past her shoulders, an ample, outstanding chest, and stunning cobalt eyes. I was taken with her. "What do you like, big guy?" she said.

"You," I said.

She didn't blink. "What do you like that'll fit in a glass?"

"Just water. The truth is I'm here on business."

"Yeah? Me, too. My business right now is selling drinks. Water's gonna cost you a buck and a half."

I told her this was in fact a police investigation. I gave her my name and asked hers.

"Cherie Boulanger," she said, glancing around uncomfortably.

"Cherie?"

"Yeah. It was Cheryl but I changed it. Now it's Cherie Boo-lahnge-ay. It's supposed to sound French."

"Cherie Boulanger. I like it. Where you from, Cherie?" Cheryl—she was Evans's hot pick.

"Maine. You know Old Orchard Beach?"

"Nice spot. What brought you to Tipton?"

She spread her arms. "Opportunity knocks. Back in May, there's this guy comes into Fresh Clam, the club where I'm dancing—I'm saving up for college, right? And he asks me do I want to make a thousand dollars a week starting on Monday."

"This guy would be Keith Quimby?"

"Yup. And I'm like, is he for real? He was totally upfront about what I'd be doing. Acting and whatever. So I thought about it for like two seconds and I said, why not?"

"You're an actress?"

"You got it," she tossed off, her storm-cloud eyes darkening. "You want a drink or don't you?"

"Sure. Get me a beer. And tell me, Cherie, is Keith around?"

She flipped a mug from hand to hand and drew off a head of foam. "He's upstairs. They're shooting."

"Really? Now?"

"Yeah, sure. They been shooting twelve hours a day since last Wednesday. Nothing wrong with that, is there?" She set down a paper coaster and the wet mug. "Buck-fifty."

"Get a message to him, will you? Tell him I need a few minutes of his time."

She clucked. "I could try, but he won't leave the set, I'll tell you that right now." She whisked herself away to the cash register. What was Evans's phrase this morning? *Road-cone tits.* Couldn't argue with that. And those eyes. She must be something on the big screen, I thought. Still, beneath her tough-chick act, she was so young and fresh, it was hard to imagine her fucking for the camera. A grand a week, though. Good money, no question. All the same, Quimby's powers of persuasion had to be considerable.

The stage was empty. The two dancers were mingling now, offering themselves more intimately, tableside. At a premium.

In a corner booth I spotted Lonnie Perkins's head of curly yellow hair. I'd known Lonnie since he was a little boy—his mother and mine had been buddies. What was he, twenty-six, twenty-seven now? Lonnie was rough-hewn, self-indulgent, something of a troublemaker but a happy-go-lucky guy most of the time. He'd been working odd jobs since he quit school at sixteen. Until recently he'd been Spud's steady hired man. The last time I'd run into Lonnie, it was the end of August, and he was in Aubuchon Hardware in Allenburg buying a set of training wheels for a kid's bike. He'd gotten engaged and moved out to Willow Grove, the trailer park east of Allenburg, with his fiancée, Stacey, and her daughter. He couldn't believe the kid was eight years old and still couldn't ride a bike. He also said he'd found some construction work, which was great, but it was seasonal, so that wasn't too cool because Stacey wasn't going to marry him until he had a decent apartment for them to move into and permanent employment. With health benefits. And don't tell him to go down to fucking Ethan Allen for a job. His dad had busted his ass down there thirty-three years till it did him in.

This had to be the fiancée sitting next to him in a Celtics sweatshirt. Pug-nosed, chubby, with henna-colored hair and silver beads through the inside curve of her ear. Two guys were sitting opposite, the smaller one about Lonnie's age with black hair cut close and round, moley eyes, the other maybe twenty years older, stocky, with a hard, brown face, paisley bandanna on his head, USM tattooed on his hairless, knotty forearm.

The moley guy gave Lonnie a tilt of the head, and he swiveled. Took him a couple drunken seconds to register my face. "Heck-torr!" He grinned and crushed out his Marlboro. "What's happening, amigo?"

"That's the bonus question," I said, and I made a smile. We shook hands. Lonnie patted the bench beside him. I sat, nodding around Lonnie at the fiancée. "You must be Stacey."

She smiled uncertainly and looked away.

Lonnie said, too loud, "I never seen you in this dump before, Heck! You're not looking for poontang, I hope."

"Never know. Some very attractive women in here."

"Hey, no shit." He beamed and gave Stacey a nudge with his elbow.

The four of them were drinking beers and schnapps. There

was a basket of popcorn on the table. The moley one and the marine were preoccupied with the dancer plying her ample wares for some college boys at the next table over.

Lonnie laughed. "You know who this is, Stace?" he shouted. "This is the constable—the guy I was just telling you about. This is LaClair's brother."

"Who?"

"Spud LaClair!" he shouted. Somebody had cranked up the music for some reason. We were right under a speaker. "The farmer I used to work for. Who they think wasted those two people up in Tipton!"

"He's the farmer?"

The stocky one in the bandanna pulled his eyes away from the dancer to take me in. "This is *who*? The farmer?"

"No, no, no," Lonnie said. "The farmer's *brother*, the *constable.*"

"He found the bodies!" Stacey said.

The music went down again. "That's wonderful," the bandanna said, turning back to the dancer.

"I got interviewed by the detectives," Lonnie half-whispered. "State Police dudes in plainclothes. This one guy, Evans—fuckin' ball-buster. How about you?"

"I talked to Evans. He seems to think Spud had a sexual interest in Gaea. I want to know who he got that notion from. Was it you?"

He pursed his lips, glanced away, and then leaned in close. "Heck, here it is. I'm real sorry if this is news to you, but her and Spud used to meet out in the sugarhouse. You know the sugarhouse." His breath was rank with cigarettes and booze. "He's got a sleeper sofa and a TV in there, like for when he's up boiling day and night. Well, so here's the thing. They used to meet in there and hump, I swear to God."

"How do you know this?"

"I friggin' *saw* them, that's how."

"When?"

"Year, year and a half ago. One of them early-spring days, when it's all drizzly and quiet, right? I'm taking down sap lines up on the ridge, and I hear this noise, like a girl cryin'. I followed it down, the sound, and goddamn if they weren't inside the sugarhouse, banging away like a pair of wild animals."

"You sure it was them?"

"Sure I'm sure. I saw 'em come out. I saw 'em kissin' and everything. I was like, *whoa*, this is serious." He sat back. "Course, obviously, that don't explain why he would *shoot* her. Him I could see. Otto. But not her."

"He didn't kill them, Lonnie. Regardless of what Spud and Gaea might have had going. He doesn't have it in him."

"I know what you mean. Because what would have been the reason, right? He would've needed some kind of motive, like if he thought Brenda was going to find out. Or if she was pregnant or something like that."

"We saw where it happened," Stacey offered suddenly, half-drunk, leaning out around Lonnie and across the plastic popcorn basket. "First thing this morning Lonnie took me up in there. It's this all-glass chalet. We saw them carry out the bodies."

I smiled at her and turned back to Lonnie. "Who're your other two friends?"

"These guys?" He paused as if to think about it. "OK, well, you probably know JJ's, that new health-food joint down in town on the river? That's Jamie's place. Jamie's my business partner—hopefully. Right, James?"

Jamie, the beady-eyed, moley one, glanced at Stacey and shook his head disapprovingly.

"What business?" I asked.

"OK, you know Keith Quimby? Guy that's behind all this here. He's moving out West, and I'm in the middle of finalizing a deal where I can take over the club, me and James. Hey,

Jamie? Partners, right? Me and Jamie Bridewater. Gonna make us a goddamn fortune."

"What, here?"

"Here, definitely! Question is, do we keep it like it is, or do we turn it into a family-type place. Tacos, ice cream, pizza . . . like what Jamie has going in town. Maybe stick a few attractions down by the water. Water slides, shit like that."

A family restaurant and amusement park? In Tipton? Somebody was playing with the young man's head. "Everybody in town'd love to see the Lodge cleaned up," I said gently, "that's for sure. But you'll never make a fortune in the restaurant business. Not here, Lon. Take it from me."

He wouldn't hear it. "Hey, man, two, three years, you don't know, Heck. This whole area's gonna be transformed. You won't recognize it. Picture a four-season destination resort. Golf, sailing, tennis, skiing . . . You're not gonna believe it."

"I don't believe it already."

"No, seriously. Ask Danny Ingalls. They got sketches and blueprints and all that shit. Truly, man. It's happening!"

A wench swooped in for the empties. "Another round here?"

"Definitely!" Lonnie said.

The marine suddenly straightened up. "Sorry, sis," he said, "but we're about to fade." He dropped a bill on her tray and slid out the other end of the booth.

Lonnie was amazed. "Marko! What's goin' on? We got an *appointment*, man! Me and James!"

"Not gonna happen." Marko frowned. "You're wasted, bro. What did we say about that?"

"The fuck I am! Marko, I'm in control. I'm in complete control!"

Jamie was warily watching Stacey, who was chewing the inside of her cheek. High degree of tension among Lonnie's entourage. And this bruiser Marko was clearly over on young Lonnie in a big way.

"Anyhow," Marko said, "there's maneuvers tomorrow, am I right? Last day."

"Not for me there isn't. I'm *done* with that bullshit. Wayne *decommissioned* me. I'm fucking retired."

This surprised me. "Aw, hell, Lonnie," I said, "you didn't go and join Wayne's wackos?" Wayne Hrushka owned Down & Dirty Construction over in Tewkesville. He was also the founding officer of the Mount Joe Militia, the county's own little paramilitary cell.

"See, that's the thing, if you're working for Wayne. You don't got much choice."

"You're working for Wayne?"

"I was. Till I got laid off."

"Nothing wacko about patriotism," Marko declared, hard through the chin, looking down his broken nose at me. "Is there?" I watched him bounce on the balls of his feet, ready to plow into me if the invitation presented itself. Half his face was lit pink by the EXIT light at his shoulder. He was one of those you'd need to flatten right off, or he'd be on you like an avalanche of jackhammers.

"Depends on how you define it," I said.

He took a step back, running his tongue over his teeth, slipping into a leather jacket. "Only one definition counts. Which is somebody that's committed to defending the Constitution of the United States against the forces threatening our basic liberties. You accept that?"

"More or less."

"Good." He zipped up, then down, halfway. "Social fabric's coming unraveled, Constable. Bill of Rights is getting fucked with every time you turn around. This country's wealth is getting sucked out by Arabs and other foreign entities. We got the UN taking over our national parks and our forests and our oil and minerals. . . . It's treason, what the federal courts are letting these internationals get away with. *Treason*—look it up in the dictionary. Soon as the people wake up, though, boom. Social chaos, brother. Big-time. Second American revolution."

I turned to Lonnie. "Don't be hanging with this numbnuts. He's only going to get you in trouble."

Lonnie looked pained. "That's the *thing*! I'm *not*!"

"Gonna be just like Bosnia around here," Marko said, "and a lot sooner than you think."

Lonnie guffawed. "It's gonna be like fucking Lake *Tahoe,* that's what it's gonna be."

"Kid's out of his gourd, Marko," Jamie declared. "Waddya say?" He motioned for Stacey to move.

I stood back while the three of them slid out. Stacey was pushing Lonnie, who looked perplexed and disappointed. "I don't get the *problem,* James," he was saying over his shoulder. "I mean, you said we got a business appointment."

"Some other time. It's no big deal," Jamie soothed him.

"I'll try and catch you tomorrow, Lon," I said. "You still go out to your mom's place for Sunday supper?"

"Sometimes . . . ," he said, distracted. "I used to, anyway."

From the door I watched them cross the parking lot to Lonnie's red Chevy S-10, his pride and joy, all tricked out with a premium sound system, smoked glass, chrome wheels, oversize tires, running-board lights, and a winch. That rig was the only thing of value he'd ever owned. He was leasing it with the help of his mother, who was almost broke herself. Now here was Marko sticking out his hand for the keys. Lonnie was balking. Marko was insisting, head bobbing emphatically. It made good sense, given Lonnie's condition, and yet there was an edge to Marko's sway over the kid that bothered me.

Stacey and Jamie got into a dark Ford Tempo, Stacey at the wheel. If the Tempo was hers, then she and Lonnie had come separately. Why?

Instead of turning toward Tipton and the state highway

south to Allenburg, both vehicles went the other way, up along the lake toward Canada. The road in that direction, narrow and rolling, hugged the shore just under the flank of Mount Joseph. Before the interstate, it was a popular scenic route into Quebec. Now the old brick customs house there at the crossing was closed, and a billboard on the line instructed travelers to check in at the Bienvenu à Canada trailer in Iceville, a mile farther on. I couldn't guess where they were headed. Unless Marko just wanted to open up that new truck on the empty pavement.

There was a cool breeze out of the north. Clouds streamed across the half-moon. I followed the porch around to the double doors at the main entry. ARROW LAKE LODGE, the etched oval doorglass read. The doors were locked, and someone had gone to the trouble of looping a chain through the pushbars on the other side. Farther along I found an unlatched window, worked it up, and scissored in.

The bright lobby was bare except for a big silver torpedo of a fire extinguisher, a pay phone behind the door, and a crock of sand for smokes. There were doors into the dining hall to one side, and doors to the recreation room on the lake side. All locked. The carpet and wallpaper were in bad shape, stained, gouged, filthy. Past the cherry check-in desk, a wide stairway curved upward toward the second and third floors, and the towers.

On the second-floor landing a broad-shouldered muscle-man in a black T-shirt rose out of an armchair to greet me. He'd been reading a paperback. He had headphones around his neck and a thick gold chain. Across his beefsteak pecs, in small letters, was the word SECURITY. The hall stretched away on either side of him, milk-glass sconces sending fans of light up the walls. The floor was crowded with the studio's supplies—stacks of lumber, reels of yellow electrical cable, stepladders, plastic crates, screens, lights, reflector stands . . .

"Man of adventure," the bouncer said cheerfully. "How'd you get up here?"

"I'm looking for Keith."

He chuckled at the idea, hitching up his jeans. "You want to see Keith, you gotta call the office, make an appointment. Just like everybody else." Boston accent.

"What's your name?"

"Who's asking?"

"I'm Hector Bellevance, Tipton Town Constable."

"This is private property, shithead. I gotta see some official papers or you're gone."

"Your name?"

"Bugsy."

"Give him the message, Bugsy, will you? I'll wait here."

The fool kept coming. "Like I said, *you're gone*. Or didn't you—"

I slipped his grab and came up into the hinge of his throat with my forearm, standing him straight for a second. Then I hooked his legs out from under him, and in another second I had his ribs pinned to the floor, his right arm wrenched up between his shoulder blades, my knee in the small of his back. He was gagging, his right cheek and ear mashed into the gritty carpet.

I bent down. "Never assault an officer. You clear on that?"

"Get— Get *off* me—!"

With this, down the hallway the old ballroom's pocket doors parted with a bang, and somebody popped out, silhouetted against the glare inside. "Steven! You schmuck! What's this crap? We're *rolling* in here—"

"Town Constable to see Quimby," I shouted.

"Jesus Christ." The doors slid shut.

I let Steven get up. Inside the ballroom someone hollered, "OK, people, break time! Ten minutes only, please. A pee and a puff."

When the doors slid back again, the porn king himself was glaring out at us. Blond ponytail, wispy goatee, striped engineer's overalls, white cotton sweater with the sleeves pushed up, black digital the size of a hockey puck on his scrawny arm. A confusion of voices spilled out around him. I could see maybe a dozen people milling about under the bright lights inside. All with clothes on.

Quimby took me in, then sneered at Steven, who was brushing himself off. "You're worthless, man. I don't even know what I'm paying you for."

"Give me a break! This asshole fucking *juked* me."

Quimby sighed and turned back to me. "What is this? A raid?"

"I have a few questions for you, Keith, that's all. It won't take long."

"Concerning what?"

"The Morganthaus."

His eyes flashed impatiently. "I been through this once already. You guys ought to get your act together."

"What did the troopers ask you?"

"It was bullshit, man. Like have I noticed any disreputable characters in here lately. I mean, fuck, that's all I *get* is disreputable characters."

I followed his swaying ponytail through another set of doors into the production suite. The walls were plastered with glossies of Keith's stable of stars. Also a large, framed photo of Arrow Lake from the air above a pair of hard-used couches. There were two phones on a magazine-strewn table, along with a terra-cotta saucer full of butts, bottle caps, and pistachio shells.

Quimby led me through another door into his office, part of what was once the girls' camp infirmary. The windows were lead-mullioned casements, now black with the empty lake and the night. On a chrome and slate table, in frames, he was showing off several citations and blown-up photocopies of reviews, also a gold-plated globe and a plaque with a director's chair engraved on it.

Straight Arrow Productions promotional posters were everywhere: *The 24-Karat Blonde, Pirates of Pleasure, Snow White and the Seven Dongs.*

"Something to drink?"

"Thanks, but no."

Keith helped himself to a can of seltzer from a small fridge. He smacked his lips. "You know, Mr. Bellevance, you sorely offended my main man Steven out there. Not a smart move. Steven's nobody you want to be on the wrong side of."

"I'll tell you what offends me, Keith. The way you're letting this fine old building rot into the ground."

He snorted. "What are you, the Village Improvement Society? Come on, there's forty people out there I'm paying to sit on their ass while I'm in here entertaining you."

"You have an appointment tonight with Lonnie Perkins?"

"Who's Lonnie Perkins?"

"Local guy who's angling to take over the bar when you pull up stakes."

"Yeah, well, I got nothing to do with that. That's Danny's business."

"Danny Ingalls."

"Right. He manages the property. He's a real estate agent."

"Working for his dad—Gavin?"

"What is this? My time is valuable, OK?"

"So who owns this building?"

"Some corporation. Hey, I thought this was supposed to be about that couple that got blown away up the road."

"Tell me about them."

Others had begun to crowd the room off the hall. He walked back to his door and closed it. "I knew who they were. Small community, you see people around."

"Around where?"

"The beach, the slopes, wherever . . . She was a hot little skier. Outstanding physique on her, too. Plus she had a foreign-type face you don't forget. Gold skin, almond eyes—Cleopatra-type."

"The Morganthaus ever come into the bar?"

He shook his head. "She was in here a couple times with another guy. Young guy, black hair, groove in his chin . . ."

"They rent a room?"

"A room? What do you think this is, a brothel? If you're wondering if they were fucking, your colleagues already threw that one at me. I guess I'm the local authority on who's fucking who. The truth is, I don't *care* who's fucking who. I hope they were. More the merrier."

"Who killed them? What do you think?"

He laughed. "What do *I* think? The Mossad, man."

"Where do you get the Mossad?"

"OK, let's put it together. She was Arab, correct? And she was involved with the Olympics, correct? Chambermaid, waitress, whatever. OK. Remember the Munich Games? Those Israeli weight lifters that got massacred? If she was somehow on the inside of that, left a door unlocked, something like that . . . The Mossad never forgets."

I went to the windows and tried looking out toward the water. It was too dark to see much, except far to the north, a few twinkling camps on the Quebec side. "You leaving Vermont, Keith?"

"Sooner the better. Headin' West."

"Selling Straight Arrow Productions?"

"Never. I'm transplanting the business. My lease here is up first of the year, and Danny's demolishing the building. Ought to make you happy. The guy's putting up a million-dollar resort spa."

"He's cleaning this place out just so he can tear it down?"

"*'Cleaning it out'?* What am I—vermin?" He shoved up from his desk to show me how insulted he was. "I'm gonna tell you something. That's the main underlying reason why I'm cashing in—this community's hypocritical attitude. I'm not up here making fucking land mines, am I? I'm not making chemical fucking *weapons*. I'm making *movies*. You people obviously don't realize it, but down through the years I have brought hundreds of thousands of dollars into this dead-ass county. Who appreciates this? Nobody. I make it a point to stop in town and buy my gas, I get my shirts done at Rich's Cleaners, I buy local eggs, milk, syrup, I go to the beach, I go skiing, I go to restaurants . . . and everywhere I go people look at me like I'm Charles fucking Manson." He opened his thin arms toward the promo posters. "I make *movies*, man. Art. Top-quality erotic entertainment. No violence, no weirdness, no kiddie shit. Just tasteful adult stories about natural human emotions. I mean, *I guarantee it,* because I write and direct every one of them myself. Let me lay a title on you, and you can see for yourself."

"Sounds good to me."

"Serious?" He was pleased.

"Sure."

Keith unlocked a storage room behind us and went inside. "What do you like, comedy? Hard-core? You like period pieces?"

"You have something with Cheryl Boulanger?"

"Cherie?" He grinned. "You know her?"

"We just met."

He chuckled. "Right, I get it. You like girl-girl?"

"Doesn't matter."

"I'm asking because that's all she does is girl-girl."

"She a lesbian?"

"She's Danny's personal cooze is what she is." He came out and handed me a shrink-wrapped cassette. *Ms. Dracula.*

"That's her first box cover. If she doesn't run away with Best New Performer for this little gem, I'll eat my shorts."

"She talented?"

"Talented?" My naïveté amused him. "It's about persona, OK? Charisma. You seen her. The girl's fantastic. Raven hair, perfect face, a body that won't quit . . . She's like a modern-day Liz Taylor, and she gets it. She knows how to use it, right?"

"She going out West with you?"

"Be the mistake of her life if she stays here."

"Danny doesn't want her to leave, is that it?"

"Yeah, but it's more of an ego thing." He sighed. "It's like, if she leaves, it reflects on him. His manhood. Danny's out for number one, and there's nobody comes in second. You know what I'm saying? The alpha-wolf syndrome. Bottom line, the girl's too smart for him. She's got a million-dollar future and she's going for it."

"Keith!" someone yelled through the door. "You better rally, man. You're startin' to lose people."

I followed him into the outer office, now pungent with pot smoke. A slew of interested gazes followed my exit.

In the hall at the top of the stairs Steven was back in his armchair reading his fat paperback.

As I passed him and started down, he barked, "Hey, you!"

I paused.

"Next time we tangle, you and me, we're gonna see a different outcome."

I turned and trotted back up the two steps to the landing.

This time Steven wisely elected not to leave his chair. His right ear was swollen, and his cheekbone was bruised and scratched. He gazed at me, nervous as a rabbit behind his flinty mask.

I said softly, "That big chain through the door-openers in the lobby? It's got to come off. Fire code violation. Make sure somebody takes care of it right away, OK?"

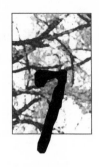

Sunday morning I fixed a quick breakfast of oatmeal, tea, and half a grapefruit and installed myself and my telephone out at the picnic table on the leaf-covered lawn. The dome of Mount Joe stood clear above the sea of fog in the valley, like a barren gray island. From the edge of the blueberry planting, with my bird glasses, I could see all the way up Otto's view cut to the A-frame. The investigators were gone. They had sealed the doors and windows with strips of red, frangible tape for the fume job. No getting back into the place now, not for days.

Information in Nova Scotia had a listing in Dartmouth, near Halifax. "Lucas Dunston here!" He was a chipper one, this early in the morning.

I introduced myself and said I was looking into Otto Morganthau's background, if he wouldn't mind answering some questions.

"To what purpose?" he wondered.

"I'm sorry to have to tell you this, Mr. Dunston. Otto is dead."

"Dead," he echoed. "The cancer?"

"No, he was murdered."

"My God! How?"

"Shot. He and his wife both. The killer is at large. That's why I'm calling."

"Of course," he murmured. "How can I help?"

I started in with a general question about his partnership with the Morganthau brothers, hoping he would prove expansive.

I wasn't disappointed. He said bitterly, "Stupidest thing I did in my life was to take up with those schemers. They sold Micmac right out from under me."

"Sorry . . . Micmac?"

"Micmac Shipping and Container. We agreed to keep my company's name when we executed the merger. A seduction in itself, I saw later."

"Otto's brother, Yves, told me your company was absorbed by another one. Is that true?"

"Absorbed!" He gave an acid laugh. "How antiseptic. They threw Micmac to the bloody pirates in the dead of night. That's the truth of it! One Monday morning I walked into my office and found myself face-to-face with a Wall Street buccaneer—with buckles on his slippers! Sitting at *my* desk! 'You are no longer involved with this firm's operations,' he told me. Micmac was *scuttled*. Scuttled and swallowed whole by Federated Can. Two hundred and fourteen workers cast adrift. Many of whom I had employed all their lives."

"And you had no inkling until it was all over?"

"Not a jot! Family-owned companies are supposed to be *immune* to the hostiles. They were a shrewd pair, the Morganthaus."

"After you lost the company, did you stay in touch with them?"

"Of course not. This is the first I've heard of them since the takeover."

"You must have made a profit on the sale, Mr. Dunston."

"We all did. Of course we did. That was the idea. Otto had built a pension fund the raiders were drooling over."

"What kind of money are we talking about here, Mr. Dunston?"

"What *kind*?"

"How much did you come away with when the deal went down? Was it millions?"

"From the takeover?"

"Mr. Dunston, I need to know what the stakes were."

"For me?"

"For Otto. And Yves."

There was a pause before he said, "After taxes, Otto took away more than two million dollars U.S. Yves and I gained between three and four. Apiece."

"Would it surprise you to hear that when Otto died, he had nothing to show for his millions but a modest vacation home and a sailboat in drydock in Florida?"

"That would surprise me, yes."

"What do you think happened to his money?"

"I'm sure I don't know. I was never close to Otto. But he was a canny one with the accounts. If I were you, I'd speak to his broker."

"Who might that be?"

He laughed. "I'm sure I have no idea."

I thanked Dunston and phoned Otto's ex in Toronto, hoping they weren't churchgoers. A man answered. Cultured voice, pleasant enough.

"Monsieur Pouliot?"

"*Oui?*"

I introduced myself and asked for Francine. A parakeet chirped in the background.

"This is Francine Pouliot," a woman said finally, in pretty, piping tones. "Let me just say before you begin . . . another inspector phoned yesterday evening. I told him I could not be of help."

"Why is that, Mrs. Pouliot?"

"Why? Because I haven't set eyes on Otto for ten years. He abandoned me, you know."

I explained that, as it happened, Otto and I had been neighbors if not friends, and so he—

"Otto had no friends," she interrupted. "He did not care for others, only himself. Otto had two children, you know. They were nine and fourteen years old when their father walked out and disappeared. He left them without a kiss. Without a word! Not one word for four years! What kind of man does that to his children? Now we learn he has been killed. It's terrible for such a thing to happen. To anyone. But he was selfish! He—" She stopped herself, then said, "I'm sorry."

"Not at all. So the last time you saw Otto was the day he left your house in Montreal?"

"Yes, exactly."

"How about the children?"

"The same. He wrote once to see if they might come to Florida to visit him. They weren't persuaded."

"Where are the children just now?"

"My son is asleep upstairs. Sylvie lives in Vancouver. She is a student there."

"I suppose you're aware the children stand to benefit considerably from Otto's estate."

"Is that so? I am told there is in fact very little to it. A yacht in poor repair and a ski chalet with a lien against it."

"A lien?"

"A bank mortgage."

"Who told you that?"

"Is this important, Inspector?"

"If Yves told you there's a lien on the property, he's misinformed you, Mrs. Pouliot. Otto owned the property free and clear, I'm sure of that."

"There is no mortgage?"

"That's right. But please, don't take my word. Have your attorney look into it."

She covered the mouthpiece and spoke to her husband.

There was a long pause before she returned to the line. "I'm sorry, I have no more to say at this time. I must hang up—"

"One second, Mrs. Pouliot. Let me give you my—"

The line went dead. I waited five minutes and called back. Her husband answered again.

"Monsieur Pouliot? Hector Bellevance. I'd like to say I'm sorry if I've upset your wife—"

"No, no, no. It's not you. It's Yves. She detests that man. Until yesterday they hadn't spoken in ten years. Now to have him meddling in her affairs again, after all this time . . . it's too much to bear."

"If you don't mind, why would Francine detest her ex-brother-in-law?"

"Why?" He paused. "I'll tell you. She believes it was Yves who drove Otto away. Out of the business, out of the family, and into the arms of another woman."

"I see." I gave him my phone number and asked him to let his wife know I would do all I could to make sure that the children received their full entitlement.

Yves didn't answer at the motel, so I tried Gavin Ingalls's office. Foliage season was such a boon to the land agents that even on a Sunday somebody was bound to be there.

"Northwoods Realty!" It was Gavin's right-hand gal, Cissy Ackerman. Cissy and I were second cousins and close in age. She grew up in Tipton a mile up the old creamery road. Went through a wild phase as a teenager, shoplifting and breaking into vacation homes, got married to a drunk, raised three kids, and had been working for Gavin Ingalls since her divorce several years ago. She was throwing him a little on the side, too, if my mother's intelligence was accurate. I didn't expect her to offer too much.

"Hector! My goodness. What can we do you for?"

"Gavin been in yet this morning, Cis?"

"He sure hasn't. Want to leave a message?"

"No, thanks. Actually I'm trying to locate Yves Morganthau."

"This about the murders?"

"Not exactly. I'm looking into the couple's estate."

"Wasn't that just awful, though? You found them, Hector, didn't you?"

"No, Spud did. It's been pretty tough on him."

"I can imagine! It's been tough on the Morganthau brother. You should see this goombah, Heck—he's half in the grave himself."

"Are they cutting a deal on the Morganthau property, do you know?"

"Who?"

"The brother and Gavin."

"That I couldn't say. They're grabbing a late breakfast down to Polly's, if you want to try and catch 'em."

I thanked her.

Polly's Diner on the highway just north of Allenburg was packed with tourists and regulars on this mild Sunday morning. Yves and Ingalls had already left, but I made it to the motel in time to catch the gray Mercedes idling in the motel office portico. Yves was inside settling his bill.

I stood leaning against his fender. Otto's brother appeared through the flashing reflection of the office door. He sagged at the sight of me, and his hand flew to his breast pocket, scrabbling for smokes.

"The State Police warned me not to speak with you, Mr. Bellevance. You have no role in the murder investigation, I'm told."

"Not true, Mr. Morganthau. I work for the Town of Tipton, and if I have to, I can subpoena you for a deposition, which would take a lot of your time and trouble. But if you simply give me five minutes right here and now, chances are we'll be all done with each other. How about it?"

He tossed his hands in the air. I led him over to a patch of lawn where the management had some plastic chairs set out under a crab apple tree that desperately needed pruning.

"Lucas Dunston tells me you and Otto betrayed him to a bunch of corporate cutthroats."

"Betrayed? Hah! Is that what he said? Lucas profited from the divestiture very handsomely. Or didn't he mention that?"

"He said you came away with more than three million dollars apiece."

Yves lit his cigarette. "Otto made a little over half that figure. And half of his return went to Francine."

"Dunston's pretty bitter about losing his company. Any chance he had something to do with your brother's murder?"

"Lucas?" he coughed. "Hardly! Staunch Presbyterian. Beacon of the faith, stalwart member of the community."

"What about Francine?"

"Never. She let go of all that long ago."

"What about you?"

He inhaled, wide-eyed, more surprised than indignant. "Me?"

"When did you learn he'd named you executor of his estate?"

He shook his head. "When I—when I received my copy of the will."

"Have you seen the autopsy reports?"

"Of course not. I understand the autopsies aren't scheduled until sometime tomorrow."

If he had this right, then they could have discovered Gaea's pregnancy only by testing her blood. Reckless of Evans to play that piece so early. And *six to eight weeks*—wasn't that what he'd said? How would he know that? "Yves, there are plenty of scrupulous realtors in the area. Why are you doing business with Gavin Ingalls?"

He took a rattly breath, gathering himself. "This is none of your concern. You know, I'm fed up with you, sir. May I suggest you seek out Otto's Florida acquaintances? Maybe there you can find what you—"

"I'll get to that." I leaned in close to him. "First I want you to tell me why you're dealing with a scumbag like Ingalls."

He relented, after a pause. "Gavin Ingalls was an associate of Otto's. Baby Micmac owned a good deal of northern-Vermont property for a number of years."

"What's Baby Micmac?"

"Our investment subsidiary."

"I see. What is Ingalls's interest in that A-frame?"

"Business, I'm sure. He's a real estate agent, after all."

"So there's an offer on the table?"

"Is this your concern?"

"Everything to do with Otto's murder and the disposition of his property is my concern."

He hesitated, massaging his forehead. "There's some interest . . . a consortium, I believe. I told them I could not consider any offer until after the probate hearing."

"They float a figure?"

"Not that I've heard."

"When they do, here's something for you to bear in mind. That A-frame's value is listed by the Town of Tipton at three hundred and twenty thousand dollars."

He said nothing.

"What's more, Otto owned it free and clear, which means his heirs ought to see a considerable return on the sale."

"I'm sure they'll be consoled by that knowledge." He shook his head, pushing up. "If there's nothing more—"

"And yet"—I stepped around to block him—"you led Francine to believe her children's inheritance wouldn't amount to much. Why did you tell her that?"

He bridled. "Now you really are overstepping your authority! I have no more to say."

"Come on, Yves! You let Gavin Ingalls wangle you into a kickback scam, isn't that right?"

His mouth worked until he could muster an objection. "That is unwarranted speculation. And I'm insulted by it!"

"I've advised Francine to retain an attorney to protect the heirs' interests. You'd better let Gavin know the deal's dead."

He paled, blinking fiercely.

"Never mind," I said, "I'll get the word to him. Now tell me about their life in Florida."

He took his time collecting himself. "I was with him in Florida for less than two days. For the wedding. Otto's best man was someone named Tucker. Randy . . . Roger . . . Speak to him."

"They were close friends, Otto and Tucker?"

"He was Otto's helmsman. He and Otto managed the excursion business together."

"What excursion business?"

"Island cruises. For vacationers."

"Really? Here's a guy with a million dollars, and he's chartering his pleasure craft?"

"He and Gaea went through that money very fast, Constable. They were touring the globe like royalty for years. Now please, if you'll excuse me, I have a long drive ahead." He threw his cigarette to the ground and walked quickly around me, giving me a wide berth.

"Drive safely, Mr. Morganthau. I'll be checking in with you from time to time."

THE East Branch Covered Bridge north of Allenburg had been a local landmark since the mid-1800s. Some years ago when the state widened and rerouted the highway, marooning the old bridge, Gavin Ingalls talked the Allenburg town officers into deeding the property to him for a dollar and consideration, the consideration being that he would preserve the historic structure on the site as a community service. He was preserving it, all right, though with a large house trailer installed in the middle of it, and a big red-and-white sign bolted to the crossbraces:

Northwoods Realty
Country Homes, Farms, and Choice Land

Cissy's rusty Ford Escort was the only vehicle out front. Her blond head popped up when the door ting-a-linged. The river glimmered through the small windows behind her desk. Rifts of vivid blue were showing in the cloud cover to the west.

"Going to be a nice day, Cis."

She glanced away. "Why, you could be right. You catch up with those two or not?" She was bleary-eyed. Hungover.

"Morganthau told me his brother used to do a fair amount of business with Gavin. Were you aware of that?"

She took her time, sensing soft ground ahead. "Well, sure, he knew Otto, but as far as any business matters, that would have been before my time."

"I guess Gavin's the man I need to talk to. Where is he right now?"

"He's probably on the golf course, Heck."

"Morganthau says some mover's already showing interest in his brother's house. You know who that would be?"

She pretended to think for a few seconds. "Well, probably Planvest."

"Planvest?"

"An investment corporation."

"From around here?"

"No, no. International."

"They're onto this one pretty fast, wouldn't you say?"

"Well, but you know Gavin—Mr. Johnny-on-the-Spot."

"How much are they offering?"

"Hector!" She tried to seem affronted. "I wouldn't tell you if I knew."

"Who represents Planvest? You can tell me that."

She pursed her lips. "I'd like to help you, but this is all private business. You better go talk to Gavin. Truly."

I walked by her to Gavin Ingalls's cluttered oak desk and started going though loose piles of papers.

"What do you think you're *doing*?" Now she was alarmed.

"I know what I'm doing, Cis. I'm looking for the bid on the Morganthau property."

She hopped up. "Get out of there! I'll call the police!"

"I am the police. Give me the figure, or I'll stay right here until I turn it up."

She fumed, fists jammed against her hips. "He's looking to squeeze a fast two, two-fifty out of it, OK? There's nothing firm yet, and that's all I know about it! Now would you get out of here?"

THE Allenburg Country Club was a scruffy nine-hole affair a few miles up Route 5 from the Northwoods office, narrow, crisscrossing fairways carved out of a big even-age red-pine plantation—ten thousand essentially worthless trees planted on good farmland as part of the benighted federal reforestation program in the fifties.

I found the clubhouse manager, Bump McHugh, snoring on a battered recliner in the greenskeeper's shack. A little dowel fire smoldered in the box stove. I didn't bother him. Bump had to be well past eighty. White hair, deep-creased cheeks, red nose. Used to run the recreation department down in Allenburg when I was a kid, taught me the rudiments of basketball. I found his reservations list on a metal clipboard in the shop. There in feathery pencil: "G. Ingalls and Guests." They'd teed off at noon.

I set off crosswise through the pine woods and before long spotted the foursome out on the second fairway sizing up their approaches. I went on ahead and waited crouched in a rocky drainage channel below the third tee. I listened to them bantering but couldn't make out the words, as one by one they cracked their drives over my head. Gavin, it turned out, scalped his, sending it diving into the rough some twenty yards from where I was watching. He appeared at the lip of the tee's plateau, wavy gray hair fluttering in the breeze, yellow slacks, white windbreaker.

He wheeled his clubs ahead of him down the wet slope. The three others motored along the cart path on the other side of the fairway. One of them was his son, Danny, lanky and sharp-faced. He'd been working for Gavin since he got out of the service, though he must have become quite the playboy these days, hanging out with Quimby, the King of Quim, living the high life up on the lake, and laying hands on the luscious Cherie Boulanger.

Gavin smacked an iron toward the flag.

"Bite!" he yelled. The ball bounded once and then rolled on across the green and down out of sight. He bounced the head of the club off his shoetop.

I stepped up behind him. "Tough luck, Gavin. Seems there's a lot of it going around lately."

He spun around unnerved and peered at me. "Jesus! Bellevance?"

"What's happening with the Morganthau property?"

He rammed the iron into the bag and kept walking. "What's wrong with you? I'm trying to relax out here! It's Sunday morning, for Christ's sake!"

"I hear you've solicited a buyer. Some investment group named Planvest."

"You're a real pain in the ass, Bellevance."

"Who's Planvest?"

He stopped. "What do you *want*?"

"I'm investigating the murders, Gavin, and I just stumbled onto the kickback deal you and Yves Morganthau have cooked up."

"You're out of your damn mind."

"That A-frame's worth three hundred thousand clear. Yves Morganthau promises the heirs twenty grand on the sale, and then you move it for a quick two-eighty, and you guys split the difference."

Gavin chuckled dismissively. "You have quite the imagination."

Someone yelled from the green. "Pop?"

He yelled back, "Stay there! It's OK, Danny! One second!"

"Otto was my neighbor," I said. "Least I can do for his family is make sure they get what they have coming to them."

"You know a person could get his nose broken for protruding into places where it doesn't belong," Gavin said, smiling.

"I wouldn't recommend it."

"Well, let me give you a little real estate lesson. You see, Constable, the value of residential property is very fluid. Price depends on marketability. And marketability depends on several factors—like where the property is located, what kind of shape it's in, and whether the previous owners just got *machine-gunned to death* inside it."

"So it's going cheap."

"The heirs are anxious to liquidate. I'm a broker, what do you want me to do?"

"Who's Planvest?"

"Some people that incorporated themselves offshore. I don't know who the participants are—and that's the way they like it."

"Who are you dealing with? Who represents them?"

He turned. "Aw, shit. See what you've done now? Now you've got Danny boy all riled up."

Danny strode toward us brandishing a black putter, a flop of brown hair dancing above his dished face. He was slim, bony, tough-looking—a hothead. I was glad to see him coming, though. I hadn't laid eyes on this kid up close since he was a runty schoolboy. I welcomed the chance to take some measure of the would-be developer who was pushing this cockamamie scheme to turn Tipton into a four-season resort.

He stopped a scant foot in front of me. His glinty, triangular eyes were too small to see into. Handsome enough, though. Pretty sure of his hands, too, or he wouldn't be in my face like this. "You're the dickhead with a badge that jumped Steven last night up at the Lodge, right?"

I hung there over him in the cloud of his coffee breath. "Better step away from me, Danny, right now," I said finally, "or I'll wrap that putter around your neck."

Danny seemed about to object, but his father seized his elbow and yanked him back on his heels. "Stay out of this, Danny. No need to get cantankerous, hear me? This's got nothing to do with you."

"Take your hand off my fucking arm," he growled.

"Don't press this guy, hear? I didn't pay the orthodontist all those years to watch you get your teeth drove down your throat."

Danny snorted, turned, and jabbed his middle finger at us over one shoulder.

"Boy's got too much of the Irish," Gavin said, blowing. "Now, are we through?"

"When did you and Otto Morganthau do business together?"

"Long time ago. He used to be a portfolio manager for a Canadian company."

"He bought property through you?"

"I facilitated some acquisitions for him, yeah."

"What acquisitions?"

"Look, that's enough. If you really want to pursue this, call my assistant and she'll set up a time. Right now I'm smack in the middle of my religious observance, OK, Bellevance?"

FROM the the trees I watched the foursome putt out. One of the Ingallses' two partners was dressed like a rodeo showman, in peacock blue, white golf shoes, white cowboy hat, long silver hair to his collar. The other was fat, in a green polo shirt and baggy khakis.

Bump was upright in the clubhouse when I peeked in.

"Hector Bellevance! What brings you way out here? You taking up small ball?"

"Perish the thought." We laughed. "Tell me, who're those two fellas out with the Ingallses, you know?"

"Lawyer named Rossi. He's one. Flashy, likes to blather."

"He the fat one or the fancy one?"

"Well, the *fat* one, that's Claude Spinney. Big car salesman. You know Spinney Saab-Olds down to Barre?"

I nodded. "What's he like?"

"Lousy golfer. Giggles a lot. They tease him a fair amount."

"They out here often?"

"Every weekend—long as the weather's decent."

"What sort of lawyer is this fancy dresser, Rossi?"

"Don't know. He's from downcountry. They got big ideas for that mountain, you know, Hector—the Ingallses do. They got some real big development plans."

"That's what I hear."

First thing Monday morning I telephoned the state medical examiner's office across the state in Burlington to ask when the results of the Morganthau autopsies might be released. The examiner's assistant assured me the procedures were scheduled for that afternoon, and the examiner's report would be available to the appropriate authorities by early the next day. After that I called Waterbury and asked someone in the crime lab whether they could estimate the stage of a pregnancy from blood chemistry. A specialist would return my call, I was told. None did.

Later, after a few hours in the garden, I was down at Sullivan's getting my mail when the van pulled in with the day's *Eagle*. Strong-Parkhurst's big piece was page one. I felt heartened by that—until the import of the headline registered.

Police Profile Hints at Local Link in Tipton Slayings

State Police say more insight has been gained into the brutal murder of Otto and Gaea Morganthau, who were found dead of multiple gunshot wounds several days ago in their chalet in Tipton. Investigators now have reason to believe that the person who murdered the couple knew the victims and lives in the area.

Lt. Brian Cahoon of the state's Bureau of Criminal

Investigation in Waterbury said that a psychological profile of the killer has been developed with the help of a special agent from the Behavioral Science Unit of the Federal
Bureau of Investigation Academy in Quantico, Virginia.
After a thorough analysis of the crime scene, Special
Agent Foster P. Singleton and Lt. Cahoon have prepared a
general description of the killer.

According to the profile, the killer "was friendly with
the Morganthaus, had been to the house previously, is
about their age, lives nearby, and is well respected in the
community."

The profile describes the offender as "unusually
strong" and says that "due to certain aspects of the
crime scene, it is believed that at some time a female
dominated the offender's life" and that "the offender may
have been under the influence of drugs and may have
been in a dreamlike state while performing the murders."

According to a source close to the investigation, police
theorize that Mrs. Morganthau may have been sexually
molested before or after her death.

Investigators now believe that "the offender attempted
to mislead the police during the early stages of the investigation." They also believe that someone else in the area
may know or suspect the offender's identity. "That person
is in serious danger," Cahoon said.

No arrests have yet been made in the case and no
weapon has been recovered. Sgt. Edmund Evans, of the
Allenburg barracks, an investigator assigned to the case,
said today, "Hopefully we'll be making some progress
very soon. We're on a roll," he said.

I drove out of the hills, down the river road, and straight
through town to the *Eagle* newsroom. The last time I'd visited
the paper I was in high school and the editorial offices were

in a Quonset hut behind the press shop, next to a lumber-yard. Since then they'd moved into what used to be Hed-strom's Funeral Parlor, a landmark on Bank Street. The main floor of the place was a maze of partitioned workstations under a dropped-panel ceiling, monitors aglow everywhere.

Wilma Strong-Parkhurst gripped my hand politely. "Very pleased to see you again," she said. Her eyes sparkled. Her fingertips were stained by her ballpoint. Even indoors, her hair stood out in wild coppery curls. I realized again, with a small shock, that I was seriously attracted to this woman. It was annoying, the way my rising blood took the edge off my anger.

She darted ahead of me, this way and that, back to her desk, where her keyboard lay tipped like a beached raft on a drift of newspapers and computer printouts. She unfolded a chair for me. I was suddenly conscious of my worn flannel work shirt and dirty overalls.

"So, what's the good word, Constable?" She propped her sandaled feet up on her desk. Under the fluorescent lights her bare legs shimmered with platinum hair.

I looked into her open face. "The word is *bogus.*"

Her smile faded. "This would be in reference to what?"

"The profile. It's a fake, Wilma, and you're a tool of the state's so-called investigation."

"That was taken from a *press release,* Bellevance. I never *saw* the actual profile."

"Did you see the release? Or did Evans call it in especially for you?"

She sat up, withdrawing those legs from view. "Sorry, but I'm not grasping your problem."

"Evans fed you the profile over the phone, isn't that right?" She rolled her eyes.

"Did you talk to Special Agent Singleton?"

"What is this about?"

"That profile was *cooked.*"

"How? What for?" She sat up, found a pen, opened a notebook.

"Any psychological analysis of a homicide scene takes weeks to produce—longer if the Bureau's involved. This one was thrown together in about twelve hours."

"OK. Why would they do that?"

"To put pressure on an uncooperative suspect."

"Your brother, to be precise. All right, do you know what makes him a suspect? What they have on him?"

"Occam's razor."

"Who?"

"Basic tenet of police science. The simplest solution to a problem is usually the correct solution."

"So you're saying Evans is pushing a hunch."

"A half-assed cop hunch, that's exactly right."

"Maybe you should be yelling at Evans."

"Cahoon's behind this one, I'll bet. But they couldn't have pulled it off without convincing a gullible reporter to write it up like hard news."

Her ice-blue eyes narrowed. "Hey, bud, when a federal agent comes all the way up here to assist the State Police in developing a psychological sketch of a local killer, let me tell *you,* the news doesn't get any harder than that."

"OK, talk to Special Agent Singleton. Ask him what specifics the profile's based on. This garbage about the killer being on drugs, in a dreamlike state, and at one time in his life dominated by a woman. That's ludicrous. What did they find at the scene that would lead them to deductions like that?"

"They never release those particulars. As you well know."

"This thing deserves a follow-up," I said, standing. "That's all I'm saying."

"All right, you got it. Give me a couple hours to see what

more I can coax out of these guys, then meet me at R and J's around six o'clock. Deal?"

We shook. I left town and headed straight back up the river to Tipton and out Canada Ridge to the farm. It was after four. Spud was down in the barn—I could hear the milking machine from the dooryard.

I pulled in under the maples and ran up the gravel path to the house. Brenda's Subaru was in the turnout next to the mudroom entry.

I walked in through the storm door and stopped in the kitchen doorway. The room looked empty. "Brenda?"

"Christ, Hector! You goddamn *fool!*" She was right there beside the doorjamb, frazzle-haired, shaking, holding a cast-iron skillet over her head. "I coulda knocked your *brains in,* Hector!"

"Calm down, Brenda, calm down."

She burst into tears. "It's just— Oh, Lord, I'm just so *scared!* I can't *stand* it."

I took the pan out of her hands and put it on the gas range. The room smelled of bacon. She leaned into me, sobbing.

"Whoever shot those people is a long way from here, Brenda."

She wiped her eyes with a dish towel. "Oh, yeah? The FBI says different. Did you see today's paper? They're saying the killer *knew* them, and he *lives* in the area, and he was a respected member of the, of the—"

"All that's nothing but a *tactic,* Brenda. They're trying to get Spud to crack."

"I knew it! Oh, God! That's what— You don't think he . . ."

"No," I said flatly. "No. Not for a second."

"But then where are they *getting* this crap?"

"Some detectives like to latch on to the most obvious solution and run with it hard as they can."

"That sounds awful damn dumb."

"Yeah. Well, generally that's all it takes."

"You mean you don't think it was somebody around here that did it?" Her lower lip quivered. She looked half her age.

"I don't think it was anyone from around here, and I know it wasn't Spud, Brenda. Somebody's setting him up, because he's the easy answer."

"So who stuck that vibrator in with his tools? He says he doesn't know how it got there. Jesus, Hector, do you believe that? The cops sure don't. What am *I* supposed to think?"

"He says he could have absentmindedly picked it up while he was in their bedroom."

"*Absentmindedly!* That's not what he told me. He told me somebody *planted* it there. 'Who, Spud,' I asked him, 'the *tooth* fairy?' "

"He didn't kill those people, Brenda. You have to believe that."

"Do I? Why? I don't know *what* to believe, and that's the truth! He's telling everybody a different story!" The baby had begun bawling upstairs. "It's got me wondering, I mean, Jesus, if the FBI wants him for murdering those two people, maybe I shouldn't even be staying here in this house. With the baby and all. Would you?"

"He needs you here, Bren. Especially now."

She slowly shook her head, chin trembling.

"Brenda—" I took her arm as she tried to brush past me. "Gaea was pregnant when she was killed. Did you know that?"

She froze. Her face drained. The baby got louder. "Get out of here, will you? Just get *out!*" she screamed.

She didn't know. I hated to pop her like that. But she was off the list.

Spud was behind the barn on his old Massey-Ferguson tractor with a bucket, trying to get his pit emptied out before winter blew in and froze the manure pile. At the sight of me he shut down his machine and hopped to the ground.

"Guess what I just *saw*, Heck. I was coming out the door there, out into the daylight, and we got these six, seven half-grown kittens? Well, they're playing around over in the tall grass by the diesel pump, and I come out and damn if this hawk doesn't come diving out of nowhere and snatch off the black one just like a hand grabbing an apple off the table. That cat must weigh half a pound, and this little hawk, he's flapping, whoomp, whoomp, trying to gain the hedgerow there, and he does, but just barely." He shook his head. "Never seen that before."

"Might have been the same young redtail I caught stooping after goldfinches at my feeder day before yesterday," I said. "Kittens are easy pickings. A bird snatches one, it'll just curl up—unlike a weasel, or a rabbit. They'll put up a fight and hurt a young raptor if they can."

But he wasn't listening. "So what's with the investigation? You having any luck getting these cops off my back?"

"Guess you haven't seen today's paper."

"Guess not. Why?"

I briefed him, then tried to assure him it was nothing, they were overreaching, it was just a ploy. "But it would help your situation considerably," I said, "if we could come up with a compelling reason why these people got themselves killed. Otherwise it could be quite a while before they loosen the screws, Spud."

"Right now, you know what? I don't *care* why they got killed. But I think he got into something, in Florida most likely. Like you said, they were hiding, only they didn't do a good enough job."

"Well, the State Police aren't about to take their show to Florida. They can't afford to, for one thing. That's another reason Evans is fixed on you."

"That's his problem."

"Which makes it our problem. Listen, remember when Wayne Hrushka screwed up their foundation? You told me Otto was pretty upset over that. How'd they resolve it, you know?"

"The foundation? That wasn't nothing. He come back up the next summer and did the backfilling and the grading. Trucked in twenty yards of topsoil—" He interrupted himself. "Wow, I just remembered something. That old antique railway safe!"

"Railway safe?"

"Otto found it up in Canada. Beautiful thing, about yea big." He described it with his arms. "Painted curlicues on the sides, big dial on the door—"

"Otto installed a safe in that A-frame?"

"He sure did. Took a while. Damn thing sat on the floor of the haybarn that whole winter—"

"It's down in the basement?"

"Wait, I remember what happened. Thing got hung up in transit. He bought it up in Ontario someplace, and there was a truckers' strike or something. Wasn't till the next summer they finally got around to putting it in the ground."

"Who put it in?"

"Hrushka did. His crew."

"What did Otto want a safe for?"

Spud shrugged. "Well, you consider they were spending half the year down in Florida. I guess it made sense to have someplace for your silver, your art, whatever. You got to keep stuff secure while you're gone."

"Did the police ask you about it?"

He shook his head. "I never even thought about it till just now."

"Who else knows about this safe? Anybody?"

"Just Hrushka as far as I know."

"Not Lonnie?"

"No. He wasn't workin' for me back then."

"You ever tell anybody else about it?"

"Not that I recall. Except Mom."

"OK. Make sure you don't. Hear me?"

He nodded.

I went home to change and check my machine for messages. There were none.

R and J's was a truck stop at the North Allenburg exit off I-91. R and J's was once praised in a *Newsweek* magazine article about road food for its Green Mountain french fries. The place was jammed. It took me a minute before I spotted Wilma's bright head of hair back in a corner booth. She was bent over her notebook scribbling as a waitress cleared away the previous party's dishes.

She glanced up as I slid in, hoisting her canvas carryall onto the table. Down one side of the bag in blurred felt-tip was her telephone directory. "You'll be glad to hear," she said into the bag as she searched for something, "that I managed to reach Special Agent Singleton before he left town, and he assured me that the profile I referred to is one hundred percent for real. All the deductions are statistically derived from observations they made at the scene, and the interpretations are based on the Bureau's extensive bank of crime data. He also assured me a profile is *never* aimed at a specific individual. The way they work, in fact, is just the opposite—they narrow the field of suspects. By *excluding* people. That's the whole idea."

"Great. What the hell else did you think he'd say? You really expect him to own up to a shabby tactic like that?"

"Hey, big fella, you're the one who told me to talk to the guy. So do I take it you're still maintaining the thing's a crock?"

I nodded. "Contemptible bullshit. But in some cases it gets the job done, or they wouldn't go to all this trouble."

She slapped the table. "Terrific, that's my angle. Let me read you what I've got so far."

The waitress arrived. We ordered beers and seafood platters.

Wilma pulled out a sheaf of paper with scribbling down the margins. "Here goes . . . 'So far, investigators have named no suspects, but as a result of the psychological profile they are now focusing their investigation on the Morganthaus' local acquaintances. One friend of the couple's, Tipton Town Constable Hector Bellevance, a former detective with the Boston Police Department, today described such police strategy as "bone-headed."'"

"Wonderful."

"'Allenburg State Police Sergeant Edmund Evans would not comment on criticisms. "This was a crime of passion," he said. "We believe the killer was on intimate terms with one or both of the victims and that he was a loner and quite familiar with the area." Police are awaiting the results of laboratory tests which could provide the basis for an arrest, Evans said.'"

"What tests?"

"DNA, I believe." She looked up. "The wife was pregnant."

"They haven't released that. Who told you that?"

She zipped her lips shut.

"You can't put that in your article."

"Not this article anyway."

Our beers arrived.

She took a gulp. "You'll be interested to know I acquired some background information on the psychological analysis. Like to hear it?"

"I can't wait."

"First off, the killer belongs to a deviant personality type known as 'organized nonsocial.'"

"Nice. I like that."

"Lieutenant Cahoon faxed me an article on this subject from the *FBI Law Enforcement Bulletin*. It's about lust murderers." She fished out some more papers and smoothed them on her placemat. "OK. With lust murderers, the deal is you basically have two types: organized nonsocial and disorganized asocial—"

"The cops must love you."

"Everybody loves me," she shot back. "Now, your organized nonsocial is your basic self-centered loner. Working class. Indifferent to society. Soft-spoken type. Good at manipulating others. Frequently the father left or else died at an early age. Usually raised by a cold mother figure. On the surface, he's vague and preoccupied. Underneath, he's methodical, cunning, and brutal. Also sadistic. Often mutilates his victims. Frequently takes a souvenir from the murder scene, something belonging to the victim, like panties—something with a sexual association—so he can relive the crime in fantasies. Commonly lives nearby. Feels guilt over the crime. Feels compelled to revisit the crime scene. Wants the victims to be found. Gets off on the excitement and publicity surrounding the investigation. Exhibits a desire to control the investigation. Et cetera." She looked up, wide-eyed. "So. Who does this describe? Anybody we know?"

"Who does a horoscope describe?"

"Come on. The killer was a psychopath. Agree or disagree?"

"Lust murderers don't use guns. They're stranglers, usually. Slashers."

"This guy was pumped up. The police think he could have been watching them screwing right before he broke in there."

"This was a contract job," I said. "Whoever did the Morganthaus wanted it to look sloppy. Like a crime of passion."

"Hit men don't usually go ransacking desk drawers afterwards, do they?"

"They might. It depends."

"If the killer was her lover, he could have been looking for incriminating letters, or pictures, or a diary . . ."

"There's no indication anything was missing."

"What about the woman's vibrator?"

"It's Evans, isn't it? He's feeding you this crap so you can bait me with it."

"You wanted details, I got details."

I found a twenty in my wallet and threw it down.

"Hold on, you!" Wilma followed me toward the exit. "This is why you came down here, remember? To round out the picture for me!"

Heads turned as we swept past.

Outside the diner she dashed around in front of me. "Listen, don't be blaming me. I just handed you everything they have on your brother. Now you can give me *his* version! Come on, lay it out for me and we'll see where that takes us!"

I opened the Powerwagon's passenger door. Wilma jumped in without a word.

The sky was purple. We took the county road west along the river and out into the hills. It was coming up on seven o'clock as we passed through Tipton village. I turned into the state fishing access and shut off the engine. Quietly, as the last light slid from the granite cliffs of Mount Joseph, I laid out what pieces I had collected from Lonnie and Keith and Yves and the Ingallses and Fran Pouliot and Lucas Dunston. She scribbled nonstop.

"I like it, as far as it goes," she said when I was done. "But if Spud's DNA portrait comes back from the lab, you know they'll indict him."

"That's a problem, all right."

"Problem! That's the ball game, Constable. He'll get thrown in jail, the wife'll split with the bambino, and the farm'll go on the block."

"DNA pairings take a while. We've got time."

"To do what?"

"Find the killer."

She opened her mouth, but nothing came out. She folded

her hands and held me with her eyes for a minute. Then, little by little, like a sawn tree just beginning to fall, she leaned toward me. Her slowness made it feel inevitable. Not only that we should soon be kissing, but that it had been fated to happen ever since we met. She took me by the back of the neck. I enfolded her in my arms. Her mouth was soft and mobile.

At last I pulled myself away, still holding her by her thin shoulders. Her eyes were closed. For once, she looked serene. I was anything but.

"This isn't a good idea," I whispered. My heart was racing. I made myself sit back.

"Goodness isn't everything," she breathed.

"No," I said. "Just the same, we'd better get going." I cranked the starter.

"Going?" Her eyes popped open. "Going where?"

"Town offices. I want to look over some title transfers."

From the low-ceilinged common room in the basement of the town
hall building I called Ella McPhetres. Ella lived way out on
the Bailey Plain west of the lake, but she agreed to come
right in to open the records room for me.

For the next hour the three of us sat there at one of the
trestle tables going through titles and transfers. Tipton's
Grand List showed half a dozen properties in the hands of
either Planvest Corp., N.V. or Stook Holding Corp., N.V. A
power of attorney in the title file described Planvest as "a
company organized and existing under the laws of the
Netherlands Antilles and having its registered office at Han-
delskad 12, Curaçao." It named the golf-course peacock,
Nathan Rossi, as the "true and lawful agent" for the corporation. There were three illegible scrawls at the bottom—witnesses and a notary. Another swoopy signature belonged to
Planvest's managing director, a Mr. H. P. H. J. V. M. de Rooij,
of the Curaçao Corporation, no doubt a shell directorship.

"They're foreign investment groups," Ella said. "They've
been buying up acreage all over the township." She tapped at
the list. "Stook Holding bought the Canadian Pacific right-
of-way along the east shore. And the old girls' camp, what's
left of it—they picked that up years ago. Here's Planvest
again. They bought the International Paper tract up the
length of Dust Mill Brook to Canada Ridge back in 1984.
That parcel alone's close to four thousand acres."

"Isn't Wayne Hrushka's place up in there?"

"Well, he's over on the Tewkesville side. But Planvest may own that, too, I don't know. They're in on the ski area expansion." She pointed. "Plus, see here. Stook Holding owns the old ash plain across from the girls' camp all the way to the cedar swamp across from the fishing access. They also bought the Lakeview Cabins, up above there. Planvest picked up Doug MacLaren's farm last spring. They got quite a few farms in Tipton and in Shadboro, too."

"What's the N.V. stand for?" Wilma asked.

"It's Dutch," Ella said. "Means 'nameless partnership.' There's secrecy laws down there that guard against disclosure."

"Who told you that?"

"Rossi. He's been doing business up here forever. Comes in fairly often."

"You have a phone number for him?"

"I have his card."

She untacked it from the corkboard on the wall behind her. Nathan Rossi was a corporate investment analyst with Weiss, Grotke, Fay, and Leiberman, 101 Hamden Street, Boston.

"No local number?"

She shook her head. Hamden Street rang no bells. No matter. There were people I could call for the word on this partnership, when and if it came to that.

"If Otto somehow got himself in the way of these corporations," Wilma was musing, "with all these millions of dollars at stake, they'd probably have good reason to want him dead."

"In the way how?" Ella asked.

"That's the question, all right. You have to wonder, what are these nameless partnerships doing, buying up half the damn town?"

"It's just investors parking dough," Ella said. "They been at it for years. I don't know what's so sinister about it."

"Come off it, Ella," I said. "This stinks. You know it does."

"No, I don't. Look, these corporations pay their taxes on time, they don't require services, they don't have kids we got to educate, they don't generate trash we got to ship to a land-fill someplace. . . . It's not that bad of a deal."

"So why are they nameless?" Wilma asked.

Ella shrugged. "Plenty of times I'd like to be nameless, Lord knows."

"Do you and the realtors and the bankers all deal exclusively with the corporations' attorneys?" I asked, leaning back.

"Just one. Rossi. That's his practice. Keep digging, you'll see."

"Rossi ought to know the identity of his clients, wouldn't you think?"

Ella rolled her eyes. "Why don't you ask him?"

"Waste of time," Wilma said. "Probably have to shove his head down the commode before he'd start coughing up any names."

Ella gave her a strange look.

"Ella," I said, "don't we have a big map somewhere that shows a breakdown of the town in titled parcels?"

She brought it out and unrolled it on the floor. Tipton Township was J-shaped. It reached from the Canadian border down around the lake to North Allenburg on the south, with Shadboro to the west and Tewkesville on the east. Most of these corporation-owned pieces seemed to be clustered along the east side of the lake and the west side of the mountain, right to the Tewkesville town line, where they abutted Mount Joe Ski Area.

"Christ Almighty, we're talking almost twenty thousand acres here, Ella. And that's just in Tipton."

"It's woods and rocks, Hector. It's not like they can dig it up and truck it away."

"Don't be so sure. Have you heard this talk about Danny

Ingalls tearing down the Lodge and throwing up a fancy resort complex?"

"Listen. In this job, I hear all kinds of pie-in-the-sky whoop-de-do. The Ingallses're already expanding the ski area, like I mentioned. They got state approval to put in a hundred-acre holding pond for snowmaking this summer— up on the old MacLaren place—and they're planning to carve sixty or seventy new trails down the back of the mountain next year. What do they have up there now, ten? Gonna be some operation. And on top of that, according to Rossi, these same high rollers that are developing the mountain are also gonna be developing the lakefront—in a big way. But I'll believe that when I see it."

"Rossi told you this?"

She nodded. "There's people around who think they got a half-decent chance. You take Okemo, Sunday River, Jackson Hole, even Aspen. Twenty, thirty years ago all of them were just dots on the map. Plus, look at the demographics. You got Montreal two hours away, Boston's three and a half. Stranger things have happened."

"Stranger than what?" Wilma said.

Ella shook her doughy arms in the air. "Come one, come all, to the Arrow Lake Four-Season Resort and Convention Center! We got your lakeside holiday village, luxury convention hotel, and Jacuzzi-equipped condominiums. Fine restaurants! Glitzy boutiques! Cafés, pubs! Not to mention your eighteen-hole Arnold Palmer signature golf course, your Jimmy Connors tennis stadium, dinosaur theme park, world-class roller coaster, plus swimming and sailing, skiing and snowboarding, and fireworks every night."

Wilma laughed. "Who in God's name are these so-called high rollers?"

"Who knows? Foreign fat cats. Danny's their front man, supposedly. He's doing all the spadework and whatnot."

"You know, this is nuts," Wilma said. "Why would 'foreign fat cats' want to pour millions into this jerkwater town? The chances of a big resort taking hold up here are pitiful. Tipton'll never be an Aspen, no way."

"Well, nothing's come in yet," Ella said. "They're probably sizing up the potential profits."

I shook my head. "If these people manage to build a resort up here, they may not give a damn if it all goes under in five years."

"What makes you say that?" Wilma was writing in her notebook as she spoke.

"Getting cash out of the country isn't especially hard. But before you can really play with it, you have to get it back in again. That's trickier."

"Jeez. You don't think that mental dwarf Danny Ingalls is running a giant international money-laundering operation, do you?" Ella said.

"He's attached to it somehow."

Ella sputtered.

"Good God, Hector, look at this." Wilma brandished a sheaf of papers. "I have four parcels of land here that these Planvest people bought from another offshore company— Micmac Investments, N.V."

We nodded at each other. Micmac was Otto. She took my hand and squeezed it.

"Ella, thanks very much for all your help. Now I want you to listen to me. Don't say anything to anybody about this. All right? What you know could get you killed."

"Oh, gee, thanks a lot!" She promised to call soon as she got a line on Nathan Rossi.

"Otto had to be in bed with these other real estate investors," Wilma said once were outside again. "But even if he was giving them trouble, why off him now?"

"Now's when it's all on the line. The Ingallses are cleared

to start carving up the mountain. The Lodge is slated for demolition. I'll bet this guy Rossi or somebody is already taking bids from half a dozen contractors and suppliers. Crunch time. The money's coming home."

"So the question becomes, where's it from."

"That's right."

"I'm glad we agree. So what's next? The Lodge? Or Gavin Ingalls's front door?"

"Neither. You know what? I need to make something up to you, Wilma."

She turned those blue eyes on me. "I like the sound of that. What is it?"

"Supper. How'd you like to come up to the cabin for a taste of the season's bounty?"

"I'd love to. But first would you mind swinging by R and J's so I can pick up my Mazda?"

I put the water on to boil and shucked corn while Wilma gave herself a quick tour of the place, inspecting my keepsakes, which weren't many. Nearly all the objects and furnishings in here, from the Danish flatware to the oak mission chairs to the gardening magazines on the glass slab of a table, were my mom's. Despite all we had accumulated in eight years of marriage, when I left the Cape all I took with me were three suitcases, my academy footlocker, and a few boxes of books and personal papers.

I opened the wine, poured two glasses, and raised a toast to Spud's innocence.

"To Spud," she said, "and may the heartless killers surface soon."

"Wilma, listen to this. You'll like this. Spud tells me Otto had a safe in that A-frame."

Her jaw dropped. "You're kidding. That's *great!*"

"Only if it's still intact."

"OK, but . . . *wow. A safe.* I bet *that's* the reason somebody's in such a rush to buy the property—before the heirs find out about it."

"Could be."

"This should take the heat off your brother, if nothing else."

"I'm not so sure. It's another key piece of information he's been withholding from the investigation."

"Hmm. I see what you mean. Also, I mean, are we positive it's really in there? Ed and the boys went all through that place. What if it's gone? Or what if they already found it and they're just waiting to see who else knows about it?"

"That's possible, too. Though I'd be surprised if Otto didn't have it pretty well hidden."

"But why wasn't there any mention of it in their will? Or in any other papers?" she mused. "Hey—maybe it *was* in the will, and Yves didn't tell the heirs about it. Maybe that's another thing he's keeping for himself out of the liquidation."

"No, the will predates the safe. Besides, even if Yves did know about the safe, he's not bloodless enough to try keeping it a secret."

"Unless *he's* the one who hired the killer." She helped herself to another ear of corn and slathered it with butter.

"I can't see it. I'm not surprised Ingalls got him to go for the kickback scam, but that just makes him a vulture. "

"And vultures don't kill. All right. So, going back to these fat cats, if they had Otto killed, then who's the next person we need to sandbag? Rossi? Or Gavin Ingalls?"

"Try 'em if you want, but the one I have in mind is Wayne Hrushka."

"The militia guy? He's zero help. Evans already went up there."

"Wayne's the one who put that railway safe in the ground. He'll talk to me, I think. We go back a ways."

"What's his angle, besides the safe?"

"He's leasing his land from Planvest."

"Really? That's worth pursuing. . . . This corn, by the way, is terrific."

"Thanks." I refilled her wineglass.

She raised another toast. "Here's to living off the fat of the land!" She was a little buzzed. "You know, Heck, every winter I say to myself, 'Next spring I'm putting in a *garden,*' and I sit poring over seed catalogs and I send away for all these exotic, mouthwatering seeds—Crenshaw melons and eggplants and kohlrabi—and it never fails, the seeds arrive and June rolls around and I end up taking them in to work and giving them away. One year I got as far as renting a rototiller, and it sat out in the rain for three days. I'm too damn busy! How can I *be* that busy? I don't even have kids!"

"Your husband doesn't pitch in?"

"Not a chance. Vic guides on weekends."

I got up to make tea.

"Hector, tell me something. Do you truly *like* living way out here? Or are you just in some kind of fallback mode?"

"It's home. I was raised here." I wasn't about to confirm her take on me, no matter how much truth there was in it. As a topic for casual discussion, my feelings and my past were off the table.

"You must miss your kid, hunh?"

I paused. Another subject I was disinclined to get into. "Who told you?"

"Spud. Little girl out on the West Coast, right?"

Spud was such a looselips. "Rosemary. She's almost two now, and she was just six months when my wife and I split up. I really never got to know her." Truthfully, I was never entirely sure Rosemary was mine. Not that I had put the question to Naomi. The issue somehow seemed irrelevant by then. In leaving, she said she would not seek child support and would prefer it if we severed all ties. I made no protest.

"That's a shame. You still in touch with your ex?"

"Not at all."

"I see. Any significant other at the present time?"

"No."

"Me neither," she said.

"What's the story with Victor?"

She sighed. "I wish I knew. Vic is a brother to me. That's the best way to put it."

"He gay?"

She shook her head. "Zero libido. And that was the quality that most appealed to me at first, if you can believe it—his imperturbability."

"Why did you marry him?"

"It was winter, and I was cold."

"No, really, tell me."

"I'd be glad to." She smiled and narrowed her eyes. "But don't think I don't know what it means when you start recounting your amours." She rose, her hands bunched in her skirt's patch pockets, and stood gazing out the kitchen window into the night. "I was in medical school in Madison, on the downside of a busted first marriage. My womanizing ex-husband was back in Santa Barbara, and I was pining for him because it was Christmastime and I was all alone and he wasn't. So anyway, Christmas Eve I'm sneaking around in the forestry greenhouse looking for some kind of potted tree I could decorate, and I literally trip over Victor. He's trying to patch a water line. A whirlwind courtship ensued. Two days later we eloped. I quit med school and we took off for the Green Mountains to live with Vic's parents and begin our idyllic life together on the family tree farm."

"You mean you married Vic two days after you met him?"

"You bet. I married Vic before we'd ever even *slept* together. How's that for a concept?"

"You're crazy."

She nodded. "I must be. Otherwise I'd be an epidemiologist working for the Red Cross out of a tin-roofed research station in Botswana."

"Is that where you'd rather be?"

"No! I'd rather be crazy."

I rolled out the first deep laugh I'd heard coming from me in a long while. I liked her. I liked her a lot—in spite of her prying and her edginess. In spite of everything. The woman definitely had *spark*. She was funny and smart. She was slender and pretty and even graceful in her own hyperalert chickadee fashion. I hadn't felt this moved by a woman in ten years.

"More wine?"

"By all means!"

I got up to find another bottle, my ears burning.

"Whoa!" she called from the living room. "*Ms. Dracula!* This thing worth watching?"

"Couldn't say. I picked it up Saturday night. Keith Quimby laid it on me."

"No! This is one of *his*? Let's check it out!" She clacked it into the machine.

I joined her with our glasses on the wingback sofa.

The tape began with a full-screen American flag rippling in a gale. Scrolling text, over a military march on the sound track, spelled out an appeal for the preservation of free speech.

Wilma hooted, "I love America! Don't you?"

Fade to black.

A few sinister chords . . . a crack of thunder . . . A dark mansion looms beneath a huge bluish moon. It's the Lodge. *Keith Quimby and Straight Arrow Productions present . . . Cherie Boulanger . . . Felix Corcoran . . . Gala Kim Long Tree . . . Juggsie Normess . . . Tony Golden . . . in . . . a Melo-erotic Spectacular . . . MS. DRACULA . . . Directed and Produced by Keith Quimby . . . Original Screenplay by Keith Quimby. Executive Producer Dan Ingalls . . .*

As more titles roll, the camera pans the treetops before closing in on one of the Lodge's tower windows.

Inside the tower room dozens of candles sputter. More thunder rumbles. Rain patters against the windowpanes. The camera pirouettes around a gilt coffin set upon a velvet-draped platform, zooming in as the coffin's creaky lid begins to rise and a woman's pale hand with black-painted nails slips through the opening. . .

"Eeek," Wilma said, clutching my knee.

The camera pans around to take in a small audience of men and women, then finds a dark and brooding character standing off to—

"Christ Almighty," I said, "it's Danny Ingalls."

"Who, that guy? In the velvet tunic?"

"Right. I hear he's Ms. Dracula's main man in real life."

"Danny? Why, the sly dog."

Danny was playing some kind of a sex-club entrepreneur. Cheryl was positively magnificent, fanged or not. She stretched languorously and stripped, going slow, haughty as a cat. Truly amazing breasts. The audience ogled her in a showy way, craning their necks and aahing, until a runty villain dressed in a brown bat costume burst into the room with a flintlock pistol. The audience recoiled as one, but Ms. Dracula glared coldly at the intruder. . . . I was intrigued.

Wilma zapped it.

"That's enough for me," she said, rising and lifting her black lamb's-wool sweater over her head. She wore no bra. "These," she declared in a nervy singsong, "are my own pink-tipped nubbins."

"Charming." I was charmed. Her skirt dropped to the carpet, and then a pair of pink-striped panties.

She was pale and freckled along the tops of her shoulders and the length of her lean thighs, and her skin had a rich peppery fragrance. Her belly was white and flat as an ironed bedsheet, and the tuft between her legs reminded me of nothing so much as a butte at sunset.

We made love on the couch and on the carpet and finally for a long while on my mother's four-poster bed under twin skylights. She was so smooth and felt so good in my arms, warm and cool at the same time, and the way she clung to me and cried out. . . I hadn't been with a woman in over a year, not since those weeks when Naomi and I knew it was all coming apart and we were desperate, even in our coupling.

We took two dishes of chocolate Häagen-Dazs out to the porch swing, and we lingered over that, feeding each other, and then I walked her down to her car through the wet, unmowed grass. I was holding the door open while she rummaged through her tote bag for her keys when, out of nowhere, I was stung with longing for a wife. A good wife. And for that sense of ordinariness and balance and comfort that I hadn't missed until just now.

"Call me tomorrow?" she said, getting in. "I'm at the newsroom by eight-fifteen."

"Sure." I shut the door.

She opened it again. A moth darted in and battered the dome light. "Look, Hector. I'm a big girl, so if you don't call, I'll be fine with that. Just watch your ass for me, OK? There's bears in the woods."

"I'll be fine. And I'll call. I'm going to need your help."

"That's nice. But listen, just because I'm in love with you doesn't mean I'm going to stand lookout while you try breaking into that railway safe."

I laughed. "You have your standards. I can see that."

"Standards hell! I have a *job,* and I mean to keep it."

"What makes you think you're in love with me?"

"Thinking has nothing to do with it." She paused. "My first husband, Gary, thought of himself as a philosopher. He liked to say it's a good thing that love is an illusion and not real, because if love were real, when you lost it, it would be gone, and you'd have to go looking for it. But since it's an illusion, you don't ever have to look for it. All you have to do is make it up again."

"Hmmm."

"I know, I know, he was flaky as a blizzard. But whatever makes it happen, when you fall in love, you know it. Agreed?"

"From my experience, I'd say so," I said.

"So there you are. What are you going to do tomorrow?"

"Drop in on Wayne Hrushka, I guess. Like to come?"

"Definitely." She started the engine. Then she grinned and added, "I'm good at that."

10

First thing the next morning I called around to the local gravel pits and ready-mix plants and building-supply yards, checking to see whether someone knew of any jobs Wayne Hrushka was on at the moment. No one did. That made the odds fair to good we'd find the old recluse at home on the backside of Mount Joe. I packed a couple of cucumber sandwiches and a liter of water, threw my hiking shoes and jacket in my pack, and headed into town to pick up Wilma.

Like a lot of vets home from Nam in the early seventies, all Wayne had wanted to do was carve out as quiet and uncomplicated a life as he could. Fade away. In northern Vermont back then, leasing an acre of paper-company land for ten bucks a month was the budget way to set yourself up in a remote spot. Wayne staked out a plateau high on the mountain. There, from plans he'd ordered out of the *Whole Earth Catalog,* he erected a yurt, one large, circular room with canted accordion sides, like a cupcake liner. It had a conical roof with fiberglass panels to let in light. He had a spring for water, a little kitchen garden, and a flock of leghorns.

During my college years, I used to trek up to the yurt at the end of the summer to score reefer to take back to Cambridge. Wayne raised the stuff in washtubs. This was almost twenty years ago. Sometime later, during his survivalist period, with dynamite and concrete and a Caterpillar D-9 bulldozer, Wayne had constructed a far more substantial dwelling on the same site—a bunker was how people described it, built right into the brow of the mountain.

About 1980, when International Paper finished logging off the southeast slope, the company sold its holdings and pulled up stakes. The Town of Tewkesville, the poorest township in the state, could not assume maintenance of the company's five-mile access road. Wayne Hrushka was the only citizen living way up there. So everybody figured he'd have to leave. That was when Wayne bought the used D-9 and began keeping the road himself. Over time he acquired more equipment and eventually went into business—demolition, excavation, road-building, a little foundation work when he could fit it in.

Not that he took any of it too seriously. If you went to Wayne with a job offer, it was because he came cheap. He wasn't in business for the money, he'd tell you quite freely, he just liked to play in the dirt. I had to drop into first gear every twenty yards to ease us over the washouts. The road ended in a rocky landing gouged out of the woods by the paper company. Along the sides, parked this way and that under the scarred trees, were several pickups, all with deep-cleated tires, most of them fairly beat, though one was a new Dodge Ram V-8 with a windowless white cap, and another a black Ford 250 with a chrome lockbox and a heavy-duty hitch. The Ford at least was local. I'd noticed it on occasion passing through Tipton. Beside me, Wilma was copying down plate numbers.

On the far side of the landing was a length of skidder cable slung between two posts. Beyond that a rutted track led up into thickening woods. Off to the right was a sign, three planks bolted one above the other to a dead white-pine tree and inscribed with a blowtorch:

POSTED

"Absolutely" No Hunting, No Hiking, No Trespassing.
Violators Will Be Violated.

A horizontal mayonnaise jar, nailed to the same tree by its lid, served as a mailbox. It contained paper and pencil stubs.

The trek in from here, I knew, was long and more or less straight, narrowing and steepening into something like a goat path at the end. You had to stick to the cleared trail—the ruination left by the logging was impenetrable.

"Hard to imagine Ed Evans climbing that trail," I said.

"Yeah. He says he just about croaked during the ascent." Wilma hopped out, shouldering her tote. I beckoned her back. She came around to my side. Laying her fuzzy forearms on the window frame, she said, "What's-a-matter, babe? You chicken?"

"Hungry." I handed her a cucumber sandwich. "But that sign there has me thinking we'll never make it up to Wayne's bunker. Not by this route, at least. Not with all those jokers up there playing army."

"You have a better idea?"

"We could try coming down on him from the top of the mountain."

She frowned, chewing. "From the knob? I don't know, it's kinda steep, isn't it?"

"We'll see. Come on."

We drove back the way we'd come, down to the Lake Road, then turned east on the Old Settlement Road among the hills, winding for miles past farmsteads gone to forest until we reached the county highway between North Allenburg and Tewkesville village. From the village, a long serpentine stretch led up to the Mount Joe Ski Area access, just a gravel track marked by a cockeyed billboard ("WELCOME TO NORTH COUNTRY SKIING AT IT'S FINEST!") set back in the puckerbrush. A mile farther we passed the cluster of milk-carton condominium units that the Ingallses had plunked down in a high meadow just below the base lodge, each unit with a carport and a lone maple sapling planted in front.

"Ed lives in there," Wilma commented as we passed the cul-de-sac.

"Ed who?"

"Ed Evans. Your nemesis."

"I thought those places were unoccupied during the off-season."

"They are, most of them. Actually Ed gets a break on the rent, in exchange for keeping an eye on things."

The base lodge was quiet. I expected maybe a few employees puttering about, but there was no one at all. From the equipment lot behind the Sno-Cat shed, we churned on up the toll road to the last tower at the top of the quad lift. After that, a blazed walking trail over the rock led to the highest point on the blunt dome of the mountain, where years ago the U.S. Geological Survey had cemented a small brass seal denoting the height of the northernmost peak in Vermont. The descent on the other side was manageable without gear, I figured, but after that, locating Wayne's compound out in all the acres of rocks and scrub on the shoulder of the mountain might take a while.

The sun at least was high and bright, and the walking was easy at first. We didn't pause until we made the ridgeline. From here you traversed a spine of rock for another hundred feet or so to the knob. I'd done it countless times as a kid. "Would you perhaps have anything to eat in that satchel?"

"Probably. . . . How about an orange?"

She dug it out and tossed it to me. We sat on a warm shelf of granite scaled over with lichens. The lavender-blue hills rippled away into the haze.

"Clear nights you can see Montreal from here—the twinkle of it," Wilma said idly. She stretched herself out with her hands behind her head. "First summer we moved to Vermont, Vic brought me up here. We spent the night under the stars." She tipped her head up at me, squinting. "Ever do that?"

"Not with Vic." I was tearing the peel off the orange and sailing pieces out into the air. They spun and fell out of sight into the brush far below. Spud and Gaea, I was suddenly thinking. Gaea in a thin tank suit that one hot day at the beach. July, it was. Flat belly, legs with the tendons shimmering like the northern lights as she walked, that corkscrew mane of hair . . . Spud was there that day, too, ragged corduroy cutoffs loose on his hips, his farmer-white hide looking all the paler for the black mat on his chest, taking a dip in the middle of the day, which was odd, but not too odd . . . They were talking, ankle deep in the cool blue lake. Why would she go for Spud? The hard, lean plainness of him. Lady Chatterley's lover. There was no accounting for chemistry, I should know. And of course there was the excitement of all they stood to lose. Their two solid, settled lives dangling in the balance. She must have been a sucker for that. Like Spud. Like half the damn Western world.

"We were married eight months by then," Wilma was saying, "and the thrill, such as it was, was gone. We'd brought up marinated chicken and a pasta salad, a bottle of wine, a few tomatoes, and we're sitting up here dining in dismal silence, so to be sociable I point out the glacial striations. In the rock, right? Big mistake. Which I compound by saying something like it wouldn't be long before the ice sheet crept on back down and put a mile-deep lid on everything we could see. This vision instantly plunged Vic into one of his famous funks. Back then, when he'd go dismal, I'd draw him out, get him to talk, make him laugh. A routine I was royally sick of. Anyway, this time what he finally confessed—and here's me, ever so slowly realizing this is the guy you *married,* you ditz—

was he couldn't stand the idea that some glacier was going to flatten the entire northern forest region and obliterate everything he might ever achieve, not just sustainable timber harvesting and the protection of ecologically sensitive areas, but also everything *everyone we knew* would ever achieve. I listened and then I had to come back with something cruel like, 'Well, what do you *expect*? We're *ants*, Victor. We're all *ants*.' He didn't speak to me until the next morning."

I broke the orange in half. "See the hawks?" A flight of broadwings, dozens of them, was gliding past at nearly eye level some fifty yards out, striped tailfeathers ruddering.

"Yikes! Look at that! I've never seen them in a whole *squadron* like that. Where're they all headed?"

"Long way from here. Panama, Bolivia, Ecuador . . ."

We listened to them. There were geese, too, somewhere far below.

To the open north beyond the lake the gray plains of Quebec stretched toward the Gulf of the St. Lawrence. As I gazed, I found myself recalling something about the Morganthaus. How they would migrate. Every year. An extravagant way of life that had charmed and amazed my mother. "Here's something interesting," I said. "For a few years after Otto built the A-frame, they used to spend every winter sailing in the islands. In May they'd bring their boat up the inland waterway, then sail up the Maine coast, around Cape Breton and the Gaspé, and on up the St. Lawrence to Quebec City. From there they'd drive down to Tipton. In October they'd go back."

"Like the hawks."

"Yes, although when the skiing was good, they'd fly back up around Christmastime."

Wilma tapped my shoulder. "Hector," she said in a soft voice, "I'm ready for dessert."

Her lust was irresistible. It transported me. Her face got so flushed her freckles disappeared. She clawed at me, she yipped and moaned, she flung her head around. The way she took over and rode me, ignoring the rock beneath us, under my bony backside . . . all of it was new to me. I liked it, I liked it too much. She kept on. I couldn't help wondering whether she was hamming it up a little, and whether it mattered. Naomi had been a languorous and inward lover—even out in the dunes. I missed her all the time, even now with this wild woman positively taking my breath away.

THE drop-off over the north side of the knob was a wall of weathered, buff-gray granite creased with veins and crevices. I had no sophistication as a rock climber, but there were plenty of handholds, and not too much farther down there was a dense fringe of gnarly spruces to break a fall.

Wilma started down first, her tote slung over her back. I followed and, after a few minutes of spidering carefully down, joined her among the trees. She peered at me. Her color was still up, and her eyes shone in the white light.

"This is the most excitement I've ever had on a date," she said.

"This is just the beginning."

"I know. That's the best part of it."

I reckoned our course as well as I could from the sun, which was starting to dim behind a sheet of gray weather moving north, the edge of the tropical storm we'd been hearing about on the radio for the past few days. The footing was precarious and noisy. We set off slides of scree with each step, but a rising, swirling wind carried the clatter off behind us.

After a time we came to an open outcropping of gray, fissured stone that dropped off gradually into a denser growth of spruce and fir. Wind coursed through the branches like water. We skirted the rock face slowly, watching for trip wires or other sensors.

As soon as we crossed below the tree line, the network of

footpaths winding through the stunted conifers told us we were close. Lichens were scuffed everywhere. Wilma pointed out two spent orange paint pellets in the leaf litter.

Soon after that I came across what looked like a piece of macaroni sticking out of the thin soil. It was a yellowed length of half-inch tubing. I pulled on it.

The tube led back in to an oval depression in the rock about the size of a bathtub. In it grew a profusion of ferns and a few sturdy little wine-colored birch trees.

"What do you think this is?" I got down and scooped my hand into the vegetation. The soil was uncompacted, loose with peat. I crumbled the stuff in my fingers.

Wilma looked blank.

"It's a planter. Somebody blasted a dimple in the mountain and filled it with store-bought soil."

"For dope?"

"Sure. Some strain that likes the altitude."

"Well, well, well. How clever."

In a short time we had turned up a dozen more basins like the first. You could pick them out just the way you'd spot a cellar hole in a hayfield, by the house-sized copse of trees that had grown up where the mower couldn't mow.

"He wasn't real ambitious," Wilma observed, "if this is all it adds up to."

"No. Hasn't been in cultivation for a good long while, either." I pulled another piece of tubing out of the humus. "Though he sure did invest some time and effort setting it up."

"*Freeze!* Right there!"

Wilma cried out and dropped into a squat with her hands over her head.

"Hello, Wayne," I said, looking around. I couldn't make out anybody in the surrounding woods, but I recognized the voice.

"That you, Bellevance?" He straightened, and then I spotted

him under the trees below us. A black cap sat low on his loose gray curls. He had an automatic rifle across his chest. "What the fuck are you doing here? This is a military training area. There's all kinds of unpleasant surprises up here you wouldn't want to find out about." He shook his head in disgust and then spoke into a radiophone clipped to the pocket of his shirt. "Scorpion One-one. It's a couple hikers. Over."

The radio spat something back at him.

"You armed, either one of you?"

"Nope," I said, patting myself.

He came toward us. He was a powerful-looking man, meaty enough through the chest and shoulders that his arms couldn't hang straight. "The girl there. Have her stand up."

Wilma rose. She was shaking. Her face had gone white.

"This is Wilma," I said. "She's a friend of mine."

"What are you people doing up here, you mind telling me?"

"Just birding is all. Searching for the elusive boreal chickadee, or maybe a Bicknell's thrush—"

"Shut up." He jabbed the rifle at me. "If you're sneaking down to try and rip off the pot plantation, then you are about ten years late, as you can obviously see."

"You're out of the trade?"

"Totally. Stakes got too high. I got enough trouble these days with my *legal* pursuits."

Wayne had been an all-state tackle for the Allenburg High Crusaders when I was in grade school. Turned down a few college football scholarships to go fight the Viet Cong. Never once regretted it, either, he used to say. I believed him back then.

"I'm looking into a recent double homicide. Couple I think you knew—the Morganthaus."

"Right. So why are you looking here?"

"Thought you might have some insights." I glanced at Wilma.

"Insights!" He thumped his rifle on the ground. "What am I, the fool on the hill? This makes the second time this week I got people walking up here uninvited. Sure, OK, Otto Morganthau. All's I did was once I poured a foundation for him. He was a picky Canuck."

"You screwed up that job, though, didn't you?"

"Aww, c'mon. This again? There was a small problem. Which I fixed."

"That right? My brother tells me all you did was you—"

"Your *brother*? That's where you're getting this?" He shook his shaggy head. "Fuck . . . That dude's in deep, Bellevance. That's why you're here, isn't it? Because they think he's the guy."

"He says that foundation you poured was over an inch off-level, and all you did was shim the sill with shingle and spray foam in the spaces."

"Cedar shims! That's exactly right! Them shims'll last longer than the rest of that fucking fish tank!" He blew out a hot breath. "You're too much. Private property means *nothing* to you. I got my constitutional right to privacy, but like any asshole with a badge you think you can trample all over a citizen's rights anytime you feel like it. And our corrupt court system backs you up!"

"Society has rights, too, Wayne. Sometimes there's a conflict."

"Society! What's that? That's bullshit. It's individuals that have rights, not society."

"I respect your opinion, and I realize this may be an awkward time, but you can give me ten minutes, can't you, Wayne?"

"Ten minutes? Fuck. Now? I got stuff going on!" He scanned the perimeter of trees.

"Wayne heads up the Mount Joe Militia," I said to Wilma.

"I heard," she said.

"You heard what?" Wayne demanded, swiveling to face her.

"I heard there was a paramilitary outfit up here on the mountain preparing for the time of social chaos after the UN and the Chinese People's Army take over the country. Good news gets around."

"I know who you are," he growled. "You're that female reporter for the *Eagle*." He turned to me. "You got balls, Bellevance, bringing fucking reporters up here." He stared at her. "You Jewish?"

She shook her head. "Atheist."

He snorted and spoke into his radio mike, "One-one. I'm heading inside the rock for thirty. With company. Confirm status and regroup. Over."

"One-seven. All units regroup. Regroup," the radio crackled. "Over."

We followed a sloping track among the scrawny spruces into a bare, weed-tufted plateau. The clearing was bordered on three sides by the regenerating woods and on the fourth by a lot of bulldozed rubble. Above that the face of the mountain, a long cliff, reached up to the knob. This was where he'd once had the yurt set up. No sign of it now. No people either. Only a slender gas pump, a small tractor, and a few ATVs and snowmobiles inside a long, low pole shed.

I never saw the bunker until we were right in front of it. The timbered entry was recessed into a great bank of broken stone like a mine-shaft opening. The door, some ten feet in, was of three-inch steel set in a steel frame. On the other side of that, the vestibule was distinctly cool. The ceiling, ten feet overhead, looked like a huge, bright waffle, each concrete indentation with its own white lightbulb. The vestibule was crowded with storage shelves, plastic trash barrels, firewood, propane tanks, and assorted junk.

Up a flight of iron stairs, through another solid-steel door, we entered an airy room of formed concrete with a high, pillared ceiling. The light came from two large plate-glass windows on the outside wall. They were full of hazy blue sky. To the back was an open kitchen. The closed double doors in the opposite wall led, I assumed, into a bedroom. A huge Sony television dominated the hardwood entertainment console. There were several overstuffed leather chairs, a sectional sofa, and four lovely double-bowl, antique kerosene lamps. It felt like a Victorian men's club. The room's centerpiece was a sumptuous pool table, and at the far end there was a stone fireplace big enough to roast a steer in.

Bypassing all these feaures, Wilma, like a kid, went straight to the view. "Hector . . . You've got to see this. It's like you're in a damn airplane." She was right. He also had an impressive collection of bonsai displayed on the deep windowsills— some thirty artfully sculpted trees, junipers and cedars, each in a footed ceramic tray.

Wayne was whistling as he cleared one end of his baronial dining table of the bottles, candle holders, cups and plates, videocassettes, magazines, cartridge boxes, and junk mail that cluttered it.

"Those your bonsai?" Wilma asked him.

"Those things? Nah. Girlfriend left 'em when she split on me. Long time ago."

"I'm sorry to hear that. You must get a little lonely."

"Never," Wayne said. "I work, so I get out almost every day."

"What was her name?" Wilma asked.

"Who?"

"The girlfriend."

"Oh, that was Beth. Beth Scoville. She's gone to fat now, if you know her." He started back into the kitchen area. "So what'll it be? Bass ale, apple cider, or V8 cocktail vegetable juice?"

"Cider, thanks."

"Cider'd be great," Wilma said. "How'd you get all the cement way up here, anyway?"

"Pump."

I asked, "You don't heat with wood, do you, Wayne?" I couldn't see any radiators or duct grates, and I knew he wasn't getting his heat from that fireplace.

"Hot water. Listen to this. I laid seventy-two hundred feet of plastic pipe in the floor here. Whole deal runs off a bank of collectors and batteries with a backup of liquid gas, which, so far, I have never had to use. I got half a mountain on top of me, which is an R factor of about eight hundred." He kicked the refrigerator closed. "Here's the deal. I designed this entire place around whatever I could find for salvage. Take the front steps—I cut them out of a fire escape on a savings bank in Hartford, Connecticut. The picture windows? Took 'em out of a waterfront hotel down in Rhode Island. Tempered glass two inches thick. Hurricane-proof. Twenty bucks apiece. Cupboards? Them I got when they demolished the Larraway School. Solid red oak, brass hardware. Cost me nothing."

"The total effect is very impressive," Wilma said. "You walk in here expecting a cave with bunk beds and hunting trophies. And it's so far *out* here, or *up* here. That's the truly amazing thing."

Wayne said, "Yeah, I don't get too many trick-or-treaters."

"But do you ever worry?" Wilma asked. "I mean, what if you had a medical emergency? Like a ruptured appendix or a seizure or a heart attack? You'd be a hurtin' puppy."

"Sure, I worry, but there's trade-offs with everything." Wayne set down a lacquer tray holding a block of cheddar cheese, a crusty loaf of seeded bread, a crock of honey mustard, and three mugs of cider. "You want to know what my biggest problem is, living up here? You'll never guess what it is."

"Wear and tear on your vehicles?" Wilma said.

"No." He bit into a wedge of cheddar slathered with mustard and said, "It's mishe."

"Mice?"

He nodded, gulping cider. "Four thousand feet up and I got a mice infestation. Can't get rid of 'em."

"You need a cat," Wilma said.

"Fucking hate cats. I need a cookbook of rodent recipes is what I need. You ever see that movie where the guy eats mice? He's a scientist up on the tundra and he's supposed to survive on what the wolves survive on. Which he finds out is mice. Eats 'em, bones and all—skin, whiskers, everything."

We chewed, thinking.

Wayne suddenly looked up. "The other day, yesterday, I had these two plainclothes troopers up here, and you know what one of them asked me?"

"What?" I said.

"Roly-poly guy. Evans. Know him? He asked me if I sold your brother a nine-millimeter machine pistol." He chuckled. "Guy's a real clown."

"I know what you mean. He's the type that likes to shock people, that's all, see how they react under pressure. So, Wayne, where were you the weekend before last?"

"Right here, man. Just like today. Had a little war game going on."

"OK. Who were the other players? Besides Marko and Lonnie."

He shook his head. "I don't give that out. You should go ask the feds. They got a grip on all the boring details—right down to our current brand of toothpaste."

"What time do these militia weekends usually get under way?"

"Around Saturday noon."

"All right. Friday before last, where were you?"

He lowered his chin to his chest and swung his limp curls side to side. "I didn't kill them two fools, Bellevance."

"They were fools?" Wilma said.

He stared at her. "How many Vermonters you know live in a glass house?"

"More than live in concrete bunkers."

"Maybe I'm a fool, too."

I reached for a piece of cheese. "But you don't actually *own* this facility, do you, Wayne? You lease the land from the Planvest Corporation."

His black eyes closed slowly and opened again. He understood we'd taken a turn. "What's this got to do with?"

"Nameless people."

"What's that supposed to mean?"

"People who want to turn this mountain into a world-class four-season resort."

"You mean the bankers, whatever?"

"That what they are? Bankers?"

"Wait, OK, you said Planvest—these foreign speculators that bought up half the fucking county."

"Are they foreign?"

"That's what people say."

"You know Nathan Rossi?"

"I know who he is."

"He represents Planvest, doesn't he?"

Wayne pursed his lips. "He's just some dick-licking accountant, far as I know."

"He give you notice yet?"

"What? What notice?"

"Come on, Wayne. Rossi's clients are gonna be plowing ski trails right through your compound here. They've got all the permits and everything. You trying to tell me this was never a blip on your screen?"

He sat back, sighing. "Well, I heard rumors, but it don't affect me—"

"They've already pulled the plug on Quimby. He's moving out West."

"No shit. You mean the old girls' camp? That's part of it, too?"

"According to Quimby."

He rolled his shoulders. "Whatever, like I say, it don't affect me. I signed a ninety-nine-year lease with International Paper. Back in fucking 1972. I'm protected."

"Like hell you are. The Ingallses are about to build a hundred-acre holding pond down on Doug MacLaren's old farm. They'll have unlimited snowmaking on sixty trails within two years. You're all done, Wayne."

"Sixty trails! Get out of here!"

"Maybe you should discuss the matter with your lawyer," Wilma suggested.

"Good idea. Or maybe I should work up a bid on the holding pond, score a piece of the action." He laughed.

"Otto was hooked up with these land speculators. Did you know that?"

His face darkened. "How would I know that?"

"I believe that's what got him killed."

Wayne lifted his hat and ran his fingers through his hair. "Now that's scary. Venture capitalists running around the woods with Uzis."

"This same Planvest Corporation's trying to close a deal on the Morganthau property before it even clears probate. You aware of that?"

"No. I wonder why that is."

"The railway safe, maybe."

After a measured pause he said, "Now there's a thought. Ever since I heard about that incident, I been wondering about his old railway safe."

"I'll bet you have. Troopers ask you about it when they came up here?"

He shook his head. "I was half-expecting 'em to, but they never did."

"And you didn't bring it up."

"Fuck, no."

"Where is this railway safe?"

"In the basement. We set a three-corner jig for it in the south wall."

"You and your crew."

"Yeah, and we were supposed to drop it in there with the form crane, like he requested, but that summer there was a truckers' strike or some shit, and the damn safe never arrived. So fucking Otto, he wanted me to take my flatbed and drive way the hell up into Ontario someplace and get it for him. Like I'm some French pissant on his payroll. Forget it, dude, I got other jobs. Whole year went by before we got back up to his place to set that thing in there. Otto wasn't too pleased about that."

"I guess not. Who else knows about the safe?"

"Nobody I know of. Just your little brother. Morganthau was back down in Florida by the time the truckers' strike ended, so your brother took delivery. Thing wound up sitting in his haybarn for months."

"What about your girlfriend? And your crew. They knew about it, didn't they?"

"Sure they did, yeah. But I ain't seen any of those people in years." He stood abruptly, yawning again to mask his agitation. "You know what? I hate to be rude, but I got stuff to attend to outside. So if you don't mind . . ." He made his two fingers run across the tabletop.

"Who was working for you the summer you installed that safe for the Morganthaus?"

"Fuck if I know. That was eight, ten years ago."

"You keep payroll records?"

"Payroll records? Do I look like I keep payroll records?"

"You don't want to make me subpoena you, Wayne."

"I don't give a shit what you do. Except if you don't get

outa here right now, you're gonna make me regret I offered you my hospitality."

"Who got Lonnie thinking he could buy into the Lodge? That wasn't you, was it?"

"The Lodge! I don't know what you're talking about."

"What does Lonnie know that qualifies him for Marko's baby-sitting service?"

"You lost me. Sorry." He cast me a look, half-amused, half-wary, a look that confirmed he was in the thing up to his ears, whatever the thing was, and he knew I knew it. My questions had proved more penetrating than he'd anticipated, and it rankled him sorely to have been caught acting self-assured. He skidded his chair back and rose. So did we. He bowed slightly in the direction of the door. "Good-bye, bird-watchers. Don't come back, or you'll regret it."

11

Like a prairie settlement, the Willow Grove trailer park sat all by itself in the middle of a brushy pasture two miles out of East Allenburg, where the East Branch snaked over a floodplain. The highway ran across the flats for a couple miles here, paralleling a raised railroad bed. Black willows lined the wandering riverbank. The park itself was as grim as they come, about a dozen single-wides in tight rows on a low rise where there once had been a ramshackle farmhouse that would get flooded out every other spring.

School was out. Kids were playing in the dirt access road, throwing a basketball at a hoop nailed to a telephone pole. Two men in torn jeans worked on a gutted motorcycle. They stared intently as we passed, the heated sort of stare I hadn't felt since I wore blue in Dorcester.

Scovilles' was a gray-green sheet-metal box backed up to the bank of the river and set on blocks. A blue wading pool in the middle of the yard was filled with yellow water and willow leaves. Black Ford Tempo in the carport—same car Stacey Scoville had been driving when she left the Lodge on Saturday night.

I pulled to the side of the road and looked over at Wilma. She was scribbling intently. "Wilma—if you don't mind, I think I'll be better off in there without the press tagging along."

She raised her gaze from her notes to my face. "I don't

mind at all." She smiled. "If this were my show, I sure wouldn't want the cops tagging along."

I had to laugh.

No one responded to my knock on the front door, but a television was on in there, so I circled around behind the trailer. The river, which you could hear muttering close by, was hidden in red thickets of alders.

A scrapwood stair led to the screened back door. Under the landing there was a chest freezer heaped with newspapers. A kid's rusty bicycle lay on top.

I rapped hard and waited, then tried the latch and poked my head into the dimness. The interior smelled of garbage and gas.

A thin little girl in shorts, with dark, straight hair, was sitting on the floor watching a video.

"Hello?"

She scrambled to her feet. "What do you want?"

"It's OK, miss . . . I'm a peace officer. Is your mother around?"

"No."

"Is there anybody home besides you?" I slipped inside.

"Beth is. She's in bed."

"She sick?"

"She works nights."

A door opened down a tight hallway. "Who is that, Megan?"

I tipped my head into view and told the woman I was a police officer investigating the Morganthau murders.

"Then what the hell're you doing in my house?"

"I'm looking for Lonnie Perkins."

"Well, he ain't here."

"He's been staying here, hasn't he? With Stacey?"

"He was, but he moved out. What you want him for?"

"Ms. Scoville, I'm Constable Hector Bellevance. I'd like to ask you a few questions if I could."

"What about?"

"Wayne Hrushka, for starters."

Beth Scoville switched on a hall light. She was a large woman, in her early forties, chenille wrap over a nightshirt. Her footfall made the floor pop. Red-painted toes, bleached hair sleep-mashed on the side, fuzzy jowls, apple-green eye shadow. Not unpretty for all that.

"Megan, you turn that off now and go play outside." She had a wheeze. "Go on now. It's warm out."

"It's gonna rain," Megan said in a flat voice.

"It ain't yet."

The girl opened the front door just enough to slip out, not a glance back.

"Special child," Beth said. "They got her mainstreamed again this year, and she don't get the kind of attention she used to, now she's in with all them chatterboxes." She sighed. "Coffee?"

"Sure, if it's no trouble."

"Two's easy as one." She filled two plastic tumblers with water, slipped them in the microwave, sat on her stool with a vinyl whoosh.

"Wayne says you and he used to live together up on Mount Joe."

"That's right. I was on disability at the time, so I didn't have to go nowhere every day. It was decent, but the one thing I couldn't get used to was all the blackflies."

"How come you left?"

"Oh, God. No, thanks. I don't want to get into all that."

I watched her face. It was soft and tender, a poor cover for her feelings. "Tell me, what do you remember about the Morganthaus?"

"Why? You think Wayne had something to do with them getting killed?"

"He helped Otto install a big safe in his basement. You recall anything about that?"

"That ain't why they got killed, is it?"

"Why not?"

"Because. The killer didn't steal nothing, it said in the paper. It was sex-related. Plus Stacey, my daughter—she's a receptionist down to Planned Parenthood. About a month ago this Morganthau woman, that got killed, she was in there to see about getting a procedure. She was by herself, if that tells you anything."

"When does Stacey get home from the office?"

"Five, five-thirty."

"She and Lonnie go out together every night?"

Beth looked into her lap. "I don't keep tabs on them two."

"You don't think much of Lonnie, do you?"

She pursed her lips. "We kinda got into it Sunday."

"You kick him out?"

"Yeah, I did, actually. Here's the thing. This summer he was working for a guy—for Wayne, as a matter of fact—but a couple weeks ago he got laid off. I already told him—I told the both of them—*nobody* mooches off me. You ain't pulling your weight, you're gone." She cocked her head. "So he's gone."

"Where'd he go, any idea?"

"Sure don't," she said on the inhale. She took the tumblers out of the microwave, stirred in some Taster's Choice.

"What do you know about the Mount Joe Militia?"

"Nothin'. That stuff wasn't part of the agenda when I was up there. It was mainly about survival. In case there was a nuclear holocaust."

"Right. But when you were up there, part of the agenda was about dope-growing, too. Wasn't it?"

She hesitated. "That'd be news to me."

"He was selling weed, Beth. I bought a few lids from him myself."

"Well, shit, what are you asking *me* about it for, if you know already? Myself, I can't smoke that stuff. Makes me nauseous."

"How much was he selling?"

"I swear I never knew nothing about that. Wayne's real good with plants. He loves growing things. He raises them little Japanese trees. You know what I mean? Bonsai?"

"He said that was your hobby."

"Me!" She hooted. "All's I got to do is *look* at a plant and it shrivels right up."

"Did Wayne ever mention the name Planvest?"

She looked blank. "Who?"

"Planvest. The corporation that owns the land he's leasing."

Now she nodded. "Well, I don't recall the name, but I do remember seein' the certificates, or whatever they were."

"What certificates?"

"He showed 'em to me one time. We were drunk. Had 'em wrapped in plastic in a ammo box."

I set down my tumbler. "What did they look like?"

"Just . . . All legalistic—you know. They had signatures and gold around the edges. They was gonna make him a rich man, he said."

"How?"

"When he cashed 'em in, I guess. Bearer shares—*that's* what he called them. Like savings bonds, only better." She shook her head, sighing. "Wayne. He was high finance all the way."

"I'll bet." If Hrushka was a shareholder, that would help explain why Otto had him set the foundation for his dream house. They knew each other. Otto was connected to the money-laundering and the landgrab, and it didn't take much to imagine that they might have tried to buy Otto out, just as they'd bought out Keith and Wayne. And that he'd refused to be bought.

"Thanks, Beth. You've been helpful." I got up to leave. "As soon as Stacey shows, have her call me. Will you, please?"

She nodded. I wrote my phone number on a pad beside the phone.

Out in the driveway Wilma was kneeling beside Megan. The girl was on her haunches scraping at pebbles with a plastic serving spoon. The wind whipped their hair into their faces.

Wilma glanced up. "Megan says Lonnie and her mom had a big fight Sunday."

The girl was clonking her ankle with her spoon. *Tock. Tock. Tock.* "What was the fight about, Megan?"

"She didn't want to go nowhere." *Tock.* "But he made her."

"Go where, Megan?"

She gave a shrug. "Camping."

"What were they fighting about," Wilma asked, "could you tell?"

"Drugs."

The trailer's front door banged open and Beth stepped out. She frowned at the sky and called to Megan, "Sweetheart, you come in here now and get a sweatshirt on."

I straightened, brushing dirt off my hands. "Megan says Stacey and Lonnie had a big fight."

"About drugs," Wilma added.

The girl tried to scoot past her, but Beth caught her by the arm at the top of the steel steps. "Damn it all, girl, what did you tell these people?"

"Grammy! You're hurtin' me!"

Wilma took the steps in two leaps and gently pried Beth's plump fingers from the girl's twig of an arm. Beth, wheezing, turned her red, stricken face up to Wilma and burst into tears.

Wilma sat beside her and draped her arm over the expanse of Beth's back.

"Beth," she said, "we can't help you if you won't tell us what's going on."

"He told me— He told me— He told me not to say nothin'," she sobbed miserably.

"Who? Lonnie?" I said.

"Not Lonnie— Marko." She fished a Kleenex out of her

pocket and blew her nose hard. "Marko Ruggles, got a gun shop out to Shadboro."

"How does Marko fit in?"

"He come by here looking for Lonnie—yesterday. Oh, God . . ."

Wilma said, "Stacey's gone, too, right? She and Lonnie took off with a bunch of drugs. Is that what happened?"

She nodded and wiped her eyes. "I'm real, I'm real worried about her. She shoulda *called* me by this time."

"You need to help us find them, Beth, before somebody else does. When did you last see them?"

"Sunday. I left for work and Lonnie was pretty much all packed, and they was watching the Patriots game. Megan says they got into it after. I don't know, but when I come home, she's alone, asleep on the couch, and today the lady at Planned Parenthood, Joan, she says Stacey ain't been to work since *Friday*."

"Would they be hiding somewhere together?"

"I don't know!" she wailed. "She shoulda *called* me by now."

I went inside and knelt between the little girl and the television. Megan dropped her eyes to her lap. She let me take her small, cold hands into mine. A ridged string of red licorice drooped out of her mouth. "Megan, when Lonnie left with your mom, did she say where they were going?"

"No, he just drug her out," she said softly.

"Did she say anything at all?"

"She told him . . . What she said was, she said, 'Fuck *you*, I don't *want* to go camping!' But he drug her down the steps."

"Did she say anything else?"

"She said, 'Tell Gram to call Jamie!'"

"Jamie?" Jamie Bridewater, the moley guy at the Lodge. "Why Jamie?"

"I don't know. She use to work there."

"At Jamie's store, you mean? JJ's? The health-food place in town?"

The girl nodded.

Wilma helped a weeping Beth through the doorway.

I got her a glass of water. When she'd calmed down, I said, "You better tell me about these drugs, Beth."

She took a deep breath and blew it out slowly. "Oh, he had a bunch of weed he was trying to get rid of."

"How much is a bunch?"

"I don't know—he had it in his truck."

"Where did he get it?"

"He never said. But if Lonnie was dumb enough to rip off Wayne . . . Jesus, Wayne'll flay him alive. That's all I can think. Because Marko come looking for him."

"And that's why you kicked him out?"

She shook her head. "No, I told you. He wasn't workin', and he wasn't lookin' to work. Plus, I got sick of swishing his whiskers out of the sink *every* goddamn morning just so I could wash my face. Not to mention him peein' all over the back of the damn toilet *every* friggin' day."

"You must've called Jamie. What did he say?"

"He said he never saw them."

"Why would Stacey want you to call him?"

"They're friends, him and Lonnie. That's how she first met Lonnie was at JJ's, and I guess she thought that's where he was takin' her."

"Why would he take her to JJ's?"

"To get rid of the weed. Jamie's got connections, if you know what I mean."

Wilma and I sped back into Allenburg. It was late in the afternoon. I left her at the newsroom, promising we'd hook up again before nightfall to exchange reflections.

"You're the cat's pajamas, Bellevance," was the last thing she said before she disappeared through the door.

JJ's was one of the upscale emporiums that had opened over the past few years in the rehabbed woolen mill and dowel works along River Street. Some New Age sort of place. Kitchenwares, imported crafts, incense, crystals, and hemp products, along with the granolas and grains, vitamins and herbs, health foods and yogurt drinks, and for the lunch crowd, mesquite-baked pizza.

It was after six. The sign in the door said SORRY, CLOSED, but through the NO PUFFIN decal I could make out three or four heads way in the back under a dropped fluorescent fixture shifting around like orbiting planets.

I hammered on the glass and waited. Jamie himself approached the door, squinting until he could see who was doing the banging. He flipped through his keys, shaking his head.

"What's happening, Constable? Little ways out of your jurisdiction, aren't you?"

"I'm looking for your friend Lonnie."

"Can't help you there."

"Any idea where he might be holed up?"

"Why? He in some kind of trouble?"

"You tell me."

"If you're looking for him, I guess he must be."

"Right. You mind if we talk a minute?"

"I'm busy. Is this about something important?"

"It's about you looking at twenty years for distribution of a controlled substance."

He frowned doubtfully, letting me see just how ridiculous he considered this prospect to be, then beckoned me in.

Under the light in the back of the room behind a half-wall, what I had taken for a pool table turned out to be a game-board on sawhorses. It depicted a medieval landscape on a painted grid. Dozens of little gamepieces occupied the field of play, pewter statuettes, all lovingly enameled. The two focused players were punks in their twenties.

"So who's winning?" I asked. "Munchkins or Hobbits?"

Neither paid me any notice. The taller, with lank, straight hair combed behind his ears and a small, slack chin, was consulting a rule book. An angular kid with eruptions on his ckeeks and a fighting knife on his belt, tattooed arms crossed, studied the layout.

Jamie's office was a low loft that overlooked the store. Two beanbag chairs and a rolltop desk stood along the wall under a blacked-out window. He perched on a stool beside the desk.

"Those boys your bodyguards or what?"

He laughed, as if this were quite a joke. "They're throw-backs, from when I used to sell cards and comics and teenage crap up on Railroad Street. A few diehards still like to stop by."

"Like Lonnie?"

"Yeah. Now and then."

"What were you doing with him out at the Lodge Saturday night?"

"All I know is he thought he was negotiating to buy the Quiver Club, and he approached me about possibly coming in on it with him."

"How the hell was he going to buy the Quiver Club? Lonnie couldn't buy a keg of beer, let alone a bar."

"Somebody was fronting him was my impression. He didn't say who."

"You were considering a business partnership with Lonnie, and you didn't know where his money was coming from?"

"*Was* I considering it? That might be a better question."

"Come on, Jamie. Where was Lonnie getting the money?"

"I never asked. I thought maybe his mom."

"Bullshit. His mom's got nothing but her social security and a piddling pension from Ethan Allen Furniture."

"Bad guess then."

"Danny Ingalls is planning to demolish that building as soon as Quimby vacates. You aware of that?"

"I honestly don't give a shit." He shifted his buns and looked around. "I'm telling you what Lonnie told me, OK? He was all excited—I mean, you heard him. He wanted me to put twenty grand in escrow for fifty percent of the club."

"Lonnie called you Sunday night."

"I believe he did, that's right."

"He wanted you to move some weed for him. That's right, too, isn't it, Jamie?"

"Christ . . ." He compressed his lips, blinking fast. Making up something, something that wasn't going to be good enough. "See, what happened is, I had my kids for the weekend, OK? And we're eating calzones and watching *Funniest Home Videos*. So the phone beeps and it's friggin' Lonnie. I'm pissed at him because he knows I don't like calls out to my house. I go, 'What's happenin', Lon?' He goes, 'Nothing much. Pats lost again.' But he's obviously wired. So I go, 'What's the problem, Lon?' and he blurts out he's sitting on twenty pounds of cured weed. I about *shit*. I mean, not only is he making this proposal on my home phone, but he's making it sound like he expects I could actually *help* him. Kid was *desperate*."

"If he's desperate, why's he calling you, Jamie?"

"I know what you're thinking, but I do not deal. No, see, here's what it is, I'm a libertarian. I believe every individual is a free entity in the universe. That's my philosophy. You want to pollute your system with drugs—crack, pot, whatever—it's your life, amigo. Plus I also believe in hemp as an industrial commodity. Hemp's got four times as much fiber as wood. You want to save the family farm in this state? Legalize hemp. OK, so knowing this about me, if Lonnie stole some stuff and he was trying to make a quick bundle, say for this sex club deal—"

"Lonnie didn't steal that shit. Even when he's desperate, he's not stupid. Somebody laid it on him—to shut him up or pay him off. Which was it?"

He managed a laugh that stuck in his throat. "Where're you getting this?"

"Marko was Lonnie's baby-sitter that night. But Lonnie got away somehow. Isn't that right?"

"I have no clue where you're coming from, Constable."

"What are you guys worried about? Does Lonnie know who killed the Morganthaus? Is that what it is?"

"You're *crazed!*" He was flushed. He slid off his stool. "I know what this is about—this is about your brother. *He's* the poor schmuck the cops have pegged for those murders, and you're just trying to—"

I reached over, clamped on to him just under the jawbone, and drew him in close. "I got my hooks in you, Jamie. In every one of you. Wayne, Keith, Marko, Danny. It's going down, this whole stinkin' thing."

"You're the one that's going down," he said through his teeth. "You're a historic artifact I'm looking at."

I thanked him for his frankness.

GLORIA Perkins lived in one of a few winterized camps in the woods west of Allenburg off a short road that twisted down to Blacksmith Pond. Hers was a dank, mildewed clapboard cottage with a studio shed attached. Carpet of pine needles instead of a lawn. Screened porch overlooking the water.

Wind chimes and ornamental doodads in the windows, dangling from the pine boughs, tinkling and clinking. Gloria had once made her living selling ceramic knickknacks at craft fairs. Maple-leaf clocks and covered-bridge mirrors and glazed plaques with inspirational verse on them. Now, by her own admission, all she did was read and drink cheap vodka. We'd last met a year ago at my mother's funeral.

I thought there was half a chance I'd discover Lonnie's rig down in the woods here, but no such luck. Just Gloria's old blue Rabbit and her venerable, dented aluminum Grumman canoe, the color of tinfoil in a campfire.

The wind had fallen off. The twilight was purple. Through the black lacework of the trees the water gleamed silver.

Gloria breezed out as I slid from the cab of my truck, waving both her arms, the door slam echoing over the water. Skinny shanks in plaid Bermudas, hair brushed out like steel wool, liverish, seamed skin, bloodshot eyes.

"Hector Bellevance!" She was overjoyed to have a guest. "*Awful* things going on up by you. They're saying Spud was involved, but I don't believe it. Spud hasn't got the stomach to put down a sick *cow*."

"He sure hasn't."

She took my arm and drew me up the steps and into the cabin. "Who do you think it was? That porno king lives up to the Lodge?"

"Possibly."

She spun around. "I was *joking*! *Quimby?*"

The place was rank with grease, wood smoke, kerosene, cat piss. She mixed me a Popov-and-ginger on the crumbly linoleum countertop. I could hear the rattle in her chest.

"Stinks in here, Gloria."

"That's Vincent. Poor baby's got a urinary something-or-other. I had to banish him to the studio."

"It's more than Vincent. This mildew'll do a number on your lungs, Gloria."

"Foo."

We carried our drinks, wrapped in pink paper napkins, though a dim interior strewn with newspapers and out onto the porch. A space heater glowed beside her wicker ottoman.

Water lapped. Bats flashed past in the pearly light. Mist pooled over the water. A loon called and the wicker crackled as she dropped into her chair.

"I miss your mama something terrible, Heck. You don't know how I miss her. How are you holding up, hey? You been through a lot lately yourself, haven't you?" Two liberal-minded, middle-aged widows living alone out in the country, Agnes and Gloria had been drinking buddies for twenty years.

"I wish this were a social call, Gloria, but it's not. I'm looking for Lonnie."

"Oh, no. What did he do?"

"I need to talk with him. Where is he, Gloria?"

"You're the second one to ask me that in two days. He's in bad trouble, Hector, isn't he? He did something. He needed money and he did something, didn't he?"

"Did you tell this other fella where he went?"

"He took the camper, that's all I told him. He said he had some good news for Lonnie, but he wouldn't tell me what it was, so I knew he was BS-ing me. I didn't say anything else. Rough-looking character."

"Good. You know where Lonnie might be?"

"No, but he's got a place where he likes to go camp up on the east side of the lake, Prentiss Point. You know where that is?"

I said I did.

"What's this all about, Hector? What kind of garbage's he got himself into?"

"I'm not sure. How has he been acting lately?"

"Different. I don't know what to say. He used to come for Sunday dinner on a regular basis." She set down her drink and wiped tears from her lashes with her napkin. Her voice was dry and thin. "But he hasn't been doing that since he left off working for Spud. Then this Sunday he blows in around noon-time and says he's taking the camper. 'The hell you are,' I say, and he gives me that look of his, so I didn't try to fight him."

"He seem upset?"

"He was wrought up."

"What about?"

She rattled her glass. "Lost his job. Again. All summer he's been up and down like a damn yo-yo. First Spud lets him go, and he's terrified the bank's gonna repo his damn Chevy truck. Then a few weeks later he got on construction. I was happy for him at first—eight bucks an hour, most money he ever made in his life. Except the fly in the ointment there was his boss. Lonnie never went in the service, you know, but this joker had him up there almost every weekend playing commandos with a bunch of broken-down marines. Lonnie didn't take to it. 'So what are you doing it for?' 'Goes with the territory, Ma.' Couple weeks later he introduces me to his new girlfriend, this horrifying airhead, but he's full of nonsense about how he's about to get a piece of the biggest development deal the state ever witnessed, and they're gonna get married, build a cabin, and buy a canopy bed and two Jet Skis. Well, a week ago, surprise surprise, it all flew to pieces, and he's just *beside* himself."

"What flew to pieces?"

"His loan didn't go through. The cosigner bailed out."

"Who was that? Jamie?"

"No, no. The Ingalls boy, Danny. Pal of that lowlife Quimby. Lives up in one of those bootleggers' palaces out at Westlook."

"And the bank was Allenburg Savings?"

"I believe so."

"May I use your phone?"

I reached Wilma at her desk and told her that Danny Ingalls

was our next pigeon. I wanted him tonight. He knew where Lonnie was, I was sure of that. And he was pluckable—if I could catch him alone. Would she like to come along?

"Sure, but how about if we eat first? I'm positively starved."

"Fine, " I said. "Where?"

"Your place. I'll cook."

WILMA made her excuses to Victor and met me at the Grand Union. Though it had only been a couple of hours, it was good to set eyes on her again. Too good. I hung in with her as she sailed down the aisles, a manic shopper, grabbing one thing and another. Outside, a tropical rain was falling.

By the time we were sitting together on the bench seat of the Dodge and she was rubbing my thigh, getting my blood up, I had to wonder whether our infatuation was amounting to more distraction than support.

"I know this is probably the last thing you want to hear," she said as we turned onto the empty highway, "but Victor just told me he thinks we should split up."

"Who should split up?"

"Us!"

"Which us?"

"Him and me!"

Right, nothing I wanted to hear. "There's a Jeep on our ass," I said. Some joker had been following us since the food store.

"There's a what?"

"Big, sporty rig. Can't make it out in the rain."

"Peachy." She turned around. "You positive?"

"We'll see. Hang on." We were on open road heading uphill toward the hospital entrance. I threw the truck into third, hit the emergency brake, and wrenched the wheel. I heard Wilma's head clonk the side window as our rear end slewed around. I let the brake off, my tires fishtailed and grabbed, and we were hammering back down the hill toward the state highway. I glanced at Wilma. Her face was in her hands.

The other rig braked as I swept by. And kept going. Grand Cherokee, light in color, Vermont tags. My side mirrors went black for a few seconds before he was back there again and gaining.

"Guy's serious," I said.

The traffic light was red at the intersection at the bottom of the hill. Two sets of taillights glowed ahead of me, waiting. I switched on my fireman's flasher, pumped the brakes, and grabbed second just as the light went green. We barreled by on the right of the vehicles and jounced through the intersection between wings of rainwater, aiming out the Old Center Road toward North Allenburg. The Jeep was maybe a quarter mile back.

"Can I throw up now?" Wilma said.

"Better not. Now comes the tricky part."

"What, we lose him?"

"Behind this seat is a pair of leather work gloves. Inside one is my Police Special." I scrunched close to the wheel so she could pull the seatback forward.

"Your what?"

"My revolver."

"Oh, God. That's what I thought." She got to her knees and managed to fish out one glove, then the other. "Here we go." She placed the gun beside me on the seat. "Loaded, I presume?"

"Yes. Thanks." I appreciated her calm.

The Old Center Road passed behind the county fairgrounds alongside the grandstand and curved gradually downhill toward the river between run-down frame apartment houses to a sharp bend just before a one-lane railroad underpass.

I swung the truck around sideways in front of the needle-eye to block the road. The idea was to put a stop to this nonsense on my terms and then have a frank chat, if possible. Or at least stall the guy long enough to catch a plate number.

"Hop out quick—in case he doesn't stop." I pocketed the .38 and grabbed a flashlight from the glove box.

We stood in the shelter of the underpass. Rain pounded on my hood and on the lid of the utility box. My flasher was a glittery blur in the upsplash.

The Cherokee rounded the tight bend in a controlled skid and chirped to a standstill some ten yards from the Power-wagon. It steamed. The high beams made a white sheet out of the rain. I couldn't see the license plate at all. He idled for a moment, then jabbed the gas twice. *Come out here.*

"Who the hell do you think that is?"

Wilma took hold of my arm and said quietly, "I know who it is. It's Ed."

"Ed who?"

"Evans."

"Evans? How do you know that?"

"I know his vehicle."

"What does he think he's doing, for Christ's sake?"

I pulled my canvas jacket over my head and walked out through the rain.

"Don't!" she breathed. "Wait, Hector, please—"

A spotlight burst on and found my face. I stopped and ducked out of the glare.

"Stay right where you are!" he yelled from behind the wheel of the Cherokee.

"What is this shit, Evans?"

There was a pause. "You're one hairy-ass dude, Bellevance. Watch somebody don't write you up for reckless endangerment and speed in excess of conditions."

"If you have something to say to me, say it. This is idiotic, tailing me around town."

"I had a crimestopper's tip that you might be planning to violate a secured crime scene."

"Who dropped that on you?"

"Anonymous."

"And that's why you're chasing me through the middle of town?"

"Wouldn't want to see you get into any deeper shit than you're in already. Try that A-frame and you'll light up the board down to the barracks."

"If I try anything, you can be sure I won't disturb your personnel. Right now I'm headed home for supper. That's the extent of my plans for the evening, Sergeant."

"That's the extent, yeah? Lois'll be disappointed."

"Who?"

"Fine with me. You go on home, get a cozy fire going, let her fix you some of that garlic-chicken stir-fry with sesame oil and red peppers. Knock back some of that cool California chardonnay. . . . Whatever plans you think you got or don't got, one thing's bound to lead to another, if I know Lois."

At this Wilma came charging out from under the tracks and planted herself next to me. "You need to *quit* this crap, Ed. Jesus! You absolutely have to *lay off*, do you hear me?"

"What crap? Crimestopper's tip, babe. Proactive policework."

"Ed, this is the same old sick shit! Don't *do* this to yourself! Don't make me go back to Larrabee."

Evans switched off the spotlight, and now I could see his face. He put the back of his hand next to his mouth in a confiding gesture. "Watch out for Lois. She's a ball-buster."

He pitched the Cherokee into reverse and roared away around the bend.

We ducked back into the Powerwagon.

I found a spare T-shirt behind the seat and dried my face with it. Wilma shook her hair out.

"So. You and Ed Evans."

She took a deep breath and said, exhaling, "I was going to tell you. But things have been happening so fast. . . . Ed and me . . . yes, but that's been over, and I mean really *over*, for almost two years, so—"

"You have a restraining order on the guy?"

"Not yet, thank God. He's been doing very well since last—"

"He's your source, isn't he? You've been trading information with that son of a bitch right from the beginning."

"He's on our *side*, Hector."

"The hell he is. He's been using you to nail Spud."

"That's not true! He doesn't believe Spud killed those people. Cahoon's the one that's all hot on the Spud theory."

"You can't trust what those bastards tell you! They'll say *anything*, goddamn it! Shit, Wilma. Did you tell him about the safe?"

"He already knew about it."

"Did you tell him about the offshores and the Ingallses' resort-development scheme?"

"Hector, give the guy some credit. He's no dummy. He lives up on the mountain—he rents from the Ingallses, for God's sake. He *knows* the Ingallses. He absolutely knows what's on the wind."

"Did you tell him about the Ingallses and Otto?"

"I convinced him there was a connection, yes. He was impressed by that. He thinks—"

"What else did you tell him? Did you tell him Hrushka's in on it, too?"

"He knows all about Hrushka. He's *helping* you, Hector. That's the bottom line. Whether you can accept that or not."

"He's over on you pretty good, isn't he, Wilma?"

"What's that mean?"

I'd had enough. Evans was milking Wilma, but if she was somehow right and he was turning in spite of himself, just maybe all this was to the good. Only I couldn't quite believe that.

I didn't speak the rest of the way home, pondering the trooper's feint at me and the import of this complicated woman stewing a foot from my hip. How straight was she? It stung to imagine she had thrown herself at me to get a story. But I couldn't quite believe that either.

Through the rain we could hear the faint sound of the phone ringing as we slogged up my muddy path. My machine picked it up.

I hit PLAY when we got inside. Nothing. Two hang-ups.

I tried the Scovilles' trailer at Willow Grove in case it had been Stacey. The little girl answered.

"Megan, this is Hector Bellevance, the peace officer who stopped by earlier today. Did your mom get back yet by any chance?"

"Yup. We're leavin'."

"Who is? When?"

"Me and my mom. We're going to Florida."

"What about Lonnie?"

"They kept Lonnie."

"Who did? Marko?"

"I guess."

"Let me talk to your mom, OK, Megan?"

"I never been on a plane."

"Put Stacey on the phone, Megan."

"She tooken Gram to work."

"All right. When will she get home?"

"Late. She runs a waxer."

"No—Stacey, I mean."

"I don't know. She said she had errands."

"I'll call back," I said.

Wilma set herself to cooking while I took a shower and shaved and changed into whipcords and a clean chamois shirt. When I came out, she was waiting with a glass of wine and a smoked oyster on a piece of sourdough.

"You're too good," I said.

"Wait'll you try my stir-fry."

"That reminds me, how did Ed know you were going to make garlic chicken and red peppers? Did you talk to him after I called you?"

"No!" She frowned. "All I can guess is he must have been watching us in the Grand Union."

"Jesus. He's a pretty screwed-up guy, Wilma."

"It's been a little awkward, I'll admit. We split up for good over two years ago, before he got made interim barracks commander. He was seeing somebody else."

"A waitress. I know, he told me. Gwendolyn."

"Exactly. This ski bunny he met up on the mountain. He claimed if I could have a husband, he could have a ski bunny. I said forget it, Jack, it's over, and he kept on calling me and leaving notes under my windshield wiper—and mind you, this was after he got *engaged* to this creature. And *then* when that fell through, as it was bound to, *that's* when it started getting really strange."

"How?"

"He started stalking me. He'd show up at meetings I was covering, or he'd follow me to the health club. It was terrible. He'd wait for me to come outside, and he'd have flowers in his fist and a bottle of this wine that he knows I like. It was positively weird, this mode he fell into. He *scared* me. I ended up having a serious talk with Sheriff Petey, who knows Ed pretty well. It seems that Ed was having palpitations at the same time. Heart trouble. The upshot was Petey got Judge Larrabee to talk to him. By summer things were about back to normal. Then pow, the Morganthaus happened and you happened, and poor Ed, he wants to close this case so bad he can taste it. But he's got Cahoon in his way. And now you. And you've got me. So he's bent out of shape again. More than anything, he wants to retire. In glory."

"I hope he does."

"You had a phone call when you were in the shower." She handed me the cordless and a slip of paper. "Female. Wouldn't give her name."

Local number, not Beth's. I punched it in.

A woman answered.

"Hector Bellevance, calling back."

The voice brightened. "Great! This is Cherie. I been trying you for *hours.*"

"Who is this?"

"Cherie! Cherie Boulanger? From the Quiver Club, remember?" She sounded half-drunk.

"Right, right. OK, what's this about, Cherie?"

"Well, you're the law in this town, right? I need to talk to you. I'm up to the Lakeview Cabins. You know where that is?"

"Those cabins are all closed up, Cherie."

"Yeah, they are. But I'm hangin' out in the main office, because these enchiladas from the industry flew in today for the wrap party tomorrow. So Keith moved me up here so I wouldn't raise embarrassing questions in their minds."

"What questions?"

"I got . . . hurt. I was working up at the Lodge today and I stepped on a rake. My eye's all swollen up, and so's my lip. I feel a little woozy, and I need some ice. And before you say anything . . . that's really what happened. I stepped on a rake."

"Have you seen a doctor?"

"No, that wouldn't be cool. What if they didn't believe me? That could throw off the shoot and everything. I *was* supposed to go back to Maine and rest. But I can't drive with just one eye. So that's why I'm up here. Could you bring me some ice? There's something I have to tell you."

"Cheryl. I'm having supper. What have you got to tell me?"

"I can't tell you on the phone! I'm not even supposed to be calling anybody! Please! The porch light's on." She hung up.

"Fine," Wilma said tautly. She flicked the knob off under the wok.

"Sorry, I can't pass this up."

"Obviously. A porn queen in distress down at the defunct motor court sure smells like bait to me."

"I'll be careful."

"Let me come. I'll wait in the truck like I did at Willow Grove."

I shook my head. "Wait here and answer the phone. If Stacey calls, see if you can find out where she's flying to and when. I'll be back in an hour."

She followed me to the closet. I slipped a poncho on over my jacket. From the inside corner among the umbrellas and hiking sticks I lifted out Reg's twelve-gauge side-by-side. I broke it open. "See? It's loaded," I said. "Mom always kept it here just in case."

"In case of what?"

"I don't know. Maniacs."

"Swell."

"Can you handle one of these?"

"I suppose." She took me by the arm. "Hector, I just want to say, please don't be upset about my sharing information with Ed Evans. I've been handling him until now—really. And we *need* Ed. He's moving your way. He can help you *beat* this thing."

"If I'm not back by ten, send out the hounds."

"Wait—" She pulled me down and kissed me.

I picked up a bag of cube ice at Sullivan's just before they closed for the night. The storm had swept on and the rain had slackened to drizzle that was softening into mist.

It was quiet and black. Every yardlight and lit window was a blur in the fleecy air. North of the village up the gap the only light was the glow of the vapor lamps in the Lodge parking lot.

Maxwell's Lakeview Cabins stood back on the side of the highway opposite the fishing access on a rise in a stand of white pine and spruce. The gravel lane was strewn with broken branches and clumps of needles. A few larger boughs had been dragged to the side. Storm-flattened, unmowed grass glittered in my brights. The drive ran between the rows of dark, run-down cabins up to the main building. Around back an orange bug light was burning in a wire cage over the door, and inside, behind the curtains, there was a dim glow.

I parked beside what I took to be Cheryl's vehicle, a blue Celica with Maine plates, got out, and stood listening. If she had heard me pull in, she was giving no sign of it. Rainwater pattered out of the trees.

I made a slow survey of the place. No sign of anybody. I went up on the porch and knocked twice. "Hey. It's Bellevance."

She parted the curtains. The door opened. An eggplant-colored welt filled the orbit of her left eye. Her lower lip bulged. It was split like a walnut. She was wearing a red down vest, dark sweatpants, and sneakers.

Before I realized I was doing it, I reached for her face. "You are going to have to have that looked at."

"So look at it," she said.

"Butterfly stitch tonight could keep you from wearing a scar on that lip."

"I like scars."

I closed the door behind me. It seemed colder inside the dank office space than it was out under the pines. The big room was musty. There was a couch piled with newspapers, a jumble of stacked straightback chairs that didn't match, and a couple dozen floor lamps—cabin furnishings. The windows were shrouded with cobwebs. I drew Cheryl over to the fluorescent lamp she had humming on a large, wooden desk. She'd been eating tuna out of the can and drinking Gallo Chablis from a coffee mug.

"I don't see a phone anywhere. Didn't you say you called me from here?"

"Unh-unh. From my car."

I tipped her chin back. Her breath was winy. The skin of her cheek and jaw was a clear pink, and her hair, falling behind her shoulders, was lustrous and black with burgundy glints. Her right eye, the one watching me, was soft and deeply blue. The contusion that closed the other eye was long. Something solid had done this, not a fist. A nightstick, a bottle . . .

I let her go. "Nobody clubbed you, you're sticking with that?"

She sighed, annoyed. "We were cleaning out the veranda boxes, me and Valerie, and if you've seen these things, they're big. They're like mini-coffins, and we were carrying one of 'em, and I couldn't see where I was going, and I stepped on this rake. Came up sideways and got me right acrost here." She traced the eggplant.

I broke the ice bag on the seat of a chair. "I don't think you should be spending the night in this cabin, Cherie. It's damp and freezing in here."

"I've been in worse places." She fingered out some ice and plopped it into her mug. "Want me to find you a glass?"

"No. Thanks. Did Keith kick you out of the Lodge?"

"No. He has guests flying in. From LA—these industry honchos. I was supposed to go to Maine, only with my eye like this I can't drive that far. At night, forget it."

"So who sent you up here? Keith or Danny?"

She said nothing.

"Let me take you into town. We'll have them check out your face at the hospital, and I'll put you in a motel for the night. Someplace with heat, a hot shower, and a TV."

"Sorry. I got my ice, I got my Chablis . . . . I guess I'm good here. But thanks. Really."

I waited for her to say more, but she was looking at the floor. She seemed to be listening to the splats of the rain on the shingles overhead.

"Suit yourself. Now what is it you wanted to tell me?"

She refocused on my face, at first seriously, but then she was tilting her head sideways, reaching for a coyness that she couldn't achieve. She extended her pointer and ran the shaped nail down my chest. I let her. "People say it's my body gets me in trouble, but it's really my mouth. I shouldn't say anything . . ." Her voice trailed off. "But the thing is, you remind me of somebody. Big, tall, handsome guy I used to go out with—coast guard. Had this mustache like Tom Selleck."

"So say it."

"Danny is ripped at you. I don't know why, but you really, really have to watch your back. He's unpredictable. He *hurts* people. He'll hurt you."

"I'm in his way, that it?"

"I already said too much. You better leave here before somebody else comes through that door."

I righted an upside-down kitchen chair and sat. "You'll have to come up with more than that if you want to get rid of me."

She licked her sore lip and whispered, "He'd *kill* me if he knew I told you, but they're into a run. It's a superbig deal, and he gets so *hyper*. And it's like he's focusing it all on you."

"What run?"

"Oh, God. He sells reefer. A lot of reefer. Once a month he ships it out. I don't know where he gets it, and I don't know where it goes."

"Who does he sell it to? These people from LA?"

"No, no, those are Keith's people. They're here for the party."

"What party?"

"They're supposed to wrap tomorrow, and Keith is throwing this big party. While I'm back at my sister's in fucking *Portland*."

"Who does Danny sell to?"

"I told you, I don't know. Really I don't. I never asked, and he wouldn't tell me if I did. It's some secret distribution system they got worked out. He's like the middleman. The wheeler-dealer."

It was definitely time for another visit to the Lodge. I told Cherie I'd be back to check on her early in the morning.

"I wouldn't recommend it. Really. Don't come looking for me unless I give you a call first."

"How come? Danny the jealous type?"

She tried to smile and couldn't. "They all are."

The temperature outside was dropping as the sky cleared. It felt close to forty. Stars streamed among the clouds. I checked my watch. Nine-thirty. All right. Go back to the cabin, have supper, and then, in separate cars Wilma and I could—

Rounding the rear of the Celica, I caught a low growl to my right. What, a damn dog? Here?

No.

Something else. Some animal under the tall pines. A rac-coon, or . . . I stopped. Too dark to see—

Before I could even half-spin around I took a blinding white crack above the ear, and the world vanished.

A deep voice. Someone calling me.

I tasted blood in my throat. I tried to cough. Thundering pain. I couldn't see, couldn't hear . . . Blazing sun all around.

"Bellevance! Listen to me! Can you feel your legs?"

"I— Where . . . ?"

My eyes opened. It was a flashlight, not the sun. I was in the cab of my truck, all cockeyed and crunched against the door. What happened? My *head*, Christ!

I tried to sit up. Water. What the—? I was in cold water. The lake. A beer can was bobbing in front of me. Rolling Rock.

"Don't struggle. You shift this crate and we're liable to slide under. Just hang loose. I'll have you out of there in two shakes."

"I can't"—I choked and spat—"move."

"I said don't *struggle,* hear me? I'll get you out of there."

The light left.

My tailbone was against an armrest. The truck was up on two wheels somehow, resting in the lake. Waves lapped against one corner of my buggy windshield. I wasn't buckled in. I might have drowned otherwise. The fishing access, that was it. Whoever clobbered me had stuffed me in here with a few beer cans and rolled me down the boat ramp.

Amateurs. Not the ones who did the Morganthaus, or they'd have done it right.

The other door popped open.

"You still there? Can you reach up?" It was Evans. "Can you stand?"

"I don't know—I—*Christ.*"

"What hurts?"

"My head . . . my ass . . . everything."

"Good. All right. You'll be OK, don't worry."

Evans panted, lips peeled back, trying to keep from falling in on me while hooking a sling under my arms.

"How's—" He huffed. "How's your ribs?"

"It's my head, mostly. I took a good swat. What time is it?"

"After ten. You been laying here a little while."

"Somebody jumped me about half an hour ago. I was just across the highway, up at the cabins—"

"All right now. All right, I'm going to boost you up . . ." He grunted.

"Cheryl Boulanger—Cherie, you know her. She works for Quimby. She set me up."

"Shut up and push out of there, will you?"

I didn't need the sling. I managed to haul myself out onto the side panel of the truck as the Rescue Squad van was pulling in, lights whirling. Behind them was Rainey Brasseur's Border BP wrecker.

The medics, three of them, wheeled me up the bank and into the back of the van. The inside of my skull was shimmering with pain as they swathed it in gauze.

AFTER the X rays and some needlework in the ER, I was helped out into recovery by a nurse and the paramedic, a Pakistani. I was half-sick. Seeing double. All the same, I was sure I'd sleep better in my own bed and asked a nurse if she would send for a cab.

The nurse raised an eyebrow at the medic, who sat me down and explained I had to stay under observation, upstairs, till the next day at least. Somebody presented me with papers to sign. The medic consulted awhile on the phone and ordered up a CAT scan for the next morning. "After the scan, then I can leave?" Not necessarily. Depended on what the scan showed. Of course.

I signed in. This was going to eat up all my savings. I'd had no medical insurance since the divorce.

Once I got upstairs, the worst of it was I couldn't sleep, and they wouldn't give me any drugs, not even an aspirin. Every half hour or so the pain would knife me out into the bright world again, like an oyster getting shucked.

14

At my bedside when I got back from the scan were Evans, looking blearier than I felt, and the renowned Lt. Brian Cahoon, veteran of three police forces and the FBI Academy, finally ready to make the most of me, now that I was another victim of this thing. Cahoon was a disappointment, squirrelly and round-shouldered with a thin comb-over and tartar-jammed teeth. Not the sort you'd expect in a cop of his stature. Though I'd put up with worse.

"Glad you came to see me," I said.

"How's the noggin?" Cahoon asked.

"Not too bad, considering I could be dead."

"I heard. Doctor says you're one lucky buckaroo."

The nurse excused himself, reminding me that Dr. Bauman would be in shortly to talk over the scan results.

Cahoon said, "Would you care to tell me exactly what you were doing up at the old Lakeview Cabins last night?"

I began explaining the call from Cheryl Boulanger, the rake-handle story, the ice she said she needed—

Cahoon cut me off. "You see the guys that jumped you?"

"No. It was pitch-dark, I'm sorry. But Cheryl Boulanger knows who they were. She decoyed me down there." I looked at Evans. "I gave you all this last night, didn't I, Sergeant? You talk to her yet?"

He clucked ruefully. "No luck so far."

"They musta been real, real good," Cahoon said, "to get the jump on a big, savvy ex-cop like you."

So now *he* was going to work me, this little rooster? "Lose the sarcasm, Lieutenant. Anybody knows it doesn't take much to waylay somebody on a dark night."

"What were you really doing at the motor court, Bellevance?"

I looked at Evans and back to Cahoon. My head throbbed. "Wait a minute. You've talked to Wilma, haven't you? She knows where I was going and why I was going there. Right, Lieutenant?"

Cahoon frowned at Evans. "Wilma?"

"The reporter," Evans said.

"Oh, yeah, the redhead." He turned back to me. "All she remembers is you got a phone call. We want the unadulterated version."

"I just gave it to you. Ask Cheryl Boulanger. She drives a blue Celica, '90, with Maine tags."

Cahoon had his thumb under his chin, stroking his lower lip with his knuckle. "You know this Boulanger woman, Sergeant?"

"She's one of those girls that work for Quimby. He's got no clue where she is."

The lieutenant wearily shook his head. He paced to the door and back, stopping at the foot of my bed. "Bellevance . . . we found the bricks."

"Bricks?"

"Two keys of pressed grass, wrapped in yellow plastic."

"What are you talking about?"

"In a garbage bag behind the seat of your Dodge pickup truck."

"Come on, Lieutenant. They set that up. Run the bricks for prints. You'll see I didn't lay a finger on them." I pushed myself up. "Hell, you guys, this thing is just *pathetic*. Only some desperate idiot would try to pull a bullshit move like this. Look, here's what you have to do. Bring in Danny Ingalls. He's the punk who's—"

"Shut up!" Cahoon shouted.

His shout made me feel sick.

"We also discovered a pile of processing residue," Cahoon said.

"What residue?" I said after a moment.

"Trimmings and stalks. Up in your brother's manure pit."

"That's overkill. It's laughable, it really is."

Cahoon looked at me, blinking. "Let me run one by you, Bellevance, OK? You went to the old motor court because certain businessmen from downcountry were meeting you there to score your fine herb. But the deal broke down, and you tried to back away. Which is when they decided to knock you over and leave you for dead with just enough product in your vehicle to get you fifteen to twenty if you lived." He smiled stickily. "How close is that?"

"No, Cahoon, that won't fly. Just locate Cheryl Boulanger, will you?" Now *I* sounded weary. "Cheryl knows exactly what happened, who did it, and why."

"Cheryl Boulanger is nothing but a *slut*!"

"She's a sex worker, Lieutenant."

"'Sex worker,'" he snorted. "What's that make you? A druggist?"

"I can prove that shit wasn't mine."

"So whose was it? *Morganthau's*?"

I fell back in disgust.

Dr. Bauman breezed in and glanced around. He was bald and slight. "You mind if I have a talk with my patient?" he asked Cahoon sharply. "In private?"

Cahoon and Evans exchanged a few words under their breath and excused themselves. Bauman closed the door behind them.

He checked my eyes and reflexes. Listened to my chest. The scan had showed nothing worrisome, but I was going to be off my feet for a day or two. If the nausea or blurred vision got worse, he'd want to run me through again. The concern, he said, was a slow bleed. That could cause an intracranial hematoma, which could cause a seizure, which could kill me. He snapped his fingers. "Like that."

I told him I'd stay, but I'd need a telephone.

He rapped his pen on a green handset next to the tissues box on my metal bedside table. PUFFS, said the box. My vision was improving.

Out in the hall the sergeant and Bauman talked briefly. Then Evans came into the room. He stood still for a moment.

"Cahoon couldn't hang. He says he'll come by and see you later in the day."

"He's such a sweet guy. Think he'll bring me an African violet?"

Evans went to the window and looked down. "I got a deputy ordered up for your room, so if you're nervous over those unfriendly people out there, don't be. Should be here any time."

"Nobody wants me dead, Sergeant. Just out of the way."

"If that's the case, which I don't happen to agree that it is, then I guess they succeeded. Anyhow, what I would do right now if I was you, I'd get my attorney primed."

"Yeah? For what?"

"This's the bad news I gotta tell you, Bellevance. The state this morning seized your property. Your brother's, too. Lock, stock, and barrel."

"That's bullshit. They can't! Not based on what these people planted in my truck! They can't make a case out of that!"

"They don't need to. You've heard about these drug-bust forfeitures, haven't you, Constable? All they need is probable cause, and bingo, your worldly goods are out the door."

My ears burned. *"Bastards."* I had to get out of this place. I had to see Spud.

"Ahhh, I wouldn't get all riled. You'll get it straightened out."

I closed my eyes and lay back in the pillows.

"No, see, first thing you do is file for wrongful seizure. Get the wheels rolling. Any half-decent attorney, you got a good shot. Me and Lois'll watch your back."

"Evans, how did it happen you found me in the lake?"

"Caught a break. I was heading back from the Morgan-thaus' place—I go up there frequently these days—and I already noticed your truck was missing. I was afraid you'd gone and done something foolish like I warned you. Few minutes later I'm headed north, and not long after that I see your rear reflectors stood up off the side of the boat ramp. I veered in for a look, and when I saw you in there, shit. I thought you were a dead man."

"Was it you who found the bricks?"

He nodded, eyeing me. "You're lucky, though. If I didn't come along when I did, you'd be down in the basement right now with a tag on your toe." He patted the bed. "Lois says to give her a jingle first chance."

"Where is she?"

"The paper, where else? Hey, and while you're recuperating here, I want you to know I am pursuing this offshore money-laundering connection."

"Yeah? How?"

"Talking to people, the usual. Only problem I have is you're talking serious money. I mean, if this is a local scenario, where's the source?"

"Those kilo bricks."

He grimaced. "Nah. You don't go financing a Vegas-style construction project with a backwoods pot plantation."

Dr. Bauman returned a few minutes after Evans left. He had his fists bunched into his wide jacket pockets. "State

Police want me to hold you a couple days for your own safety. They're telling me whoever attacked you might be back. This true?"

"I doubt it." I sat up. "I need to get out of here, Doctor. Now, if possible."

Bauman drew in his jaw. "No way. Like I told you before, you're here at least until tomorrow. And when I do release you, by the way, I'll expect you to have somebody with you who's going to look after you, somebody I have clinical confidence in."

"Sure thing."

Five minutes later, dressed in my damp, muddy clothes, I slipped out of my room and down the hall to the elevators.

I skirted the lobby and hopped on the shuttle from the hospital entrance down to the strip mall on the edge of town. I got off at Burger King and tried to buy a grilled-chicken sandwich before remembering that my wallet was gone. I ended up walking a hard half a mile to the newsroom, sticking to the railroad bed and the weedy bank of the river, out of sight of the highway.

Wilma drove me straight out to Tipton. We found the cabin doors front and back boarded over with sheets of new plywood. Taped to the front of the house was a printed poster: "NO TRESPASSING. These premises have been seized and sealed by the United States Drug Enforcement Agency. Entrance by any unauthorized person(s) is prohibited. 21 U.S.C. Sec. 881(a)."

Wilma smacked the sign. "This is outrageous! Who do you know who's a lawyer? I know some good—" She stopped. "What are you doing?"

I was prying the plywood off the doorframe with a garden trowel. "I need my shotgun and something to eat."

"You don't want to go in there! It's a disaster area, Hector. I saw it come down, and it was horrific, believe me."

The twin-barrel was gone, naturally, but I did find my mother's old Pentax camera, and a quart of yogurt, a wedge of cheese, some bread, and a few bananas, and came back outside. "Now all I need is a weapon."

"Join the Mount Joe Militia."

"I should. They're onto something, you know that? Hell, when the state can come in and seize everything you own without due process of law . . ."

I suddenly realized she was crying. "You're right," she sniffled. "This country's *fucked*."

I held her. "What's wrong?" The top of her head came just to my chest. "Are you scared?"

"No, I'm exhausted." She pushed back to look up at me. "Last night I was scared. I have never been more scared in my whole life. I don't know what time it was—one, two—I woke up and you still weren't back, and I didn't know what to do. Call Ed? Wait? Go home? Then I look out the front windows and whoa! There's crisscrossing light sabers in the mist above that little pond—the imperial hordes! Swarming up the hill! I freaked! They started beating on the door. Bam, bam, bam, bam, bam. 'Agents of the federal government!' and—*crash,* there they are, exactly like a cop show but a lot louder, these great big bruisers in DEA windbreakers. I walk right up to them like I'm in full command of myself, and I go, 'Would you people mind telling me what this is about?' Forget it. These boys tell you *nothing.* First they frisk me and then they drag me through the mud and throw me in the back of an unmarked car, and it's *freezing* and I've got no jacket, no sweater . . ." She blew her nose. "Then Ed shows up and says the EMTs have taken you to the ER. You've been clocked, but you're conscious and stable. I wanted to go see you, but Ed said I had to wait for that rodent Cahoon from the Crime Lab to show. OK, great, I think, here's my chance to tell him the whole thing about the nameless partnerships. Except he's not interested in that. He's interested in one thing and one thing only—the pot farm scenario, about which I know zilch, which he isn't buying, so it's six in the morning by the time I get out of here. I wanted the trooper to take me straight to the hospital, but he said no visitors would be allowed until they got you stabilized, so I had him drive me downtown to write the story."

We'd been walking down to her car as she talked. I stopped and looked at her.

"Don't be that way, Hector. Somebody had to cover it. You give me a statement and I'll play it up in a sidebar."

I opened the passenger-side door for her.

Up at the farm we found the dooryard between the kitchen and the milk house just a gumbo of leaves and mud. The Subaru was gone. Brenda had no doubt packed herself and the baby off to some friend's apartment in Allenburg. Spud's unregistered wreck of a Cutlass was pulled up to the side porch under the bony maples. Other than that, things seemed normal enough, heifers taking the sun in the lower pasture, pigeons flapping, lilacs gone to seed, lawn shaggy and rich with leaves and mushrooms.

We let ourselves in. Spud had his head in his arms on the pine kitchen table, all inside himself, the way he'd been when I found him at the Morganthaus'.

"We've got ourselves a situation now, haven't we, Spud?"

He raised up and stared blankly at us. "Yesterday before breakfast she asked me when the hell was I gonna shave. I said tomorrow, I guess. But now I just got through looking at it, and I believe it's got to the point where it's easier to let it grow out." He found a liter of diet Coke on the bench beside him and took a pull.

"Grow it out then." I sat on the bench opposite. Wilma slipped in beside me.

Spud cocked his cap back. "You took quite a pop."

"That I did."

"Hospital called a little bit ago. Said you left against doctor's orders."

"That's right. How are you doing, Spud? You seem kinda shaky."

"I'm fed up. I'm finished. It's like a nightmare where nothing makes sense, but it keeps getting worse and worse." He jabbed his place mat so hard the top jumped off the sugar bowl. "Nezzie Holmes sat me down here and told me flat out they'd be taking it all, *all*—house, machinery, everything but the goddamn cows. And I haven't done nothing *wrong*! How can they *do* this to me?"

"It's a bad law. If there's cause to believe your property was used in the facilitation of a crime, the law says the government can help itself, no questions asked."

"What law?"

"Comprehensive Crime Control Act of 1984."

"What's the cause?"

"The pot by-products somebody dumped in the pit last night. That constitutes evidence of the cultivation of a controlled substance with the intent to distribute."

"But it's not *mine*. I mean, it's obvious! Even Brenda told them that. There's no way in hell they can prove I grew that shit."

"They don't have to. The way the law's written, once property is forfeit, guilt is presumed. That means it's up to us to prove we *didn't* grow it."

"How do we do that?"

"Have it analyzed. I'm pretty sure it's indoor weed. Shouldn't be too hard to show it wasn't grown on this farm anyway."

"That won't prove we didn't grow it someplace else."

"No, I'm working on that part."

"Who's doing this to us, Hector?"

"Same people that put the vibrator in the sugarhouse, I guess."

He swayed in his chair. "That was Lonnie."

"Lonnie?"

"I mean— He didn't put it there. But he sure as hell told them where to look for it. Or how else would they find it? Barely took 'em two hours poking around."

"How would Lonnie know about that vibrator?"

He shifted on the bench, embarrassed. "He knew we used to meet there. He had the hots for her first. That's how it got started."

"You *both* watched Gaea?"

He nodded and swallowed. After a while he said softly, "He started it. We'd see her, you know, from the woods. This was way before anything happened between her and me. One time after that, I was dumping off a load of manure for her compost, and we talked, and one thing led to another. See, she just wanted me . . ." He lowered his head to the table. "I kept it a secret," he said into his arms, "but Lonnie got all pissed when I wouldn't go watch her anymore. Last summer one day—it was after haying—we was drunk, and he wouldn't believe me when I finally told him what was going on. I shouldn't have ever told him nothing, the dumb shit, but we were drinking beer, and I don't know why I did it, except for being proud of it and sick of Lonnie talking about her, so I told him. Only he still didn't believe me, not till I took him down to the sugarhouse and showed him the vibrator." He took a deep breath and blurted, "Then he tried to *blackmail* me, the stupid shit. In the spring I *had* to let him go. I didn't have the money to pay him, and he knew it, but he still cursed me out. Looking back, I think it was more stupid-ass jealousy than being let go. He said if the bank repo'ed his truck, then Brenda would find out about Gaea. I told him if he ratted me out, I'd beat the skin off of him with a rubber hose."

"You ever mention the Morganthaus' safe to Lonnie?"

"Unh-unh. Only people I mentioned the safe to, besides Brenda, was you and Sergeant Evans."

"*What?* You told me just yesterday the police never asked about it!"

"Right, and they didn't! But soon as you reminded me of it, I called him."

"*Why?*"

"Because! If you think about it half a damn second, you might suspect that what's in that safe could save our asses!"

"Christ, Spud, you never listen to anybody—"

"Evans *appreciated* it. He thanked me and he said it was significant information."

"What else did he say?"

"Same as you. Don't tell anyone else about it."

"I'd trust Ed's instincts on this, Hector," Wilma said.

I was already out the door.

Marko Ruggles's lonely place of business was out on the winding
highway toward Shadboro village. It was a shingled-over
modular building with a big satellite dish beside it. When I
was in school, there used to be a filling station and a Fire-
stone tire dealer on this spot. The only remains of that were
a broken concrete apron and a ramshackle clapboard garage
way in the back under the pine trees.

A molded plastic sign beside the road said RUGGLES WEST-
ERN WEAR AND GUN SHOP. Out front was that sturdy black
Ford 250 Wilma and I had seen parked at Wayne's landing
and a dragonfly-green Geo. We circled around back for a look
in the shed. The doors were padlocked but crooked, permit-
ting enough light for us to make out Lonnie's red-hot Chevy
S-10 inside.

The entry bell tinkled. The merchandise in the main room
was mostly cowboy boots, colorful pairs set out on shelves
row upon row. Satin shirts and fluffy square-dance dresses
hung from racks of steel pipe. A china cabinet was filled with
a selection of Western belt buckles. He had customers, a
young woman straddling a cowhide bench helping a moon-
faced boy slip into a red boot with silver fringe.

Marko, minus the bandanna, came through a doorway in
the back. He had more boots for the kid to try. He hesitated
half a beat at the sight of me in my bandage and ruined
clothes. "Be with you in a minute, Constable."

Wilma was occupying herself examining some robin's-egg-blue boots with eagles stitched into the sides. Marko gave her a sidelong look as he set down his boxes.

"Nothing in a three," he said to the woman.

"Frankie wants the red ones," his mom said, obviously unhappy with the kid's stubbornness.

"Ah, well, two pair of socks till he grows into 'em, he'll be fine," said Marko. He took the box up to the front and ran the woman's card. "I'm surprised to see you up and around," he said without looking at me. "I heard on the radio where you mixed it up with some rough hombres last night. Said you're in the hospital."

"I'm looking for a side arm," I told him.

He pursed his lips. "I could handle that. What do you carry now?"

"Nothing. This is an emergency situation."

"Yeah? Related to the sex murders?"

The woman turned from the rack of earrings she'd been studying and stared at us. Little Frank, strutting around in his new boots, caught his heel on the carpet and fell headlong into the belt-buckle cabinet, sending it into the wall. It would have toppled back over on top of him if Wilma hadn't bounded over the bench and caught it. The buckles clattered and chinked inside the case.

Marko hustled over. "No harm, no harm," he said. He handed the woman her charge card and a slip to sign.

The boy started whimpering. His mother took him by the sleeve and towed him out of the place. Marko held the door. "Have a good one," he said. "Superwoman," he said, winking at Wilma. "Nice job."

He followed us into the back room, where the guns were laid out in three large display cases. Paramilitary magazines sat in stacks on top. A large poster on the back wall, framed in crossed muskets, read:

Firearms stand next in importance
to the Constitution itself.
They are the American people's
liberty teeth.
—George Washington

Marko scratched his fuzz as he considered the inventory. He walked around behind one of the cases, stooped down and unlocked it, and lifted out a large, nickel-plated semiautomatic. He held it in both hands. "I wouldn't venture into harm's way with nothing less than this here. This is the industry standard in a big-bore pistol, the Colt .45 M1991 A1. The hands-down classic. Its stopping power and reliability are unsurpassed by any gun ever made." He laid the gun on a chamois cloth. "And for backup I would recommend a .22 worn on the ankle." Some salesman.

"You have one of those you can show me?"

"Sure. Walther TPH. Got one in stainless with a Cordura rig." He nodded at Wilma. "Females go for these." He placed the smaller gun beside the .45. "Also very reliable and very comfy to carry."

I looked over the Walther. Sleek little thing. Suddenly I felt woolly-edged. I was sure I ought to sit down to keep myself from fainting. I leaned on the gun case, breathing slow, and it passed.

Marko was whipping through pages in a catalog. He spun it around for me to read, pointing. "You might be wise to also invest in some Kevlar undergarments. I can get you the best deal anywhere, plus I can have 'em all here by the time your paper clears."

"You'll have to waive the background check, Marko. I need the guns today."

He studied the counter. "This some kind of a sting, or what is it?"

"No, I'm the law, remember? This is a police emergency. My friend will be paying."

Wilma didn't blink.

Marko tried to grab back the .45, but I clamped my hand down on his wrist.

"I'm taking it. I made that clear."

He let the gun go.

I picked it up and checked the magazine. Empty. "You wouldn't have a shoulder holster for this monster, would you?"

His eyes were like stones. He was a man who wasn't used to holding his rages in, the kind who always turned vicious once he got the upper hand. "Fine," he said softly. "Here's what I'll do. I'll sell you the two pieces, rigs and all, for nine seventy-five."

Wilma snapped her plastic on the glass.

"That's good of you," I said. I wedged the heavy Colt into my jacket pocket and kept the solid little stainless Walther in my palm. It reminded me of a cigarette lighter.

"Extra magazines?" Marko was looking through a drawer for the nylon holsters. "Anything else, as long as we're doing this?"

"Yeah. Tell me what you did with Lonnie Perkins."

He went still. "What I *did* with him?"

"Where is he?"

"Should I know?"

"His Chevy's out back."

"I'm storing it while he takes a vacation, OK? He didn't want to leave it at the airport."

"Vacation where?"

"Mexico. Him and his girlfriend."

"Marko, listen up. Withholding information in a felony investigation is a felony. You get straight with me or I'll take you in right now for obstruction."

"You fucking asshole, you got no jurisdiction on this side of the mountain."

"You've been misinformed."

"I'm inviting you to leave. Now." He was pointing a small blue-black automatic at my nose. "First, set those two hand-guns on the counter real easy, and back away real slow."

"You into the drug-running, too, Marko? Or do you just do Wayne's shitwork?"

"Let's go, Hector," Wilma said.

"What did you do with Lonnie?"

"*Get out.* I wouldn't want to have to shoot you for a gun thief."

"You're too smart to kill me. Or you would've killed me last night. You need to finesse this somehow."

"You got an inflated opinion of yourself."

"Where's Lonnie?"

"Lay the guns on the counter and *get the fuck out.*" He gestured with his own gun, sidling out from behind the case. "Right *now!*"

I didn't move.

"*Hector . . . ,*" Wilma urged through her teeth. "Come on . . ."

I turned to her and gasped. "*Jesus!* Your *mouth!*"

Wilma's jaw dropped and her hands flew to her chin.

Marko glanced her way. I whipped the chunky Walther at his face.

He fired once—*blaow*—as I tucked and went for him. With my shoulder under his arm I lifted him up into the display case. His back broke the glass and the frame. We slid together to the floor.

Before he could catch a breath I rose and hammered his fat slab of a cheek, one heavy blow. He grunted. Blood sprang from his nose. "You tried to shoot me, you gun-crazy moron." I hammered him again. "Let go of the weapon."

"I can't!" I had all my weight on his right shoulder. I slammed him in the eye. He yelled. I slid my knee off. The blue-black gun tumbled from his fingers.

"Where's Lonnie?" My eardrums rang from the shot.

"I— I don't know!" he hissed.

I twisted his collar tight.

He went white. "Let me— Let me—" He pounded the floor with the heel of his hand. I snugged my knee into his groin. He shut his eyes. His mouth gaped. His teeth were bad.

I bent close. "You want to breathe?"

He struggled. I squeezed. Mucus and blood bubbled out of his nose into his wrinkled-up eye socket.

"Where's Lonnie?"

"Let—me—*ch-hakkk.*" His lips were blue.

"Talk to me, hear? Or I'll kill you right now." It seemed I could have. I was caught up in it, my cracked head screaming at me. "I'll rip out your windpipe with my fingers."

"Gok—" he crackled.

I squeezed.

He flailed his free arm, bleating.

"You getting straight with me?"

He stopped thrashing and shuddered. I let him have air. He gasped and gagged, grabbing for his throat. He vomited.

"Jeez-zuss," Wilma breathed behind me. I swatted Marko's pistol across the floor and told her to take it and point it at him. She did.

When I stood up, my vision and balance drained away. "Watch him," I told Wilma. I groped for the wall. But Marko was too wrapped up in his own pain to notice.

When I could see, I slipped around the gun case and pocketed a fistful of .45 hollow-points from a box. I filled my jacket pocket and thumbed eight rounds into the Colt's magazine.

Marko rolled to his side and pushed up. Gingerly he tested his cheekbone with two fingertips. He swore under his breath, wiped his face with his shirtsleeve.

I squatted beside him. "Now. Where is he?"

"Wayne took him," he croaked.

"Where to? The mountain?"

"No, it's all shut down."

"Those kilo bricks you planted on me last night, that was the same weed Lonnie was running around with. Right?"

He gaped at me, licking blood. His eyes blazed pink through the tears. "I didn't plant *nothing*. Listen, we caught up with them two out at Prentiss Point, two, three days ago. Wayne grabbed Lonnie out of his sleeping bag by the ear like he was a little kid. He had me take the truck. We left the shit in a bag by the side of the road—no lie. Wayne called Danny and told him to come get it. That was the only time I ever saw the stuff."

"How did Lonnie get his hands on it?"

"I don't know."

"Danny a dealer?"

"He ships for Wayne."

"Where to?"

He grimaced and shook his head. "They got it all compartmentalized. Wayne doesn't even know."

"Where do you fit in?"

"Cover. Protection."

"You mean Wayne organized a militia unit to cover a dope-growing operation?"

"No! That was totally Wayne's baby, the dope part of it. The rest of us in the unit, we never gave a damn where the bankroll was coming from. The end justifies the means."

"What end?"

"Survival. What else? Freedom."

"I guess Wayne had you people suckered pretty good."

"You don't know shit."

"He's kicking you off the mountain, isn't he?"

"He don't want to leave. The mountain don't belong to Wayne. There's this waddayacall . . . like a *syndicate*. He's only one vote."

"Who are the others?"

"I don't know. They don't advertise."

"Who are they?" I bopped him with the gun butt.

"OK!" He covered his head with his arms. "Keith Quimby. Danny and his dad. Couple others I don't know who they are. But they got no connection to the militia, just like we never had nothing to do with the plants. It was compartmentalized. They set it up that way on purpose."

"Must have been a sizable operation. How huge was it?"

"I don't know. . . . I'm hurtin' . . ." He shook his head and groaned. "Tell her to quit jiggling that Glock in my vicinity."

"Chill, scuzzball," Wilma said, but she lowered the gun.

I squatted. Marko's bruised, fuzzy head felt connected to my own head by a web of pain—my right hand, too, the one gripping the big auto. "How much shit was he pushing out?"

"That wasn't it. It was about *quality,* not weight. He was raising clones. Little bushy mothers. It was like a mini-jungle in there."

"In where?"

"The fallout shelter."

"Underground?"

"In the mountain, yeah. High-tech-lab type of situation— with these special lights and cooling fans and drip lines and all this. He cloned 'em, cured 'em, and bricked 'em up right there in the lab. Never seen anything like it."

"Who moved the bricks off the mountain?"

"He did. Supposedly Danny took it from there."

"OK. Get into the bathroom. Go on." I grabbed a set of nickel-plated handcuffs out of the case and fastened his wrists around the hot-water feed under the wall sink in his tiny, piss-stinking bathroom. As we left, just as a precaution, I reached into Marko's big black pickup and yanked a handful of wires out of his CB set.

THIS time the old paper-company landing was empty of vehicles. We trudged up a logging trace through thick, regenerating stands of aspen, birch, and pin cherry. In time we came to Wayne's equipment yard. He'd enclosed his machines in a corral of boulders—a blue Ford ten-wheeler, a six-wheel dump truck, a flatbed trailer, a Case backhoe, and the old Caterpillar D-9 cocked up on its blade, all of them battered and rust-pocked except for the Ford. Beyond that, between cedar posts, was a sheet of buckled, gray plywood emblazoned with red stenciling:

"Absolutely" No Trespassing
Military Training Area
Danger !!!

Wilma balked. "This really is a little extreme, isn't it, us charging up here? I mean, we already have enough to sink this whole thing. Why not just let Evans and the feds handle the rest?"

"We don't have enough."

"Of course we do! Let's run what we have past Ed and Nezzie Holmes. If we do that, I promise you by this time tomorrow the feds'll be all over this mountain like flies on a hog."

I kept walking. "By then there'll be nothing for them to find. As soon as Wayne hears Marko's been yodeling, he'll have that grow lab torn to pieces and burned. I'd like to photograph it. And I need to find Lonnie."

"Christ, Hector. You're not going to quit until you get yourself *killed*."

I turned around. "If I quit now, they'll kill me anyway. On their time, like they did the Morganthaus. You, too, most likely."

Her eyes widened. "Now there's a jolly thought." She clomped grimly along behind me the rest of the way, saying nothing.

The road leveled out after a while and crossed a marshy swale on a causeway of crushed rock. On the other side of the causeway it wasn't much more than an old skid road, furrowed and littered with junk wood. As the trees thinned and the slope steepened, this track dwindled to a root-laced footpath.

The path crested and ended at an outcropping of granite. There we came upon an ornate arbor gate, of all things, welded out of rebar. On either side of the gate Wayne had installed a wrought-iron spike fence eight feet high. Quite a feature, as imposing as it was incongruous. It curved away in both directions, disappearing into the low growth. "Where do you suppose he scavenged this baby?" Wilma muttered. On the outside, the fence was augmented along the bottom by a four-foot coil of concertina wire.

The arbor gate offered no buzzer or bell, just a plain latch handle with a heavy, rusted rasp jammed through it, as if in a makeshift attempt to stop the gate from rattling. Dried morning-glory vines woven through the gate's high arch twitched in the wind.

Beyond the gate was the rough, weedy plateau Wayne had created by blasting away the granite incline. We could make out the bunker back there below the rock face—or rather we could see its windows, that row of large, blank recesses in the bank of rubble.

"It isn't locked, I don't think," said Wilma, reaching for the handle.

I took her arm. "I wouldn't try that, not unless you want straight hair for the rest of your life." I cupped my hands. *"Yo, Wayne!"* I shouted. *"Trick or treat!"*

We waited.

Nothing. The wind massaging the stone.

We followed the fence upslope, looking for a less formal passage through it, or around it. In time we came upon a smooth rock face, which I reckoned to be the backside of the last steep pitch to the knob, the top of the mountain. The fence ended here, and the concertina wire spiraled up and over it like a giant Slinky. Between the coil of bladed wire and the nearly vertical pitch of rock was, what do you know, another gate. Nothing elaborate like the first one, just a section of fence torched free and fitted with two sturdy hinges and a Kryptonite bike lock.

Inside, springwater sheeted down the broad rock face, gathering at the base of the drop to form a stream that snaked underneath the fence and spilled away through the woods, disappearing among the boulders, down and down toward the lake.

I stretched. My right hip felt bruised where the gun in my jacket had been knocking against it. I took it out.

Wilma eyed me as she crouched next to the brook to fill a Sierra cup. "What are you gonna do, blast the lock off?"

"Wilma, this is it."

"This is what?"

"The Yellow Brick Road."

"The . . . ?"

"The Ho Chi Minh Trail." I stepped into the shallow flow and squatted. "Look here. See how the moss is torn, and the bottom's been gouged up?"

"So?"

"He's been hoofing the product off the mountain right down this water course."

She followed my eyes. "To the lake, you mean?"

"Why not? That lake's been an avenue for contraband ever since the first white man took a piss in it."

"But . . . that's wild. That's smuggling. Just like back in

Prohibition when there used to be whiskey-runners with high-power speedboats."

"Something like that."

"Except why would you go to the trouble of smuggling it into Canada when the hot market's domestic?"

"It's just a guess. I could be wrong. Maybe these friends of Quimby's from LA—"

"Shh!" She held up her index finger.

Someone was whistling. Scraps of a cheery tune penetrated the breeze, not far off, on the other side of the fence, coming our way.

"'Three Coins in the Fountain,'" Wilma whispered.

"Gotta be Wayne. Ducking out the back door."

She nodded. "How opportune."

We slipped back into the trees to wait for him, keeping a clear line of sight through a screen of branches. I hefted the Colt and thumbed off the safety. Wayne came into view before long, picking his way down a steep defile. He was alone, dressed in full mountain camouflage except for his black DOWN & DIRTY CONSTRUCTION cap. He had no rifle. We watched him as he paused at the gate to hawk and spit and hoist his baggy pants with his thumbs.

He groped for a set of keys in his pocket. I extended the Colt and lowered the front sight toward the middle of his chest.

When he came through and turned to refasten the lock, I rose. "*Freeze.* Right there."

He jerked and dropped the U-shaped lock. "Fucking shit, what's this now?" he drawled, lifting his arms into the air.

"Hector Bellevance. Stay just the way you are, Wayne. Don't move."

"Bellevance, you goddamn scumbag. You scared the *piss* outa me. What are you doing?"

"Returning the favor."

He glanced around. "You actually holding heat or you trying to be funny?"

I rose a little more so he could see the .45. About ten yards
separated us.

He looked pained. "Awww . . . This is asinine. What is this?
You're fucking *trespassing* again!"

"Stretch out on the ground. On your belly."

"You're out of your tree, Bellevance. You know what this
is? This is *rogue-cop crap*, ambushing me on my own fucking
property like this. You got no legal reason to draw down on
me—"

"On the ground. Now."

He studied me sourly, rocking his cap tighter on his curls,
weighing his options. He wasn't going to be pushed. But
he wasn't about to chance making this too difficult for me
either—at least not until he could reckon just how much he
had at stake. So he got down, first one knee, then the other,
and spread himself out.

I stood over him. He stank. "Where're you going, Wayne?"

"Nowhere."

I kicked him in the hip. "Where?"

"You cocksucker—cut the shit! I'm going to a party, all
right? Keith Quimby wraps his last film tonight, and everybody's getting down."

"You pretty tight with Quimby?"

"I got lots a friends my mother wouldn't approve of."

Between his shoulder blades under his field jacket I found
he was carrying a sizable piece of handheld artillery. I yanked
the jacket over his head, knocking his cap off, and tugged the
thing out of its harness. Chrome-finished semiautomatic
with rubber grips, a scope, and a fluted barrel that had to be
ten inches long. The muzzle opening was huge.

"What's this for? Rhinos?" I stepped back out of his reach.

"Personal protection. You got no legal right to take it off

me." He rolled over and sat up. "That's my— Aw, Christ," he groaned, "not her again."

Wilma had slipped out of cover behind me. She had twigs in her hair.

"Relax, fella, I'm a neutral observer."

"You're a fucking parasite is what you are."

"Who you calling a parasite, you misanthropic, paranoid drug pusher?"

"Mouthy bitch."

"We're looking for Lonnie," I said. "Marko says you snatched him after you heard he was running loose with a certain amount of your bricked-up produce."

"Marko, Christ. He'll say anything. He's delusional from the war. You oughta see all the pharmaceuticals he's on."

"Where's Lonnie?"

"They got him under house arrest. I don't know where. What are you pickin' on Marko for?"

"Marko set me up last night. He cracked me in the head and stuffed two bricks behind the seat of my truck and pushed me into the lake. I might have checked out right there if Sergeant Evans hadn't come along and found me."

"No . . ."

"I'm afraid so. The troopers took the bricks. And now we've got the DEA swarming all over Tipton, checking out the local economy."

"*Don't* tell me that. . . . Fucking A."

"Yeah, he really knows how to get attention," Wilma said. "He also went up to the farm and dumped a load of trimmings in back of Spud's cowbarn."

"Load of trimmings? What trimmings?"

"Stems and leaf," she said. "You should know. He got it from you, didn't he?"

Wayne ran his palms down his face. "You're shittin' me, you gotta be. This didn't really happen."

"It happened," I said. "State Police, DEA, Border Patrol, AG's office, they all got into it. Even ended up seizing my place, plus the farm, everything but the damn animals."

"Of all the stupid, dumb-ass . . . I fucking *trusted* that dickhead." He let his head fall between his knees. "Listen, it wasn't Marko set you up. It was Danny. He had the bricks."

"Well, hell, if Danny's throwing shit over the side, he must be having connection problems."

"You're too smart for your own fucking good."

"Where does this streambed come out, the old girls' camp?"

"What streambed?"

"This one right here."

"How do I know? The lake."

"Where's Lonnie?"

"I don't *believe* this," he whined. He buried all his fingers in the curls behind his neck.

"We won't be leaving here until you tell me where you've got him hidden."

He was quiet for a moment. When he looked up again, his face was flushed. "Here's the deal. Give me back my fifty mag, and I'll give you my best guess on where they took young Lonnie."

"Throw in a tour of the grow lab and I'll go for it."

He tucked his chin in and swung his gaze to Wilma. "I'm telling you, the fucker's too damn smart for his own good."

"I hope not," she said.

"First the handgun, Constable. Gesture of trust." He beckoned for it.

So I gave it to him. In a smooth, practiced motion, he flipped it over his shoulder into its custom harness. "There," he said, snuggling into the weight of the thing. "That's better."

16

My youthful excesses with smoke were decades behind me, but between the restaurant scene on the Cape and my years with the BPD, I knew enough to know that indoor growers these days generally worked small-scale. They had to make the most of their biggest investment—lamps, and the power it took to run them. The limiting factor was how much juice you could draw without somebody's catching on. Wayne supplied his own, that was true, but I didn't see how you could drive more than a few of those four-hundred-watt, metal halide lamps with solar-charged batteries.

As it turned out, he used generators, in vented, sound-proof chambers. He was proud of the setup—it had been the achievement of his life. For eleven years he'd been cranking out pressed cola bricks, at the rate of forty or more a month. They wholesaled for two K a kilo.

"Out of *here*?" Wilma squeaked. We were looking through a small doorway into a dim, low-ceilinged space no larger than a school bus. The entry was in the back of the main vestibule below the bunker, through a short, square tunnel.

"Yup. It was about density, right? Picture a green froth. Knee-deep and wall-to-wall."

Wayne swept his flashlight around the room. Dismantled metal scaffolding and sheets of corrugated fiberglass were piled on the floor. Otherwise it was empty. The chemical tang in the air was the last tangible vestige of the presence of marijuana. The hefty lamps, the fixtures and hoses and fans and nutrients, the whole growing operation—there was nothing left of all that.

"You were doing this for *eleven years?*" Wilma said. "Who was *buying* it all?"

"You'd be surprised. Discriminating people from all walks of life."

"I mean who was handing you the suitcase of cash every month?"

"Nobody. Didn't work like that."

"So how did it work?" I said.

"Come on, Bellevance, you already figured out that part. All the money got invested. Offshore—for profit protection."

"Wait a minute . . . Tell me you never had any qualms about producing powerful drugs that little kids can get wasted on." Wilma was indignant.

"To me it wasn't about morals. Or the law. It wasn't even about whether you have the natural right to get blasted on quality reefer. It was about free trade. OK? Exchanging desirable goods for value. A simple, time-honored, human practice. Went beyond political bureaucracies—way beyond."

"So who are these corporation guys?" I pressed him. "Besides Ingalls, Quimby, and you?"

"Totally anonymous." Wayne smiled. "Keeps everybody nice and safe."

"Until one guy fucks up," I said.

"Even then," he said mildly. "Or else we wouldn't be having this conversation." He switched off the flashlight. "So you got your tour. About young Lonnie, he's at the Lodge. Danny's sitting on him."

"What for?"

"That part I don't know. You liberate the guy, maybe you'll find out."

THE parking lot was half-full of cars—including Cheryl's blue Celica and four white stretch Lincolns on the lawn in the shade of the pines. The Lodge itself seemed quiet.

We strolled in. Light country dribbled out of the Quiver Club's Bose speakers. The dance floor wasn't open for business. The tables were empty. Nobody was at the bar.

"What makes these joints seem scuzzier in broad daylight?" Wilma said, frowning.

"You've been in here before."

"A few times, yeah," she said.

"Not with Victor."

"Not with Victor, no."

The lone bartender was a buzz-cut slacker with a ring through the middle of his lower lip who said his name was Wes.

"Kindly tell me where I might find Keith," I said.

"Keith's on location."

"What location is that?" Wilma asked.

He eyed her. "I don't got a shooting schedule. You want to see Keith, come back tomorrow."

"How about Danny? He upstairs?"

"I wouldn't know."

"I need to talk to him about his role in an assault."

"What assault?"

I told him.

"That was you?" Wes laughed. "Shit, some plainclothes dick was in here about an hour ago on that same thing. Said there was drugs involved and all kinds of weirdness."

"What else did he say?"

"Nothing. He was looking for somebody."

"Who? Cheryl?"

He hesitated. "What is this? She didn't file charges did she?"

"Some reason why she shouldn't?"

"She signed a waiver. Everybody signs waivers going in. You get hurt on the set, whatever, the company's not liable."

"I told her I'd come and check on her. She's upstairs, isn't she?"

"I doubt it. I can call and ask."

"Ask who?"

"There's a security guard holding down the fort."

"Who's that? Steven?"

"You know him?"

"We go way back." I turned to Wilma. "You still have that nice little nine-mil you picked up at Ruggles's gun shop?"

Wilma felt around in her tote bag and pulled it out. "Sure do."

Wes's eyes went wide.

"Good. You stay here and make sure Wes minds his own business. If I'm not back in half an hour, call Evans."

Wes was blocking the kitchen's swinging door when I got around the bar. "Sorry, this is employees only. Federal law."

I took him by the jaw and banged him into the doorjamb, stretching him up to his toes.

"Anh," he grunted, eyelids clenched, lip ring jiggling.

"Where's Cheryl right now?"

"The tower!"

"Which one?"

"Danny's!"

"This shouldn't take long," I told Wilma.

The kitchen smelled of bleach and garbage. The steel surfaces were yellow with grease. Out in the main hall it was quiet. Multireel film cases with FedEx labels stood near the double doors. I slipped upstairs. The second-floor hallway was littered with movie junk—shipping cartons and coils of yellow cable, wood crates, light stands, banged-up equipment cases with stenciled numbers. This was new since the last time I'd been up here.

The Lodge had two towers. The one to the east was shorter and round with a conical roof, while the west one was capped with a balustrade, like a widow's walk. I'd be in the west tower if I had the choice, so that's where I was headed. I checked doors along the way. The ballroom, where he'd been shooting last time, was shut and locked. The suites along the front of the building were also locked. No voices anywhere. No music. No cigarette smoke. Nothing. Everybody, it seemed, was where the action was.

I took the Colt out and started up the narrow stairs. The last flight opened onto an L-shaped landing with three dark-stained-oak panel doors. The first one was it, by the condition of the carpet. I rapped twice. Twice again.

A man's voice: "Danny?"

"Steven, let me in! Now!"

The chain rattled off. I shoved as the door opened. The muscleman backpedaled into a sky-bright, curving room. "What the fuck—? You can't just come—" He choked and swallowed, seeing the .45 pointed at his head. Cheryl, curled up into a corner of the leather sofa, burst into tears.

"Sit on the floor and put your hands on your head, both of you."

They did. I looked around the space. A glossy black AV setup on one wall. Opposite, the tower windows were full of the sheen of the lake.

"I'm *sorry* about last night," Cheryl whimpered. "I really, really am. They *made* me do it!" She was wearing a deep purple velour sweat suit that almost matched her shiner.

"Shut your *mouth!*" Steven yelled at her.

"Who made you, Cheryl?"

"*Cherie!*" Steven bellowed.

I scissored fast over a low glass table and cracked him on top of the head with the butt of the handgun.

"*Fuck!*" He covered his head with his arms.

"Enough out of you, shithead." I stepped out of his reach. "Who, Cheryl?"

"Him and Danny! I had to do it. Or else Danny'd be more pissed at me than he was to start with. They were waiting for you in the trees."

I turned on Steven. "You know, I'm disappointed in you. I thought I had taught you a valuable lesson—about assaulting officers."

He sneered. "You thought wrong."

"You almost *killed* me."

"Yeah? My mistake."

I crouched so I could look him in the eye. "Your *luck,* Steven. You still have the chance to step away from this stupidity and find yourself a decent life."

Steven said nothing.

"Where's Danny right now?"

He was giving me that flinty look.

I stood up. "Cheryl?"

"I wet my pants," she whimpered.

"Where's Danny?"

She was dabbing at her good eye with her sleeve. "He's at the shoot."

"Where's that?"

"Westlook. One of those camps."

"OK. Now where's Lonnie?"

She glanced at Steven. "In there," she breathed, pointing with her chin toward a closed door.

"Alone?"

She nodded. "They gave him something. He crashed about two minutes after he got here."

I edged over and kicked it open. *"Lonnie!* Come out of there."

I looked in. He was lying on his back across a huge sun-washed water bed. Basketball shoes still on. I could hear him roughly breathing. *"Lonnie!"* I shouted. He'd been beat up pretty bad.

Steven bolted for the open door. I swung around, too late. Nothing I could do but listen to him thunder down the stairs. I should have locked us in. Clumsy, Bellevance. You always were a straight-ahead clumsy damn cop.

"Better keep running, Steve!" I yelled out into the hallway. "I catch you again and you'll do time!"

Cheryl said, "I need to use the bathroom, OK?"

"Sure, go ahead."

I went back to the bed and gave Lonnie a shake. He groaned softly. His cheek and jaw were webbed with dried blood.

"Lonnie! Wake up, Lon! Come on!"

He groaned dully and his lips twitched.

I tapped on the bathroom door.

"One minute, please."

"Cheryl, tell me. Is there a fire ladder up here, would you know?"

She came out of the bathroom in a flowered silk wrap tied with a green cord. "If there is, I have never seen it."

She'd brushed out her hair.

"Danny hit you often?"

She touched her eye. "He only hits people when he's pissed."

"What did he use on you?"

"Karate."

"Next time I see him, I'm going to lay him out. My promise to you."

"Yeah, well, it's not me he's pissed at right at the moment. It's you."

"All the more reason. Why did he slug you?"

"Oh, God. He got all bent when I told him I was leaving the area just when he's about to turn this place into the next Aspen."

"You're going West with Keith?"

"Damn right I am. Fifty thousand bucks a film, plus a new Miata. I'm actually pretty stoked. Would you believe I've never been out of New England?"

"Good luck to you, Cheryl. Which camp are they using for the shoot?"

"The last one on the cove. It's set back in the trees."

I found a phone and punched in the Town Office.

"Ella, it's Hector. Tell me, who are the owners of the northernmost of those old bootleggers' cottages out at Westlook?"

"*Hector?* Where *are* you, Hector?"

"Never mind. Just look that up for me."

"You're supposed to be in the hospital! What in blazes is going *on* in this town, Hector?"

"I'm getting to the bottom of it. Look that up, will you?"

"Keep your shorts on. I think it's one of those . . . OK, the Collins place—what they used to call Raven's Roost. Yup, I'm right, it's an offshore. Stook Holding owns that one, Heck."

I thanked her.

"Wa-hooo! Help's on the way, Constable," Cheryl called out. "Look out there!"

Through one of Danny's high windows, down the shore I could see two flickering blue racks coming hard out of the village. Evans and company.

Getting jammed in here would seal it for us. They'd grab me up in good shape, and Danny Ingalls and the rest of his so-called syndicate would have all the time in the world to scrub clean.

No ladder hooks under the sills. The windows, broad, double-hung panes, lifted easily, though, the sash weights still smooth. But I couldn't see a fire escape, just a short slope of mossy shingle and a litter-filled rain gutter. How had the B and B owners gotten by with this? The ground was four tall stories down.

I took Cheryl by the arms. "Listen up now, Cherie. When

those troopers bust in here, I want you to yell out, 'He's in there!' and point to the bedroom. OK? Later, when they ask about me, just say, 'Oh, him? He left a long time ago.'"

"You left?"

"I'm leaving. I'm going to climb out onto the roof. Close the window after me."

"I don't get this. I thought *you* were the police."

"If they ask any more questions, don't say anything. Understand? Just say you want to see your attorney, OK?"

"OK. . . . But I don't have an attorney."

"Well, you'll have to get one."

"You mean, they're gonna arrest me?" Her good eye brimmed.

"No, no. Cheryl, listen, you're a key witness. The state'll gladly cut a deal for your cooperation. You won't go to jail, I promise." The gravel popped under their tires as they barreled through the main gate. I started out the open window.

Cheryl grabbed my jacket. "Hold it! You can't do that. Here, let me show you something."

"What, the widow's walk?"

"No. Come on."

I followed her out into the hall to a door across the way. It was a walk-in utility closet. "First place they'll look, Cheryl."

"Hang loose." She pulled the light cord. An upright vacuum cleaner. Cedar shelves covered with dust and mouse droppings. Mops. Cases of empty champagne bottles on the floor. "Look over here."

Around the corner there was a lever handle in the wall. She grasped it and turned. A large bin door fell toward us. I peered in at blackness. Laundry chute. About three feet square.

I stuck my head inside. Cold air streamed by my ears. The shaft was lined with sheet metal and seemed to go straight down. I could hear a distant rumbling down there, the furnace maybe.

An old leather strap held the bin door at a forty-five-degree angle. A good yank popped that.

I told her to shut the door after me.

"I will. Good luck. You're bleeding, you know."

I fingered my bandage. "Thanks."

"Good luck," she said again.

I felt my way into the shaft, reaching for the back wall of the chute with my foot. I pushed till it gave. Not too much. It was coated with dust. She closed the bin door.

Could I crab to the bottom? Sure—long as I didn't bust through a weak spot, or another door. A fall would probably kill me. So I wouldn't fall.

I positioned myself crosswise in the shaft like a cocked spring, legs bent, backbone and both hands splayed behind me against the sheet-metal wall. Shifting my weight, I let one foot slip and then the other, then my hands, a few inches at a time. The walls popped and creaked. Sweat trickled into my eyes. Dust sifted down.

I made progress. Slowly.

After a couple minutes, though, my forearms began cramping. My thighs trembled in spasms. I had to stop, braced in the shaft, to try to shake out one limb at a time. That only made the taut leg worse. It got so I couldn't move except in little bursts, down a foot, rest, down, rest, down, rest . . . My palms were on fire.

When the sole of one shoe finally met air, I pulled both legs in, pushed myself straight, and managed to land flat on my feet. Something wooden cracked and gave way under me. I fell onto my hands and knees. Dust rose around me. I straightened one leg, then the other. The spasms eased. I opened my eyes. I was on the cellar floor, kneeling in what appeared to be a smashed cart. I was all right.

The churning furnace was the only noise I could hear. I stood up. Blood ran into my ear. Must have sprung some stitches. I dabbed my head with my jacket sleeve.

The dank air was threaded with the odors of mildew, rotten hay, sewage, and cold stone.

A brownish light filtered in through a pair of well windows that were half-buried in pine needles. Overhead was a rough-board subfloor. Sheaves of metal-clad wiring ran along the huge joists. This room, the old laundry, was partitioned off from the rest of the cellar. Arrow-Wind Camp's ringer washers lined the yellow wall like a platoon of squat aliens. There were stacks of dust-coated furniture and boxes of dishware and moldy linens.

The large, windowless main room was a good deal dimmer than the laundry space. I could just make out a broad, open stair that led up to the first floor. In the other direction, somewhere on the back wall, I was sure there ought to be a sloping passage up to the bulkhead doors on the lake side of the building. But after a few minutes groping all along the rough wall, stumbling around stacked firewood and other junk, I couldn't manage to locate the opening.

I finally found my way into the furnace room on the east side of the building. It was comparatively uncluttered. I was hoping maybe it still had a coal chute—the building was old enough—but no such luck. Along the outside wall were two hot-water tanks and several leftover rolls of pink insulation. The furnace was fairly new, a hot-air job dating from the B-and-B remodeling.

I was about to go back and try to bust out one of the well windows in the laundry room on the back side of the building, but just as I reentered the main part of the basement a string of bare lightbulbs came on as if I'd tripped a switch. The heavy door at the top of the stair crashed open. I scuttled back into the furnace room and worked myself in between the hot-water tanks.

No one was coming down.

Then I heard a man pleading in a panicky voice: ". . . long do I have to *stay*—"

"Till we *get* him, I said!" A sharp, deep voice.

Another whine from the first one. He was strung out.

"Wait there now. *Wait.* I got something for you . . ."

A gunshot. The hollow crump echoed in the stairwell. A body fell hard, tumbled once, and stopped. Something clacked and skidded across the concrete floor. Upstairs, the door quietly clicked closed. The lights stayed on.

I waited a moment before easing out toward the light, wiping a film of sweat and cobwebs off my face with my hand. Salt burned in my head wound.

The body was hung up a third of the way down, one leg hooked around a post. The rest of him lay headfirst, his loose blond hair streaming with blood.

Christ Almighty, it was Lonnie. At the foot of the stairs lay the gun that killed him. My gun. The old Smith, stolen out of my truck last night.

Which had been established. Hadn't it? Hell. I couldn't remember mentioning the gun to Evans. This looked bad. I ought to pocket the thing right now. But if I got caught carrying it, I was cooked. Besides, it had the shooter's prints on it. But whether it had the shooter's prints on it or not, touching that gun would spoil the scene, and I couldn't do that. A few scruples were still ingrained. No, this little setup was going to have to play out however it would, without my meddling in it.

Who shot him, then? Steven? Danny? Did they know I was down here? Could Cheryl have ratted me out? One thing at least was clear: I had the bastards in some kind of profound panic, for them to risk blasting poor Lonnie in the head with the police right outside the damn building.

All at once, in the bare-bulb glare, on the far wall I spotted the way out, a plain cross-braced plank door painted the same yellow-gray color as the walls. I had to roll a number of giant, moldering, straw-filled archery targets out of the way to get to the four-by-four in brackets that secured the door.

Mold spores had me sneezing over and over, into the crook of my arm.

The bar lifted free of the brackets easily enough, but it took a minute or two to work the swollen door open, hauling and scraping it an inch at a time over the concrete. I drew it shut behind me the best I could.

It wasn't the bulkhead opening. Better, it led into the original root cellar, a wide passage with slanted, debris-filled shelves on either side. The tin-sheathed hatchway at the far end opened straight into the ruined greenhouse. It was a jungle of bindweed, sumac, glass, and red clay potsherds. Overhead the few pieces of glazing still in place were black with sap and leaf litter.

The Lodge loomed above the mock orange hedge just behind me. Toward the east end of the building one set of rack lights played in the pine boughs. The other cruiser was probably out front. If they didn't find me or Lonnie right away upstairs, they'd seal the place and start a room-to-room. The cellar would likely be last—unless they got tipped to it.

I made for the shore, heading down the broad lawn at a good trot, praying nobody would glance out a north window. Down the shoreline all the way to the village, the lake lapped a hard, flat strip of grayish sand. In the other direction, beyond the camp, the shore was rocky and overhung with cedars. At the reedy lip of the beach I came upon three sun-bleached, green fiberglass canoes turned over in the unmowed grass. Paddles inside.

17

The east shore ran north under the face of the mountain. From the Lodge to the border, a distance of eight miles, it was too rough and steep for any construction—with the picturesque exception of the six-acre cove at Westlook. The cove was maybe a mile from the line where Fern Brook emptied off the mountain. There under a bank of hemlocks and beeches were five extravagant cottages, all built during Prohibition. Whiskey-runners, trying to outdo one another, had lavished their fortunes on balconies, cupolas, slate roofs, ornate chimneys, copper weather vanes, leaded-glass casements, and Italian-marble mantelpieces. Down through the years these gems had found their way into the hands of the wealthiest Allenburg families. No surprise that one would belong to the Ingallses, with the titled owner listed as one of these hidey-hole corporations.

I paddled along in the lee of the near shore, where the water was quiet. Twenty yards out a good fair-weather chop was running, and beyond that whitecaps danced as far as I could see. To the south off the state beach a few windsurfers jiggled against the willows that grew on the bank below Sullivan's and Lake Street.

Mallards scooted on ahead of me into the next cranny among the rocks or took to the air. I stopped once to rest my arms and rinse my face in the cold water. After a while I heard noises from upwind, first a halyard ringing against a mast or a flagpole and then a sort of humming, which after a moment I recognized as an amplified voice. I tucked the canoe in between two boulders, climbed out, and began pulling myself up among the trees toward the highway cut.

About halfway up, I looked back down through the tops of the trees and was able to make out part of the stony margin of the cove. The camps themselves were hidden from view. Before long I intersected the gravel road down, a narrow lane that sloped through a few switchbacks to an open parking space where a varnished sign read:

WESTLOOK—PRIVATE
Overnight Parking by Permission Only
Police Take Notice

Footpaths from there led down through ferns and woods to the enclave. Quimby's crew had taken the place over. RVs crowded the parking area. Other vehicles lined the lane as far up as I could see. There weren't any people nearby except for a few young women who were busily unloading food, folding tables, and cases of wine from a catering-service van and trundling them down through the woods. I followed.

Below, at the edge of the grassy clearing that fringed the cove, generators hummed. Rivulets of black and orange cable ran over the ground. Lights and reflectors stood around in front of the more exposed cottages, where a crowd was gathered.

"May we have . . . *quiet* please!" Some exasperated woman with a bullhorn. "*Quiet* on the set! *Quiet!* Thank you! Traffic control? Are we holding up traffic on the highway? Please? Roger? Holding traffic? Sheriff? Holding traffic north? South? Fine. Fine and thank you. . . . OK. *Ready. Sound?* And . . . and . . . and, we, are, *rolling* . . ."

"Roll-*ing*!" someone echoed far off.

The caterers and the technicians all sat still. A sizable audience of onlookers sat in folding chairs near the water. The wind washed through the trees. From up on the highway, in the stillness, I thought I could just hear a two-way radio sputtering. I ducked back into the woods and circled around, climbing steadily until I reached the highway's blue-stone embankment.

Up on the highway in the direction of the village, a white Montcalm County Sheriff's Mercury was pulled up against the guardrail, red lights whirling. Sheriff Petey Mueller had his walkie-talkie in hand and half his big ass hitched up on an orange sawhorse in the middle of the empty highway. His job, evidently, was to keep the sound of passing cars from spoiling Keith Quimby's erotic extravaganza.

Over the treetops, across the lake, lay Quebec. This was the stretch of water the whiskey-runners had traversed to their considerable gain when Reg was a young boy. On the far shore a fringe of waterside camps and docks and boathouses was barely visible through the spray. . . . Then it hit me. If the militia was providing cover for the production end, as Marko said it was, why couldn't the movie business be doing likewise for the distribution end?

It was too neat. And it was all going down right under Sheriff Petey's fat red strawberry of a nose.

The amplified woman announced, "*Cut. Cut* and *print*! That's a wrap! It is now chow time, people. We break down and set up for the sunset farewell sequence at five-thirty. We'll need Brooke, Rachel, and Gregory. Release traffic. That's a roger. Let 'em go, Moe. . . . Sheriff . . . Roger, ten-four and out."

When I got back down, the hustling caterers already had a dozen cloth-covered tables arrayed on the mossy shelf right near the shore—and they were setting them with real china.

The late light was spectacular. It seemed they'd been shooting on the center cottage's wide, mossy lawn, and using the northernmost cottage as a retreat for the actors. All the others were shuttered for the season.

Down on the cove's shingle beach, a few techies were dismantling the light stands and reflectors that surrounded a sailing ship's dory nosed into the shore. A crowd of actors in knee britches and wigs and some production-crew people stood chatting near the camera, which was anchored to a little flatbed trolley. Keith was up on the trolley conferring with a string bean in a leather cap—his cinematographer, I figured. I was able to pick Keith out by his ponytail and white sweater, but I didn't see anyone else I recognized. No Danny, no Steven, no Wayne Hrushka.

No boats either—other than the dory they were using for the movie. As the crew and the onlookers gravitated toward the banquet, I slipped over to the last cottage and entered by the sunporch. The rattan carpet was clotted with mud. In the country kitchen a coffee urn and cases of soda and juice drinks were out on a table. The place was a shambles—worse than the Lodge. I wolfed down a bagel, trying all the doors until I found the one off the pantry that led to the cellar. It wasn't locked. Dirt floor. Firewood, paint buckets, some rusty garden tools, a rowing machine covered in dust thick as fur, nothing much else.

Through a fine kitchen window framed with stained-glass panels, I observed the crowd outside. Quimby, clearly in a jovial mood, had one arm around the neck of one of his beauties. There in a black jacket, slouched in a lawn chair talking on a cell phone, was Danny. His old man, Gavin, was nearby in a group of half a dozen other movers I didn't recognize, the people from LA, no doubt. They'd been drinking and watching the shoot.

Danny got up and started urging them all toward the eats,

waving his arms. "Yo! Soup's on!" When they were up and moving, he hung back to speak quietly to his father. Then, rather than join the guests and crew, he started back this way along the shoreline. If he came in here, I'd have the prick alone finally. But no. I watched him disappear into the soft-wood trees at the end of the cove, where the shingle beach ended. Taking a leak maybe.

It was more than a few minutes before he reappeared. When he did, he was striding hard, just the way he'd come at me on the golf course that Sunday morning. He went straight to Gavin's table, and they had a short exchange of words, heads together. Gavin patted the back of the empty chair beside him, encouraging Danny to sit. He balked. He seemed wrought up over something. Yet a second later he gave in. The caterers were pouring the champagne.

I left the house and circled out through the dense trees. Just ten yards in I came to a churned-up path that seemed to run between the lake and the highway, tracing a brook. Fern Brook. The other end of Wayne's Yellow Brick Road. I followed it down until I reached a small, muddy clearing on the shore. Under a shaggy canopy of cedars, a shingled boat-house was built out over the lake on concrete piers. In back of the boathouse someone had laid down a corduroy of wooden pallets to walk on. The door was padlocked.

I stepped out of my trousers and field jacket and bundled them up under my arm. The .45 was in my hand. The water was numbing and the rocks slippery underfoot, but I managed to totter out crotch-deep, to where I could fit myself in under the wall of the building without getting soaked.

All I could see at first were scraps of reflected light jiggling in the rafters. There was a small, regular *creak-creak, creak-creak, creak-creak* sound, as if the waves were nudging something in the slip. A tarp covered it. I imagined a mini-submarine.

I hoisted myself, ankles throbbing, out of the water and onto the narrow catwalk around the boatslip. I unhooked a corner of the tarp. A large winch stood underneath. A simple motor-driven spool like one you'd find on a fishing boat, slowly turning, creaking, reeling in a rusty cable through a sliding chock.

Easy enough. All you needed was a similar setup on the Iceville side, and you could move almost anything back and forth through the dark belly of the lake with no risk at all. They were at it right now. Waiting for a delivery. That's what Danny was agitated about.

The time to bust this thing was now. Right now. But I couldn't do it alone, not a chance, not in my condition. It was way too big. No, the smart thing to do was hike to the highway and get Sheriff Petey to radio the barracks—

Danny was back. I could hear his voice under the wind and the slap of the water. He was right out back—and he had company. Gavin? He was grousing about something.

I rehooked the tarp and eased myself into the knee-deep water alongside the winch at the back of the boatslip. I stooped down and waded in under cover of the catwalk. But for the cold, this wasn't too bad. They'd have to be looking for me to find me. Then again, if they noticed the wet planking, they might just do that. I thumbed the safety off the Colt. My hands were stiff, and it was hard to suppress my shivering.

The padlock rattled. Someone coughed. The door opened out into the green day, the space overhead brightening to gold. The winch creaked monotonously on. Little wind-driven waves splashed the piers.

A big guy with heavy shoes edged out along the catwalk to peer at the cable. I could see him, a wavering image, his black cap reflected in the water. Wayne. He'd got down here a good deal faster than I figured he would.

"It's movin'. So what's the problem?"

"Now it's moving. But it's been stop and go, stop and go. I never seen it do that before."

"Ah, you're an old lady. It's just the lake is all riled up from that storm. Don't worry about it."

"Yeah—don't worry! Thanks to you, I got a pack of troopers going through my place of business. They come out here, it's gonna be ugly."

"Nah. You wait. Soon as they find the constable, they'll be happy."

Danny kicked something. "I still don't see why you couldn't just leave it alone. It was working perfect!"

"*Perfect!* You asshole—you threw them the product! Who told you to do that? That was totally fucking over-the-top. All you were gonna do was take the guy out. Break his legs for him. But, no, you had to get fancy."

"Hey, don't call *me* asshole, you motherfuck. I already *told* you, that was the crazy man did that. You know this all goes back to him, this whole thing."

"The fuck it does. He couldn't have used the shit if you didn't lay it on him. Right?" Wayne hawked and spat into the water. "And let's don't forget who it was thought he could screw Morganthau out of his dividend. And who demanded we put a paranoid, stupid little cunthound like you on the board? Your fat fucking father, man, *that's* who it goes back to." He leaned out over my head for another look at the dripping cable. "Stay here. When the box docks, come and get me."

The space dimmed when the door banged shut. The lock rattled.

Danny stewed. I heard him muttering to himself. He paced. He kicked the winch frame. *"Fucking shit-fucking thing!"*

A moment later he had his cell phone out, trying to make a connection. He waited, then snapped it shut. "Fucking *shit!*"

I wasn't in good shape, either. Trembling nonstop, chattering, seized, too, now with cramps. I had to bend and massage my calves with my free hand.

All at once, while I watched, the cable sliding out of the water a few feet in front of my nose turned from rusty red to a shining, tarry black.

Danny perked up at this. "Whoa, whoa, whoa, here we *go,*" he sang.

In a moment a rubber collar emerged from the lake and caught in the chock, and with that the winch motor cut out. The creaking ceased.

A large blue crate lay in the shallows. Made of fiberglass, with sled runners underneath it. The cable was shackled through rings at both ends.

Danny got down on his hands and knees to reach for it— then went suddenly still. He'd seen me. My feet, my reflection maybe.

I didn't stop to think. I lunged and snagged his bony arm with my left hand, took him, and yanked him headfirst into the slip. He squealed and thrashed in front of me. As he came up with a gasp, I drove the barrel of the Colt hard into the back of his skull. He collapsed facedown into the water.

I sloshed out from beneath the catwalk and unfastened the box's steel clasps. On the inside of the lid, small raised letters identified the crate as the product of MORGANTHAU CON-TAINER, LTD. MONTREAL, P.Q., CANADA.

Danny's hip bobbed against my knees. I took him by the shirt and shoved him behind me, out of sight under the catwalk. Pink lake water slopped into the box. I unfurled the thick inner plastic wrap. The sunlight caught on a magnum of Mumm Cordon Rouge champagne. It lay nestled in a bed of U.S. currency. Packets of twenties, hundreds.

I closed it and refastened the clasps. I wanted to float the box away with me, but I couldn't free the damn thing from the cable. The shackles had screwed-in fasteners, and with my stiff fingers I couldn't manage to get them started.

I sealed the blue box back up and waded out of the boathouse, barely able to feel my legs. Petey Mueller, I was thinking. Get to Petey's radio and tip Evans to this before Wayne or somebody came back and got it cleaned up. They were eating. How much time did I have? Twenty minutes? Thirty? That much or more. It was enough.

But it took a good fifteen minutes' bushwhacking through the softwoods before I even broke out at the foot of the highway embankment. I scrambled up through the clattering stone to the pavement and had to rest my shaky legs before starting on down the empty highway toward Petey's car, a mile or more to the south. My head throbbed. Most disturbing, the center of my vision was going out on me. I could see things only if I looked at them sideways. Not good at all.

The sun was low across the lake. The wind was falling, the air sharp. I was badly chilled. It took all my will just to make myself keep moving through the blotted-out world. I jogged, half-stumbling, along the shoulder of the highway.

Topping a crest in the road, all at once I was within sight of the Westlook drive and the sheriff's pearl-white Merc. It had been joined along the guardrail by Wilma's Mazda 626. Right on her bumper was Ed Evans's unmarked Caprice cruiser.

I scissored over the guardrail, sending rock into the scrub below, and passed the sheriff's empty car in a crouch until I could see Wilma in the front seat of the cruiser having a heated conversation with the big sergeant.

Neither of them noticed me as I approached. I rapped on her window.

"Hector!" Wilma yelped. "Where the hell did—"

Evans popped out his side of the car. *"Don't move."* Sweat

was beaded out under his hat brim. He sidled right around the car with his gun aimed at my head.

"Spread your hands out on the roof. Now!"

I did. He found the .45 in my pocket and took it. He opened the back door.

"Now get in this vehicle! Get in!"

I got in.

Wilma clambered up to see me through the mesh separator, her face set in a grimace. "Hector! It's *so good* to see you. But, God, you look like shit! How'd you get out of that building?"

"What are you doing here, Wilma?"

"Hector, Hector . . . Oh, my God. They found Lonnie in the Lodge. Somebody shot him. He's dead, Hector. I buzzed up here to try and get a reaction out of Quimby and whoever else. But Ed caught up with me. As you can see. So here we are."

Evans put his gun away and slipped in behind the wheel. "Sorry to treat you like this, Bellevance, but you are a *very* wanted man. Cahoon found your friend Lonnie Perkins with his brains blown out. By a .38 Smith & Wesson Police Special."

"My gun was stolen out of my truck last night."

"Yeah? How come you didn't report it?"

"I guess I overlooked that piece. I was in a bad way, as you'll recall."

He clucked.

"They're down there looking for you," Wilma said grimly. "Cahoon thinks you busted out of the hospital so you could get to Lonnie before they did."

"You got only yourself to blame for this, Bellevance," Evans said. "Shit, you were in protective *custody*. You were safe in the hospital, but you didn't listen to me, and now you're set up for the *long* fall."

"You listen to me, Evans. Danny Ingalls has been smuggling Hrushka's reefer across the lake with an underwater cable. It's going down right now, right below us. You come with me and I'll show it to you."

"*Smuggling?*" Evans cut his eyes to Wilma. "He serious or delirious?"

Wilma stared at me.

"I'm serious. There's a crate full of cash sitting in Danny's boathouse. Come on, Sergeant! We can bust this thing open right now, you and me. *Let's go.*"

I groped for the door handle. There wasn't any.

"Sheriff Petey's already down there," Evans said. "You sit still. You done more than enough. I'll go check out the boathouse." He threw his door open.

"You're gonna want backup."

"Yeah, well, Cahoon and them'll be screamin' in here before too much longer." He paused. "Only trouble there is as soon as the lieutenant latches on to you, that's the ball game. He won't go no further."

"Evans, please. For Christ's sake, don't blow me off this thing. Let me go with you. Come on!"

"Hector! God," Wilma breathed.

"Forget it," Evans said to her. "He's in no kinda shape. Look at him." He paused, thinking. "All right, babe, here's what you do. Take Bellevance to my place. Clean him up, make him some noodle soup. Then the both of you sit tight till you hear from me. OK?"

"Sounds good to me," Wilma said. "You OK with that?"

I didn't have the wherewithal to resist.

"Better move it," he said.

She helped me into the Mazda. As we sped off, I turned to watch Evans lope alone down the gravel lane toward the cove.

We took the Radar Road east over the ridge to avoid the Lodge. It was a shorter route to Shadboro, in miles at least, than if you went by way of the highway through the village.

"So who do you think killed Lonnie?" Wilma said, banging the Mazda over the washboard. "I hope to God it wasn't you."

"Did anybody else pass through the bar before the troopers showed up? Say Danny? Or a bodybuilder with swept-back hair?"

"I don't think so. A couple of limo drivers came in and took a table."

"Did you hear a shot?"

"Nope. State Police came charging in maybe twenty minutes after you went upstairs. They told me to get out of the building and not to leave the parking lot until we had a chance to talk. I said I'd be very glad to talk."

"Did you?"

She shook her head. "They all went upstairs. Wasn't more than ten minutes after that Cahoon showed up, and then half an hour ago they found Lonnie. He was down at the bottom of the basement stairs. So was your .38. After that, boy, were they lathered up. Cahoon ended up concluding you must've escaped out the back somehow. That's when I split. They want you bad, Hector."

Evans's SkyHawk condo was one of two dozen units

Ingalls had thrown up around a scummy artificial pond, all with slot windows and metal prefab chimneys. Vacant in the off-season.

Wilma parked beside his tan Grand Cherokee and hustled us inside—to get to the bathroom, she said.

It was a stale, cramped one-bedroom smelling of cigarettes. I looked around while she went to pee. Stained green carpet, bare walls. A pine bookcase beside the door held heaps of magazines, an aloe plant in a Folgers coffee can, a wooden bowl of loose change, keys, matches, a few shotgun shells. On top of a paint-spattered boom box was an old Peterson's *Field Guide to Animal Tracks,* still with its dog-eared, blue dust jacket.

Franklin woodstove, small vase of wildflowers on top of it, foam slab of a couch with cushions frayed and askew, dirty pillows and an army sleeping bag stuffed into a corner, television and VCR on a rolling cabinet, newpapers kicked around on the floor. Balled socks. Plates of crumbs. Saucer full of butts. More magazines. I picked one off the coffee table. *Guns and Ammo.*

Wilma brought a box of bandages and cotton balls out of the bathroom.

She sat me on a stool and slowly stripped off my hospital bandage, wincing. Looking down at the gummy floor, I told her I was finding it harder and harder to understand what she'd seen in Edmund Evans.

"You don't want to go there, Hector."

"He's a pig, Wilma."

"He's no housekeeper, that's obvious. Hey, I wouldn't want to show you my humble abattoir either."

"He's a bully, too."

"Granted."

"It wasn't just sex, was it?"

She frowned. "It was sex, of course it was sex. But look,

Ed's also a shrewd, determined person with a messed-up past. Not unlike mine. You don't want to hear about it. Beat up by his old man, no friends as a kid, did lousy in school, wounded twice over in Nam, ex-wife went bonkers, daughter's a floozy, up-and-down career, unappreciated by the force, and on and on, numerous health problems, emotional problems, alcohol problems, woman problems . . ." She trailed off. "He's a disaster in pants."

I went back to the pine shelves and picked up the Peterson's guide. Inside the cover it said, "Noël 1965, Otto— Je t'aime . . . —F." I thought I'd recognized it. Otto kept several of these guides on his fireplace mantel at the A-frame. He had them for butterflies, trees, wildflowers, insects, edible plants, ten or more. Evans had helped himself, the light-fingered jerk.

I showed Wilma.

She clapped the book shut. "Half you cops are a hair away from being crooks."

"No excuse." I wedged the book into my back pocket.

"So now you're gonna steal it back?"

"This the snow bunny?" A framed photo on the TV had preserved the goony smile of a young blonde in a halter top leaning against an apple tree, a sprig of Queen Anne's lace behind one ear. Big chest, peachy skin, dumb—the eyes too round and close together.

"What snow bunny?"

"The one he tossed you for. The fiancée."

"No, no. That's Amy-lynn. Ed's daughter."

The floozy. There was a sort of sad resemblance when I looked again.

She drew me back into the dining nook and sat me down to daub my head with soapy water. Two mugs stood on the table with dried coffee in the bottom. An empty Sara Lee coffee-cake pan, more butts in it. Marlboros.

"Ed doesn't smoke, does he?"

"Ed?" She wrinkled her nose. "Not to my knowledge."

"Whose are these, do you think?"

"Couldn't tell you."

I pushed her off and went for the telephone in the kitchen. In the directory I found the listing for Brasseur's Border BP out west of Tipton, the wrecker service that pulled my Powerwagon out of the lake.

"Rita?" Rita was wife and partner to Rainey Brasseur. "You still have my pickup on the lot?"

"We did. Two fellas from the state come up this afternoon and impounded it. Took it off on a flatbed."

"Where'd they take it?"

"Waterbury. You probably heard why."

"Tell me."

"They found a lot of dope behind the seat, Hector. Rainey was there."

"They find anything else?"

"Buncha beer cans and a loaded gun. From what Rainey told me."

I thanked her.

"What do you think you're doing?" Wilma said, following me into the bedroom. It was dim, blinds drawn.

Big water bed, smoky mirror behind it, green satin sheets. Dirty sheepskin rug. Dustbuster vacuum lying beside the bed. Black shoes lined up along one wall. I switched on a little gooseneck lamp on the nightstand: quartz clock radio, black RadioShack phone. I tugged open the drawer.

"You getting some kind of peculiar kick out of this?"

Dental floss dispenser, few packets of Trojans, scissors, pliers, sunglasses, address book, pencils. I thumbed through the address book. Nothing of interest far as I could tell. Random scrawls and doodles on the cover. I dumped the drawer on the bed. Marbles, more shotgun shells, stopwatch on a lanyard, packet of E-Z Wider rolling papers, and a rolled-up baggie. I opened it and took a whiff.

"Did you know Ed smoked pot?"

"What? No."

I twisted the lamp toward the open closet. Uniforms, jackets, slacks, neckties on hangers, shoes and boots on the dusty floor, big white basketball sneakers. Boat shoes. Couple cans of tennis balls. Prince racket and canvas shotgun case leaning in one corner. Shelf on top had folded sweaters and a pearly white motorcycle helmet. Nothing else.

"Would you mind telling me what you're pawing around after?"

"I'll know when I find it."

"This is perverse of you, Hector."

The surface of his long, low bureau was strewn with junk: old mail, paperbacks, Canadian coins, buttons, a spark plug, a hunting knife, a roll of electrician's tape. Under a murky-looking mirror he kept a scuffed leather cuff-links box. I lifted the lid. Right on top was a piece of blue paper folded around a pink index card. The card had a scrap of old newsprint stapled to it. The paper was an invoice. For a "Rail Road Vault, Elk Co. #233," from Kitchener Commercial Salvage, Hamilton, Ontario. Date of purchase, August 16, 1985. Price: $1,175.

"What do you make of this?"

"I—I have no clue."

I buttoned it into my pocket. "Better keep looking."

I opened the top bureau drawer. Socks and underwear, tray of blazer buttons, marine insignia, medal boxes. Fancy chrome handcuffs. Middle drawer was T-shirts and shorts. Bottom drawer was dress shirts. Something underneath them . . .

"Those are Ed's scrapbooks."

"You've seen these before?"

"Sure."

I took them out.

First one had a cardboard cover. Clippings—sports stories out of the newspapers. A few pages of baseball cards in plastic slips—all Red Sox. Grade school class pictures, three of them, black-and-white, Little Falls Elementary School, Worcester, Massachusetts. A Great Dane on a lawn. House on a lake somewhere, a boy in a sandbox, on a JC Higgins bicycle, blowing out birthday candles, showing off his Little League uniform, Mason Lumber.

"No family," I said.

"Ed had a miserable childhood. His aunts pretty much raised him."

Cars. A red TR-3, a junker 'Cuda, a pinstriped Firebird. Ed in a blue football uniform, big pads, foam neck ring, number 78. Ed standing in front of Baskin-Robbins in a clown suit and blue high-top sneakers. Ed in a cream jacket and plaid cummerbund and a slender, white-necked girl in a strapless pink prom gown, under a high-school mural of pilgrims marching down a gangway. Eight-by-ten of Ed in a marine dress uniform, white hat clamped under his arm, in love with himself.

I flipped to the war. Scrawny guys in fatigues. Sweat. Jungle. Blasted terrain. A bunk bed. A field of helicopters, two of them burning. Ed in a hospital bed smoking what looked to be a joint. Ed shirtless at the controls of a crawler. Tucked into the back was a small folded map printed on crackly paper. I opened it. It wasn't in English. Cambodia by the shape, a long smear of soot across the paper.

Last scrapbook was a hodgepodge. His cop career. Clippings. Police academy diploma. Rotary Club luncheon program with Ed listed as speaker. News story about the flood downtown a few years ago. Photos of the flooded police barracks. Ed in a fishing boat. Ed at a hunting camp in a measly beard, red flannel undershirt, shaggy hair, posing with a buck strung up on a game hook suspended off the end of the camp porch. I recognized the place.

"Ed ever show you this picture?"

"I don't know. Boy, now *that* was a long while ago. Look at those sideburns—"

"That's Wayne's yurt, Wilma."

"That is?" She looked more closely. "Oh, my God . . ."

"This was taken not too long after he built it."

"Shit . . ." Her face, already pale, went white. Even her lips lost their color. *"Wayne and Ed?"*

19

"You had no idea?"

"No! He's such a *cop*." She slumped to the bed.

"Nam buddies, most likely. They go back quite a ways."

"But seriously, how could he be connected? Ed's *broke*, for one thing. Look around this dump—his ex took *everything*. He's got nothing."

"Got a new Jeep."

"Yeah. You know, last summer when he bought that tank, I jokingly asked him how he swung it. He said he got it 'for services rendered,' haha. 'Services rendered *to whom?*' I said. And he said, 'The powers that be, 'Pine, the powers that be.'"

"'Pine'?"

She sighed. "Short for *porcupine*. He used to think I was a prickly bitch."

"What powers did you think he meant?"

"Quimby. That's all I could figure."

"Quimby! What favor could he do for Quimby that would get him a new car?"

"So it was the Ingallses then?"

"More likely. Hell, he was hiding Lonnie Perkins. Right here. Till Lonnie either ran off or Ed moved him to the Lodge."

"You don't think *he* shot Lonnie?"

"Didn't he get to the Lodge before Cahoon?"

"Yes. By ten minutes or so. He didn't come in through the bar, I know that—" She stopped. *"Jesus . . . ,"* she breathed.

"Wayne told Ed I was headed for the Lodge. All Ed had to do was get Lonnie down there and make a corpse out of him. With my .38. They had me walking into my second setup in twenty-four hours. These people don't quit."

"Shouldn't we think about getting out of here?"

"You have Marko's gun?"

"It's in the kitchen." She jumped up. Her face was flushed again behind her freckles, though her hands pulling on mine were clammy. "Come on, Hector, let's just go. We don't need—"

Too late. Shoes scraped up the stairs outside. I shoved the scrapbooks in under the shirts and closed the drawer. "If he'll let you go, then go," I said softly. "Go to a phone and call Cahoon."

I stretched back on the wobbly bed.

Evans was coming through the living room, heavy on his heels. "What am I . . . I'm not interrupting something funny in my own place, am I? Hunh?"

"He's out of it," Wilma told him.

He stopped beside the bed. "Is he?" He snuffled. "Shit. He say any more about smuggling?"

"He's been real woozy. I'm thinking I should call an ambulance. Did you find this boathouse?"

"He that bad?" Evans picked up the bedside phone and punched keys.

I breathed deep and slow. My heart was racing.

"Rebecca? This is Evans. I need a Rescue unit right away. I'm at my place. Pine Tree Court. . . . No, no . . . Yes, you do that. Thanks plenty. I will."

"Did Cahoon show up at Westlook?" Wilma asked.

"Yeah, he sure did. He was all outraged Bellevance here slipped the net. I couldn't even talk to him."

"You tell him about this underwater smuggling thing?"

"He wasn't paying attention. Those boys were on a tear, though, babe. I mean, if there was anything down there, he'll damn sure find it." He groaned. "I am wiped out. This has been one wicked day!"

"You didn't tell Cahoon about the boathouse?" she whispered.

"Wilma, like I just said, if there's any reality to it, they'll nail the shitheads. Cahoon's all over that cove."

"Did *you* find it?"

"Find what?"

"You didn't call the Rescue Squad, either, did you?"

"Wilma. Look. Cahoon wants this fella. In the *worst* way. I'm gonna sit on him right here—at least until he improves."

"I'm fine," I said, sitting up.

Evans reeled back a step. "It *lives.*" He laughed.

I reached for the phone. "I need to make a quick call."

"One sec." Evans pulled out his black pistol and unplugged the phone. "Before anybody makes any calls . . . You are in custody, Bellevance. OK? Now you know you have certain rights, which—"

Wilma was heading for the bedroom door.

Evans moved to block her way. "You're not leaving, babe. You're a *witness* to this."

"I know. I'm getting my tape recorder."

"You're staying right here."

"What, am I in custody, too?"

"That could be arranged."

She tried to push past him. He grabbed her arm and threw her back.

"You *pig.*"

"Bitch. You been going through my kit and caboodle in

here. You been going through my *shit*." He kicked an open drawer. "Look at that. What's that?"

"You're the connection, Ed," Wilma said. "Aren't you? You're the link between the Ingallses and the fool on the hill."

I lay back in the sloshing mattress. Now neither one of us was about to stroll out of here.

"The way you used to hang out at Quimby's, I figured you had to be squeezing more than free drinks out of that scuzzball," Wilma went on, "but I thought that was the extent of it."

"There's certain things a man in public office has to be discreet about."

"Like drug-smuggling and murder?"

His pudgy face went hard around the nose.

Then, *bang*, the front door flew open and crashed against the bookcase. Something fell off onto the floor. No one came into the room.

"Hi, honey, I'm home!" Hrushka.

Evans allowed a quick glance behind him. He yelled, "Get in here and shut the fucking door."

I craned my neck. He walked in slowly, short of breath. He was holding that oversize silver handgun, its ten-inch barrel pointed upright beside his ear.

"Cut the cowboy shit," Ed barked. "And put away that howitzer. I have this handled."

Hrushka stopped in the bedroom doorway. He lowered the gun and covered the room with it. "You takin' *hostages* now, or what is this crap?"

"Ed's trying to figure out how to kill us," Wilma said.

Hrushka chuckled. "Yeah, he's got a real talent for that."

"Bellevance beat up on your militia mouthpiece," Evans said in disgust. "The shithead laid out the whole structure. Named names and everything."

"Don't mean nothing. Marko's deluded and deranged. You seen that fucker's medications?"

"He got into *Westlook*, Wayne. He saw the machine. He opened the goddamn cashbox!"

"Machine? Box? These words mean nothing to me."

Evans sat back, exhaling through his nostrils. His eyes were wild. "OK. Where's the green? You got it with you?"

"Eddie, Eddie . . . ," Wayne soothed. "You're fretting again. What happens when you fret? You do drastic things you're sorry about later. Marko's got a mentality problem. He can be finessed. Meanwhile, the mountain's clean. The *lake* is clean. Fucking Quimby's on his way around to tidy up the other side. What more could you ask?"

"You asshole! These two people can't be out there knowing what they know!"

"Why? Myself, I am not too concerned about getting busted because of what people *know*. That's just words—it's unsubstantiated. They need hard physical evidence and they aren't gonna find it."

Evans nodded toward Wilma. "You wait till she puts it in the paper for everybody to read."

"Mail me a copy in Rangoon."

"They go, Wayne. This is the final crisis. We got it under control. We can deal with it."

Hrushka came over to the foot of the bed. He had the gun pointed up above his shoulder again, supporting the elbow with his left hand. He looked us over, Wilma sitting on the bed, me lying next to her, Ed standing spread-legged a few feet off, his western shirt so tight you could see his undershirt between the snaps.

"What a mess," Wayne said to Evans. "How did it ever get so messy, Ed? I keep asking myself this question."

"You know how! Morganthau was going to go to the *state*."

"Was he? According to who?"

"According to *Morganthau*! Danny heard him say it!"

"According to Danny."

"Going to the state with what?" I said.

Wayne sighed. "Danny didn't like the Morganthaus. He wanted Otto cut out. That's more like what it was."

"You don't know shit," Evans said.

"Who killed them?" I asked.

"The kid!" Evans said. "Lonnie, the dumb punk."

"Was it Lonnie?" Wayne looked at Evans. "We'll never know for sure, will we, Eddie. Now that Lonnie's been smoked. And Lord Shitbrain along with him."

"Danny's *dead*?" Evans hissed. "How?"

"Blew off his protection. Just like poor Lonnie, I imagine."

"Lonnie had it coming for days. One way or the other. It was a foregone conclusion. That would've sealed it, if it wasn't for this asshole here."

Hrushka took a step closer and said softly to Evans, "It was you, wasn't it? Whether you pulled the trigger or not, it was still you. You wanted that fucking glass house."

"What? What's *with* you, Wayne? You trying to put me wrong in front of these people? What are you doing?"

"It was *you*. You took and used my herb for your own self-ish purposes. Everything was going perfectly smooth and fine until you started fucking with it, you and shitbrain Danny."

"It's *still* fine. Eliminate these two obstacles and it's back to how we planned it. Except for Danny getting caught in the backdraft."

"And these two obstacles."

"I gave the guy a *choice*." He turned his flushed face to me. "You coulda stayed safe! You and your brother would've got off on the cultivation *and* on the Morganthaus. Now you're too contaminated to live."

Wayne drew the gun down in front of his nose and he stared at it vaguely. "It's so hard for me to believe," he mused, "the way our elegant operation is shaking out. With *murders*, and this *double-crossing* shit. It's pathetic. It was so perfect for so long. . . ."

All at once Wilma was on her feet and flying past Hrushka out through the doorway.

"Halt!" Ed barked, swinging his muzzle around. Wayne was already on her heels. When he herded her back into the room, she had the canvas tote from the kitchen.

Evans said, "She's got a tape recorder in that bag."

Wayne motioned for it. Wilma rummaged the recorder out and thrust it at him. He kept motioning. She handed him the bag. He groped around in it, as she flung herself onto the water bed.

"Whoops . . ." Wayne extracted the Glock she'd taken from Marko. "Nice piece." He looked it over and placed it on the bureau. "No more dance moves, girl, understand? That shit'll get you dead. We want to avoid that if we can."

He walked closer to the sergeant, the outlandish .50 held alongside his ear again, like a duelist's flintlock. He tightened his lips, drew a quick breath, and lashed the barrel down onto Evans's right wrist.

Evans's head flew back. He bellowed. His gun clonked to the shag. Wilma covered her face.

"Nnn, nnn, nnn, nnn . . ." Evans, on his knees, pressed his forehead into the bed, hugging his cracked wrist and grunting.

"Hate to put the hurt on, Ed, but I'm out of options." Wayne stooped to retrieve Evans's weapon.

The sergeant reared up, eyes squeezed shut, cheeks streaming with tears. "My fucking *arm*—"

"Suck it up, Ed. You'll recover."

"Why did you—" he panted, *"why did you—"*

"I got something I want to try. Bellevance, I'm gonna let you have this piece here." He picked up Marko's gun.

Evans rocked on the floor. "What the hell are you *doing*?"

"You'll love this, Eddie. Champion frame artist like you. Here's what I'm gonna do. I'm gonna give the constable here

the means to arrest you—for dereliction of duty and whatever—"

"Wayne, no!"

"Wait, wait . . . This is good. After I give him the means to
arrest you, what I'm gonna do, I'm gonna give you the means
to resist arrest—"

"Jesus God," Wilma said.

"Don't move!" he yelled at her. "Now. If Bellevance is as
quick as Marko says," he went on gently to Evans, "he'll get
off a couple shots. Unless you *don't* resist. But you *got* to
resist, right? Or else you're all done, fried for life."

Wilma moaned and started to cry. "This is *nuts,* you guys."

"It's a cockfight. One of you's gotta kill the other one." He
sighed as if moved by the idea. "Meanwhile, I'm gone. Which-
ever way it plays out, the poor pitiful police are gonna have
themselves a royal field day untangling the motivations."

"Wayne! Don't *do* this!" Evans pleaded. "We can get
clean! We wait till dark and take these two up the hill. They'll
disappear!"

"You remember my ironclad motto? 'Remain above the
fray'?"

"Wayne! We're a team, Wayne! Everything I did, if I made
any mistakes, it was for *us!"*

"How about you, Bellevance, you down with this plan?"

"Not too."

"Better adjust. Now. We all set?" He snatched up Marko's
gun and tossed it underhand to the bed. It snagged in a fold
of a thermal blanket. "There." He motioned to me. "Now you
pick that up, Constable. Nice and easy."

I didn't reach for it. He wanted me to have clear odds and
no choice. He wanted me to kill Evans for him, so he could
sky with clean hands and nothing to tie him to the smugglers
but his footprints in the mud. The Ingallses had bought him
out, like they'd bought out Quimby. And like Quimby, he'd

be heading West. The Ingallses would close out their offshore accounts and trash my poor town with drug money.

"You best take it, Bellevance. Because Eddie's getting his heavy-hitter back in two seconds, and he's the best pistol shot I ever saw. Only not left-handed. . . . That's another break for you."

Ed sat back, cradling his right arm against his ribs like an infant. He gathered himself and pleaded, "Bellevance, listen to me now. Lonnie killed the Canadians. The murder weapon is laying in the chest freezer behind his girlfriend's trailer. You were supposed to find it in there, which would have put everything right . . . but you never *looked*. But so what, the main thing is Lonnie *deserved* what he got. He stomped in there all coked up and he executed those two people, you were right about that. You and me together can make the case against the kid, and both of you, you and your brother, fly away free. But you shoot me here and you'll go to jail for a very long time."

"I won't shoot you—as long as you don't touch your gun."

"Careful, Bellevance," Hrushka sang. "Ed ain't a man to be trusted. Never was."

Hrushka was backing out of the room with his silver cannon leveled at us in one hand and Evans's black auto, grip extended, in the other.

"Ready, Eddie? Heads!" The gun pinwheeled through the air. I grabbed up Marko's Glock.

Ed reached out and caught his own gun.

"Point that this way," I said, "and you're dead."

He didn't look at me. He was sitting cross-legged with the flat of the gun resting on his left knee, half hunched over the useless arm in his lap.

The front door opened and closed.

I said, "Place that gun on the floor and then slide back away from it."

"We got to talk."

"Put down the gun, Evans. This is where—"

"Bellevance! Bellevance . . . *Listen to me.* You're gonna have to be a lot more reasonable about this—"

He swung on me. He might have shot me, but Wilma dove at him from his blind side. He got off a round before she bowled him over. I launched myself over her, going for his good arm. I flattened him.

Wilma rolled away. Evans was howling. I had my weight on that broken right wrist.

"Wilma! You OK?"

She lay on her back beside me, nodding, breathing hard.

Evans was retching. As I started to ease up off him, he heaved and bucked under me. I wrapped my arm around his throat and squeezed. A shudder convulsed his torso.

He went limp. I pushed off him.

He was dead.

I figured I'd broken his neck, but when the medical examiner got through with him a day later, it turned out he'd had a massive stroke. More mercy than he deserved.

I ran to the front door and threw it open, keeping cover behind the jamb. But Hrushka and whatever vehicle he had come in were long gone. The sun had just set. The sky was golden and streaked with pink ribbons of cloud. Wilma came up.

I turned and pulled her to me.

FROM Evans's condo I telephoned the Sécurité Quebec. They and the Mounties had no trouble rounding up Keith Quimby at the Iceville end of the smuggling channel, a log fishing camp owned by Planvest, N.V. The winch on that side was concealed in a trough that ran under the main floor of the camp itself, with no outside entry. Four blue crates packed with Wayne's premium bricks were still inside the cabin. The bricks were wrapped in yellow paper with gold-embossed seals at the ends that read: JOLLYWOLF HYBRID/USA.

Soon as it was federal, the FBI and the U.S. Attorney's Office grabbed up the case—to Lieutenant Cahoon's relief. He had enough to deal with, in atoning for his blunders. Not that anyone in a position to blame him did so (nobody had Evans pegged for what he was), but Cahoon was sorely humiliated just the same. His pride had taken a sucker punch. And yet it wasn't until after I had spent the rest of that night under police guard at the regional hospital that he and Nezzie Holmes came up to offer me their "sincere regrets and no hard feelings." Holmes wanted to assure me that my brother and I would have our property returned by the end of the day. Spud's machinery, too? He'd do all he could, he promised, and did I need a lift home to Tipton? On the way, he let me know he'd be naming Wayne Hrushka as Danny Ingalls's suspected killer. Hrushka had ample motive, and Holmes had a dozen witnesses at the wrap party who'd observed a big guy in fatigues slipping away toward the boathouse with Danny the last time he was seen alive. It was nothing I felt inclined to comment on. He added that Rossi and the Ingallses were stonewalling, sealing themselves off— for all the good it would do them. Keith Quimby was already talking a blue streak, painting himself as a legitimate artist and businessman who'd been hornswoggled by his treacherous executive producer (Danny) and a collection of local lowlifes.

Investigating officers from two governments would be combing bank records and gathering depositions for months. After Keith and Jamie and Marko cut their deals with the prosecutors, they would have plenty to offer about the Ingallses' operation. With that leverage Holmes would get Nathan Rossi to turn. Lots of questions would go unanswered, of course, and lots of answers would go unconfirmed, but in a sworn affidavit Rossi would assert that it was Gavin and Marvin Ingalls who set up Wayne with his mountaintop lease—at Ed Evans's instigation. Gavin Ingalls, Hrushka, and Evans, it turned out, were war buddies. They had all fought with the Twenty-sixth Marines during the siege of Khe Sanh.

Keith said the Canadian contact was some faceless gangster known to Danny as the Priest. How he had hooked up with Wayne was a story no one knew, but it was the Priest, apparently, who had persuaded the mountain man to go high-tech. Through the eighties, as zero tolerance took hold in North America, the market for boutique marijuana in urban Canada became hugely profitable. Gavin Ingalls came across with the funds Wayne needed to outfit the grow lab, Jamie flew to a cannabis aficionados' trade fair in Amsterdam to score some exotic seeds, and young Danny engineered the underwater shuttle. Once they had it up and running, the hard part would be closing it down again. Wayne's Jollywolf Hybrid acquired a decidedly appreciative following north of the border. The Priest took everything Wayne could produce. Gavin recruited Otto to mule their swiftly accumulating cash out of the country. And later on Danny sold all of the others on his grandiose scheme to get it back in again.

All except Otto. A big resort would have spoiled his view. To say nothing of our quiet town. Presumably he'd had his fill of big resorts during his years of romping through the tropics, or else what was he doing living back in the woods? Forget it, he told Danny, he wasn't selling, he wasn't moving. This take seemed about right to me, although Keith suspected Otto was trying to position himself for a bigger payoff. Whatever it was that made Otto balk, Danny handled it by having the Morganthaus taken out, like some provincial crime boss.

The Ingalls brothers would be indicted by a grand jury for

drug-trafficking, smuggling, money-laundering, and bank fraud. Gavin would eventually get twenty-five years, Marvin five to ten. Rossi would plead to lesser charges. Keith, Jamie, and Marko, in exchange for their testimony, would get off with suspended sentences. Wilma's story on the whole crazy business would run for three days in the *Boston Globe* and get her nominated for a Pulitzer Prize. What pleased me most was that the state would seize all the corporate holdings, and by spring the legislature in Montpelier would be discussing proposals for an expansive state park.

As for Wayne, if he managed to melt into the American landscape never to be found, that would seem to me less a travesty of justice than a credit to his ingenuity. Not to mention his bankroll. I forgave Wayne nothing. But I couldn't begrudge him his personal triumph. He'd played the game for the highest stakes and come away with the jackpot. Without killing anybody. No mean feat, considering the way it all flew to pieces in the end.

20

By the time Wilma made it out to the cabin, I had most of the garbage cleared away and the furniture put back where it belonged, and it felt good to be just sitting on the porch with my iced tea, just sitting for the first time in days.

I met her in the grass. We embraced without a word. She'd run up from the car and her chest was heaving.

"I'm on deadline . . . so I've only got . . . till two o'clock . . ."

I took her hands. "We're not finished."

"I know. Wait, we aren't?"

I took her up onto the porch and handed her Otto's old Peterson guide. "Look up *elk*."

She went to the index.

"Ed was a shrewd guy," I said. "You were right about that. Not many people would have guessed where Otto had recorded the combination."

"'Elk, Wapiti, 271,'" she said. She found the page. "Jeez . . ."

A penciled notation was across the bottom. She read, "'NYSE, Aug. 16, 1985, closing: 3 Roper, 2 ConAgr, 1 USFG . . .' These are stock issues . . ." She closed her eyes. "OK, wait, I think I get it—he found the numbers in the newspaper and used them as a code."

"Right. That's what the page of newsprint attached to the receipt was about. Ed came across it somewhere in Otto's files."

"How did *you* figure all this out?"

I shrugged. "You coming? Spud's waiting up at the A-frame."

She ran down the steps after me. "You can't open up that safe! Not without somebody *official!*"

"I'm official."

"You know what I mean. . . . I mean *Holmes!* Hector, stop. I mean, goddamn it, you could ruin the evidence. . . . You could get *arrested!*"

SPUD'S rust-eaten Cutlass was parked in the turnaround above the A-frame. Most of the maples around us were wind-stripped, so that it seemed a month might have passed since I was last here, rather than just a week or so.

The deck door was open. The sun was streaming in. It was quiet.

"This place is gorgeous," Wilma whispered.

Gaea's blood still stained the tiles around the oven, webbed in the places where her body had lain. Cahoon's fume job had left powdery traces on the stovetop, table, counter, door glass, everywhere. And of course the place still smelled sweetly of death.

Spud met us there in the kitchen. I took him and pulled him to me. He went stiff as a tree. I didn't let go. After a few seconds his neck and shoulders gave a little. Our heads touched. He grazed my ear with his whiskers pushing himself loose.

Wilma was examining Gaea's cookbooks.

"Power's off," Spud said. He cleared his throat. "Bring a flashlight?" I handed him my Maglite. He nodded and took it. "So, was it Lonnie shot them then?"

"Drugged up, I guess he could have," I said. "We'll never know for sure."

"Brenda says she can't imagine Lonnie doing it."

Wilma laughed. "But she can imagine *you* doing it?"

He scowled. "Don't get me going now. We're on eggshells, me and her."

The smell of fuel oil eddied around us as we descended the stairs. Pine paneling, gray carpet. Two scarcely used Windsurfers were tipped up on the edges of their blue and purple hulls. Four bikes hung from hooks in the ceiling.

Spud led us through Gaea's plastic-draped darkroom to a workbench that hardly looked used. The red vise bolted to it was brand-new. Behind it was a Peg-Board for hand tools. We lifted the bench out of the way, swung the Peg-Board aside, and Spud lifted out a four-by-eight section of paneling.

"The Elk," Wilma breathed, awestruck. "How lovely."

"Don't make nothing like they used to, do they?" Spud said.

It had a black steel door and a polished dial the size of a pie plate right in the middle. The dial was calibrated 0 to 100. Below the dial in gold leaf an elk stood on a crag, surveying his domain: THE ELK VAULT CO., 1886 HAMILTON, ONT."

I slipped on my gloves.

Spud aimed the flashlight. Wilma held the Peterson guide. I ran my finger down the agate-print column of stock quotes and found Roper. It had closed at twelve.

Then ConAgr. Thirty-four. OK.

"Three turns to twelve, two to thirty-four . . ." Right, left, right . . .

Working slowly.

The lever came free in a buttery arc, first try. I looked at Spud. He winked, delighted as I'd ever seen him. I pulled and stepped back.

"Oh, baby," Wilma said.

The inner panel, within a gold-leaf border, was a vivid landscape hand-painted in enamel. A wilderness panorama, the Yukon or the Northwest Territories. Snowy mountains above forests and grass plains. Through the middle came a river of elk, appearing first as a brown trickle, like a strand of wool, winding through a notch in the mountains, then zigzagging down and down from snow to rock to bush, tiny as fleas all the way, finally coming straight at you across the plains under a veil of dust torn by the wind. In the foreground they became distinct animals, bulls, cows, and calves, fording a white, stony stretch of water.

I unfolded the recessed thumbkey and turned it, unlatching the panel.

Inside was an arrangement of cubbyholes, two rows down the left side, all empty. In the middle were four steel shelves, also empty.

Except for the top one. In back I found a leather portfolio and a few vinyl-backed ledgers.

I unzipped the portfolio and drew out a sheaf of gilt-edged certificates, more than a dozen, on heavy linen paper. "Bearer Shares," in large letters. "Micmac Investments, N.V." Signatures scrawled at the bottom.

"That's where the money is, right there!" Wilma said. "Stashed down in the Caribbean."

"What money?" Spud said.

"Otto's piece of the action," I said. "No telling what they're worth. Several thousand dollars apiece. Probably a lot more."

The vinyl ledgers were embossed on their covers with a single word: *Starlight*.

They were cruise logs.

Wilma held the light on the lined pages as we flipped through. Gaea had kept the books in French, in a fine hand. She had preserved the details of every charter—dates, weather, ports of call, maintenance records, repairs made, diesel fuel and materials purchased. Even menus. She'd entered the manifests of the guests and crew as well, including, on their inaugural cruise to Curaçao nine years ago, Gavin Ingalls and Nathan Rossi.

"They were moving the drug money," I said.

Spud made a face. "Come on. You telling me you can just load a bunch of cash money on a boat and cruise to South America?"

"Caribbean used to be pretty wide open if you knew your way around."

Wilma tapped her finger on the vinyl. "Why do you think he stuck these logbooks in here?"

"If Otto ever needed to incriminate the Ingallses, the books would back him up."

"U.S. attorney's going to be real tickled with all this, that's for sure," Wilma said.

On the right side of the safe was a smaller snug-fitting panel door with an ornate design on it—red and gold enamel curlicues.

Inside was a stack of shallow steel drawers with recessed handles. The top one moved heavily.

Rows of plastic disks like poker chips, set on edge.

I fingered one out.

Each disk contained a Canadian Maple Leaf coin. One troy ounce of pure gold. I pulled the drawer out all the way to count them. Fifty or so.

Each drawer held about the same number.

"What do you think," I said, "five, six hundred ounces? More?"

Spud said, "How much are they worth?"

I looked at Wilma. "What's gold going for? Three hundred an ounce? Four?"

"Somewhere in there," she said. "Not a *huge* amount."

Spud snorted. "It's enough."

"It's enough to get by on. But it's not a *fortune*."

"It's enough to get killed for," Spud said.

I slid the drawers in. "It wasn't the gold. It was the shares. Danny wanted to buy Otto out the way he'd bought out Keith and Wayne. Otto wouldn't come to terms. He didn't have to—he had too much on the Ingallses. They knew it, too."

"Good a guess as any," Wilma said.

AFTER some awkward small talk up in the parking area, Spud managed to ask Wilma if she would please leave out the part about a sexual connection between him and Gaea when she got around to writing up her article.

Wilma folded her arms. "Now why should I do that?"

"Because it's a personal matter, number one, and number two, it's got nothing to do with them getting killed."

"Spud," she said, "I don't think you realize how huge this story's going to be. Gaea died pregnant. And Otto wasn't the guy. Those are significant facts. And they're bound to come out at some point."

"Why? It has nothing to do with what happened to them!"

"Sure it does," I said.

"How?" he demanded. *"How?"*

"Lonnie knew from Stacey that Gaea was pregnant, and he knew you were sleeping with her. Otherwise, he and Evans never would have tried to frame you for the murders. And if he hadn't done that, they just might have got away with the whole damn thing."

He considered this. Then he said, "Heck, here it is. Me and Gaea talked about a lot of things. Personal things. But never once did she say a single word to me about drug-smuggling or money-laundering or *any* of this foolishness. You know why? Because she was never a part of it, that's why. Or she would've told me. And after being shot up bad as she was, which was enough all by itself, she doesn't deserve getting her name dragged down in the paper. Neither do I."

"Were you in love with her, Spud?"

He stared at me, wooden-faced.

"Did she love you?"

"What the hell difference does it make?" He snugged his dirty red Massey cap onto his head with two hands. When I said nothing more, he added, "I guess she would've broke it off sooner or later. Either that or drove me bat-crazy. Or both." He turned and got into his car.

I leaned down. "Brenda deserves the truth, Spud."

"If she wants the truth, she'll ask for it. If she doesn't, she won't. I don't want to see it flung in her face, is all." He paused. "Because I know one thing. If she ditches me, she'll be ten times worse off, her and the baby, living on food stamps in some shithole in town."

"She won't ditch you."

"She will if all this garbage gets in the paper." He glared at Wilma.

"You'll make it, Spud, whatever Brenda does." I was thinking, hell, with Otto gone, he could sell the farm's development rights to a land trust. He'd be fine.

Spud was about to say more but changed his mind. We stood there while he cranked the key four, five, six times, patiently, staring off into the sugar maples. With the leaves mostly down here on the heights, the lemon light of October was streaming through all around us, every gray twig and tree trunk glowing.

The engine caught. He revved it hard. "Solenoid," he said. "Always something."

Exhaust hung in the air as we shuffled out along the leaf-deep lane. Wilma waved her arms at it. "So," she said, "you gonna sue the State of Vermont?"

"Me? What for?"

"Damages! Hector, jeez, they trashed your house! They trampled down half your mom's blueberry bushes!"

"I'll think about it, but I'm not real big on litigation."

"Could be a pretty penny in it for you."

"There are some very pretty pennies sitting right down below in that old vault."

She let out a laugh and took my hand. After a pause she said, "You're kidding, right?"

I just winked at her.

ABOUT THE AUTHOR

DON BREDES is the author of two previous novels. He lives in the hills of northern Vermont with his wife and daughter.